RUN IS

W9-BPQ-802

"TERRIFIC...
WHAT WINTER DOES HERE IS OPEN A NEW
SCHOOL: HOW TO WRITE THRILLERS WITH
A PACE THAT TAKES YOUR BREATH AWAY."
—ELMORE LEONARD

RUN IS
"STARTLING, UNFLINCHING,
UTTERLY IMPRESSIVE...
ORIGINAL IN EVERY WAY, *RUN* IS A MASTERLY
REDEFINITION OF THE CRIME THRILLER, ONE IN
WHICH DOUGLAS E. WINTER HAS DISCOVERED
A VOICE THAT SEEMS TO COME FROM HIS HEELS."
—PETER STRAUB

RUN IS
"APOCALYPTIC...
FULL OF HALLUCINATORY EFFECTS."
—THE NEW YORK TIMES BOOK REVIEW

RUN IS
"LIKE STEPPING ONTO
A SPEEDING TRAIN."
—THE WASHINGTON TIMES

Raves for *RUN*

"**[A] startling, unflinching, utterly impressive novel-as-thriller.** Instantly, I mean from the first paragraph, *RUN*'s language jumps off the page and sears itself into the reader's consciousness. . . . I had to go on reading it until three in the morning, when I reached the final sentence. I don't think that has ever happened to me before."　　　—Peter Straub

"**With *RUN*, Douglas E. Winter . . . ups the ante for thriller writers everywhere.** *RUN* has the hard, sharklike sheen of a Richard Stark novel and the bullet-riddled kineticism of early John Woo. Plan to stay up half the night."
　　　—George P. Pelecanos, author of *Shame the Devil*

"Winter's **high-firepower** thriller about schemes inside of schemes is **all adrenaline**."　　　—*Los Angeles Times*

"**Apocalyptic**. . . . Winter shows an amusing ability to turn descriptions of firearms into demented arias, and a talent for cooking up interlocking conspiracies . . . full of hallucinatory effects."
　　　—*The New York Times Book Review*

"The **breakneck pace** . . . is more than matched by the action in this high-speed caper novel. . . . The pace is unremitting, the language jumps off the page **like freshly ignited dynamite** . . . a terrific first novel by a writer of real promise."　　　—*Booklist*

Continued on next page . . .

"**Relentlessly paced,** this chase novel impressively captures the frantic energy and emotional panic experienced by an East Coast gunrunner forced to flee both his own gang and the law. Written in rough, gritty street vernacular . . . Winter sets a torrid tempo for his electric narrative . . . a memorable debut novel." —*Publishers Weekly*

"**A crime thriller that turns on dime after dime** and hurtles into a night of **sheer poetry.** Winter devises an artificial language of hoods and tough guys that insists that every syllable carry its freight of menace . . . aglow with originality . . . has echoes of John Huston and W.R. Burnett's masterpiece, *The Asphalt Jungle* . . . Second to the lingo, the quality of the narrative lies in Winter's impressive command of guns, which amounts to a lyrical depiction of weapons. . . . As often happens in hugely showy first novels, **Winter will have a tough time topping himself.**" —*Kirkus Reviews*

"**You don't read this book: You eavesdrop. . . .** Winter's twists seems as inevitable as breathing. . . . [A] supremely ironic, sardonic, bloody visitation into the American Dream . . . [Winter's] debut novel joins the very short list of best first American language novels ever." —*Philadelphia Inquirer*

"**Opening RUN is like stepping onto a speeding train.** It wastes no time building momentum, and when it reaches the end of the line, it keeps on going anyway. . . . Douglas Winter's uncommon conversational prose style, awesome powers of description and profound understanding of literary pace set this debut novel apart. . . . From its first page, the book pulls the reader in with the urgency of its plot . . . breakneck speed . . . harrowing . . . unsettling . . . powerful. . . . The ending is the kind that sticks in the reader's mind for days afterward— in other words, the best kind. It raises questions about guns, freedoms and the roots of America's increasingly violent society. Most of all, it raises questions about good and evil. . . . Mr. Winter's language is vivid and explicit. The images he describes are so real that the words alone are enough to make the reader shudder. . . . This is an edgy novel, full of powerful descriptions. However, far from glorifying violence, the book presents it in all its gritty ugliness. Every detail is there, including the ones guaranteed to make the reader squirm . . . a complete, utterly terrifying picture of a violent American subculture." —*The Washington Times*

"**Don't walk—RUN.** . . . If you're a fan of thrillers and you can read only one all year long, make it Douglas E. Winter's debut novel, RUN . . . a high-powered, blood-and-guts story . . . hip and street-smart. . . . It whines and threatens like a chain saw from the opening to the harrowing climactic shootout. . . . RUN is both entertaining and darkly disturbing. **They just don't get much better than this.**" —*Greensburg Tribune Review* (PA)

ALSO BY DOUGLAS E. WINTER

Prime Evil (editor)

RUN

DOUGLAS E. WINTER

AN ONYX BOOK

ONYX
Published by New American Library, a division of Penguin Putnam Inc.,
375 Hudson Street, New York, New York 10014, U.S.A.
Penguin Books Ltd, 27 Wrights Lane, London W8 5TZ, England
Penguin Books Australia Ltd, Ringwood, Victoria, Australia
Penguin Books Canada Ltd., 10 Alcorn Avenue, Toronto, Ontario, Canada M4V 3B2
Penguin Books (N.Z.) Ltd, 182–190 Wairau Road, Auckland 10, New Zealand

Penguin Books Ltd, Registered Offices:
Harmondsworth, Middlesex, England

Published by Onyx, an imprint of New American Library, a division of
Penguin Putnam Inc.
This is an authorized reprint of a hardcover edition published by Alfred A.
Knopf.
For information address Alfred A. Knopf, a division of Random House, Inc.,
299 Park Avenue, New York, New York 10171

First Onyx Printing, February 2001
10 9 8 7 6 5 4 3 2 1

Copyright © Douglas E. Winter, 2000
All rights reserved

Grateful acknowledgment is made to the following for permission to reprint
previously published material:

BMG Songs, Inc. and Universal-MCA Music Publishing, Inc.: Excerpt from "Cock
the Hammer" by Senen Reyes, Louis M. Freese, and Lawrence Muggerud.
Copyright © 1993 by Universal-MCA Music Publishing, Inc., a division of
Universal Studios, Inc. (ASCAP); BMG Songs, Inc. (ASCAP); and Cypress
Phuncky Music (ASCAP). All rights on behalf of Cypress Phuncky Music
administered by BMG Songs, Inc. International copyright secured. All rights
reserved. Used by permission.

Donovan (Music) Limited: Excerpt from "Hurdy Gurdy Man" by Donovan Leitch.
Copyright © 1968 by Donovan (Music) Limited.
Copyright renewed. Administered by Peer International Corporation.
International copyright secured. Used by permission.

 REGISTERED TRADEMARK—MARCA REGISTRADA

Printed in the United States of America

Without limiting the rights under copyright reserved above, no part of this
publication may be reproduced, stored in or introduced into a retrieval system,
or transmitted, in any form, or by any means (electronic, mechanical,
photocopying, recording, or otherwise), without the prior written permission of
both the copyright owner and the above publisher of this book.

PUBLISHER'S NOTE
This is a work of fiction. Names, characters, places, and incidents either are the
product of the author's imagination or are used fictitiously, and any resemblance
to actual persons, living or dead, business establishments, events, or locales is
entirely coincidental.

BOOKS ARE AVAILABLE AT QUANTITY DISCOUNTS WHEN USED TO PROMOTE PRODUCTS OR
SERVICES. FOR INFORMATION PLEASE WRITE TO PREMIUM MARKETING DIVISION, PENGUIN
PUTNAM INC., 375 HUDSON STREET, NEW YORK, NEW YORK 10014.

If you purchased this book without a cover you should be aware that this book is
stolen property. It was reported as "unsold and destroyed" to the publisher and
neither the author nor the publisher has received any payment for this "stripped
book."

A well-regulated Militia, being necessary to the security of a free State, the right of the people to keep and bear Arms, shall not be infringed.
—Second Amendment,
    Constitution of the United States

Cock the hammer it's time for action
—Cypress Hill

once upon a time in virginia

So we're shaking down this Dickie Mullen guy, and the guy's your usual suburban shoot-shop owner, talks the talk about home defense and hunting season, spreads out copies of *Guns & Ammo* and *Soldier of Fortune*, sells crappy .38s to concerned hubbies and housewives, and all the while he's dressed up in the red, the white, the blue, it's the grand old fucking flag. They're taking away our constitutional rights comes out of this Dickie Mullen guy's mouth about as often as those fine patriotic words We take VISA and MasterCard. This guy couldn't defend a house against cockroaches and he wouldn't know a ten-point buck from a heifer, and right about now he's talking his talk at the lee side of the counter, an overfed gnome with capped teeth and a lame smile, and I really don't want to be here but the numbers didn't add up for the third time in as many months, and this upsets Jules, and the shop's on my beat so this upsets me. But what upsets me more is that this Dickie Mullen guy is talking a Hefty Bag worth of trash about this and about that, he is talking about anything but the numbers and why the numbers didn't add up, and I wish he'd come out and say it. Just look up out of the lies and say:

Hey, all right, okay, I've been skimming here and scamming there, but I need the money, owe the money, got to have the money. I got a wife, I got kids, I got a mortgage, and a little from a lot don't matter, can't matter, just should not matter.

Then he ought to say, and say very loud:

And after all, you are reasonable men.

I look at Trey Costa, who's leaning into a hardwood trophy case at the back of the storeroom, right under the deer mounts and a rack of lever-action center-fires. Trey slips the sawed-off from under his raincoat, tips the barrel back over his shoulder, and starts cat-scratching its snout against the glass of the trophy case. Screech, screech, boom.

I look at Renny Two Hand, who just told this Dickie Mullen guy, owner and operator of Safari Guns in the Triland Mall in this bright little suburb of Dirty City, that there's no time for new lies. That's when Two Hand shoved the really meaningful part of that wicked Colt Python .357, a nasty handgun if I say so myself, to a spot two inches below the guy's belly button.

And while I'm taking the time to look, I check

out myself, courtesy of the mirror behind this Dickie Mullen guy's head: solemn-faced and empty-handed. I do not draw down unless I'm going to shoot, but if looks could kill, dear Safari Guns, with its wondrous selection of overpriced foreign product, Taiwanese knockoffs, and well-oiled calendar girls in camouflage and string bikinis, would be redecorated in red right now.

The look I'm giving this Dickie Mullen guy, the stone-cold thing that looks back at me from the mirror, takes years of practice. If you can fake the sincerity, you're halfway home. So when I try on the face, now and again, I do want to laugh. But today it's there on its own, and I'm not laughing, this is not a laughing matter. Because, after all, there should be no doubt:

We are reasonable men.

Which is why I hit the spineless fuck in the face.

His head snaps back and red spit leaks out from between those too-real teeth. On cue, Renny hoists his pistol from gut level and points it down on this Dickie Mullen guy's dome.

Now that we have his attention, it's time to talk.

Hey, pal, I tell him. I say this one time. So listen up and listen good.

Here's what I tell this Dickie Mullen guy.

I tell him:

You have the right to remain silent.

I tell him:

3

If you choose to speak, anything you say can be used against you in a court of law.

I tell him:

You have the right to talk to a lawyer before we ask you any questions.

I tell him:

You have the right to have a lawyer with you during questioning.

I tell him:

If you cannot afford a lawyer, one will be appointed for you before any questioning if you wish.

You have all these rights, I tell him. And, if some cop says so, maybe even a few more. But what you don't have, pal, is the right to fuck around with me.

That's when I hit him again. And then I nod, and then Renny cocks the hammer, and then I happen to believe that Dickie's little dickie just pissed his pants.

You got a nice business here, I tell him. And you ought to keep it that way. But hey, you've been selling off the books.

I look down into the display case of pistols and I cannot believe the crap this Dickie Mullen guy is peddling. Just like I cannot believe that Jules Berenger and I are selling it to him.

You want to keep out of trouble, pal. You don't need this shit. If the state cops or the ATF come sniffing round here, then my friend with the gun

4

comes sniffing round here, and sooner or later I have to come and pay you a visit. Not that I don't like a friendly chat now and then, but I'm about done with the talking. So you keep things in order, pal. You sell your stock over the counter and you send in those little forms to Treasury. You know why?

He hesitates, shakes his head: No.

I cannot believe this guy.

Because it's the law, dumb shit. It is the fucking law.

I pass him a handkerchief.

Now wipe your face off.

He looks at the hankie like it's an alien life form. Then he gets the idea and starts mopping down. First the split lip, then the forehead, then he starts on his pants. Guess he gets to keep this one.

You got a wife, right?

Yeah, he says, but when I give him the look he locks eyes with me and says it right: Yes.

You got kids?

Yes.

And a mortgage?

He looks at me funny but not for long. Then: Yes.

I point to the front door. So, I tell him. You don't open up today. You leave that CLOSED sign hanging there, and you take the rest of the day off and you go home. You tell them all—the wife, the kids, the mortgage—that you love them. And then tomorrow—well, tomorrow you come in here and you turn that sign over to OPEN, and, hey, it's like they say: Tomorrow is the first day of the rest of your life. You got me?

Yes, he says.

I fucking hope so, I tell him.

But worms like this one never learn. Never. Guy probably cheats on his tax returns, cheats on his wife, maybe even cheats on his poker buddies. Next time this happens, and sooner or later there's gonna be a next time, he's gonna skim a little bit less, he's gonna hide a little bit more, the guy's gonna think he's getting away with something, and you know what?

That's when I'm gonna have to kill him.

one a.m.

Renny Two Hand's in the hot seat, drinking Bud Light out of a bottle and snaking a new cigarette from the battered pack on the bar. Some achy-voiced rock-and-roller, a dead guy, is droning on and on and he's not even in tune with these dentist-drill guitars. Five one-dollar bills are tented on top of the bar, and Two Hand is looking point-blank into the dancer's snatch like there's no tomorrow.

You ever pray? he says.

For what? I ask him, and he just looks right through me and says:

You ever pray?

Shawnee, that's this dancer's name, ha-ha, she lets down that witchy-woman hair, and she works her way over to me, and she wants me. I know she wants me because she smiles, a little sly smile, and then the little wink as she strides on past, high heels clicking in time to the beat. So she wants me. Yeah, right. She wants me to lay a little more green on the bar, and when I do, I get some good old hippy-hippy-shake, and then it's walk on down the line to the next guy, and then the next and the next, still smiling, still winking, still shaking, still wanting. Sweet kid, probably studies psych or sociology at George Mason University and dates a fraternity boy when she isn't giving blow jobs in the alleyway out back.

I'm leaning my head toward Renny Two Hand, trying to imagine what he's really saying to me through a night's worth of cigarette smoke, drugstore aftershave, gutter rock guitar, and the cheap talk of the Dauphine Steak House, and that is when I hear the cough. It's a nasty cough, the kind of cough that sort of stands right up and says: I'm a Glock.

Sitting on my cozy stool, nodding away to the music from the band with the dead guy, minding my own business and a lot of the naked lady who's strutting her stuff atop the bar, trying to think real hard about Bud Light instead of tomorrow, and with that cough in my ear, I realize there's no escaping a simple fact:

Guns are my life.

So I grind out Renny's Chesterfield and take a spin on the bar stool and there's this damn fool backpedaling away from one of the tables out on the dance floor. His chair's tipped over, and he's pushing a Spandex-bursting waitress out of the way with one hand and waving a Glock 19 with the other. Asshole.

Not that I don't like the Glock 19. It's my weapon of choice. Right about now I'm carrying two of them: one out in the glove compartment of my Mustang, the other one tight to the flat of my back, snug in a Bianchi holster.

Nice construction on the Glock. It's the original polymer pistol; some folks, the dumb ones, thought you could walk it through airport security. The G19 is compact, weighs thirty ounces loaded with a fifteen-round magazine, and the trigger pulls as smooth as taffy. Maybe it's just the cough that bothers me. Hearing it when it's not my own. That annoys me. Like shooting one of the Beretta 80s, those little .22s that sort of spit when you squeeze them. Or the MAC-10: On full auto, sounds like a cat pissing.

I used to like my weapons loud. Let's face it, when the shit goes down, so deep that it's time to shoot—well then, you ought to make a statement. The old Springfield 1911A1, standard-issue Army .45, spoke up with a bull roar, scared the shit out of anybody, anything. Which was helpful, since it's a bitch for anyone but a pro to score hits with old Slab Sides from more than about twenty feet. But that four-five talks like it looks: big and mean. I keep mine in a footlocker, way up in the attic, with a pair of my old fatigues, a picture of my high school sweetheart—that bitch—and a map of the provinces. That's where it belongs: put to rest, another buried dream.

Don't even think about it, I tell myself, and then I say it aloud to Renny Two Hand, who's finally fallen out of the beer-and-babe fugue and noticed that something's going down. He looks from the asshole on the dance floor to me and then down to the cuff of his right pants leg, which no doubt hides a heavy something with a barrel and a trigger and, if I know Two Hand, a high-capacity magazine. I snag his jacket, ready to hustle our happy asses to the fire exit and out of this non-sense. Trouble is something you just never need.

So through the huddle comes this well-armed asshole from the outland, Manassas maybe, wear-ing torn jeans, standard-issue black Metallica T-shirt, a flannel overshirt, and about five too many beers. He shakes his sloppy blond head and slow-dances back into the jukebox. That band with the dead guy—now I remember, it's called Nirvana—starts singing in double time. Little wrestling around, then cue the scream. So the asshole's got a Glock. Full magazine, maybe, and he's shot one time. Could be lots of bodies rolled out of the place by Springfield EMS, but that one's beyond Vegas odds; no way he's serious. Drunks are rarely serious about anything but fighting or fuck-ing, and like most drunks this asshole isn't much capable of either.

By now the piece is pointed at the linoleum.

The first of the bouncers, a skull-shaven Marine probably moonlighting out of Quantico, makes his appearance, gives him the old okeydokey take-it-easy routine. Hands up, smile and a nod, smile and a nod, one step closer, one step more.

The jarhead gestures to the ceiling and when the asshole looks up—told you he was an asshole—the Marine whales him with what the boxing announcers like to call a solid right to the jaw. Down and out for the count. Stick a fork in him, this one's done.

I look over at the table where the commotion started and there's another spud there, another black T-shirt, another flannel shirt, another pair of jeans, and he's looking at his left thigh like it just sprouted an eye and winked at him. He's saying oh momma oh momma and wiping blood back and forth in his hands like it's grease.

I look at my watch, which reads nigh on one in the morning. Last call for blood and alcohol. A black-and-white ought to be wheeling around any minute now. So:

Th-th-that's all, folks.

Ren, I say, let's call it a night.

Yeah, he says. A night.

He pulls back the last of his Bud Light and shrugs himself up off the bar stool. It's hard to believe he can walk.

I drop a fiver on the bar for dearest Shawnee, she shakes her tits at me, and we're gone.

Sucking cold air on the blacktop parking lot, shaking out the smell of cigarettes, I'm taken with one of those *Twilight Zone* thoughts, and this time it's the idea that, while we were being entertained, the mighty suburb of Springfield, Virginia, slid into a deep black hole. Then I realize the power is out along Backlick Road and its rat maze of mini-malls. And how much I hate the dark.

I steer Renny toward the Mustang. A couple beers, that's all. The age-old promise, man-to-man. So we had a couple beers, did our business, traded the keys, and seven p.m. rolled into nine, and we had a couple beers again, and round about eleven the bottles and the dollar bills formed up ranks on the counter. A nice drunk, until the coughing fit.

I try to remind Renny about Thursday, about why we traded the keys, but he's giving me the Ren routine, hands waving out at nothing in particular, clearing the cobwebs, no doubt searching for the clever exit line. An unshaven and gimp-kneed Shakespearean. All the world's barrooms and parking lots are a stage.

Ah, the smell of blood after midnight, he finally tells me and the parking lot and the black, black sky and the red-and-blue lights of the police car whirlybirding down Franconia Road toward us. It's the smell of—

There isn't a pause; it's a gap. His face goes loose, and he takes a long look back at the

Dauphine Steak House like he's left his best friend, which is me, inside. The silence doesn't stop. I stand there until it's just too much.

The smell of . . . what? I ask him.

His face comes back at me, a full moon that shines on with nothingness. Then:

You drive, he tells me. He hooks his fingers into his belt, hoists his jeans, and wobbles on to the car.

That's my partner, Reynolds James—aka Renny, aka Two Hand, aka The Wrap—for you: Always starting something but never getting it done.

another morning
after

How did you sleep? Mom asks me.

Like a rock, I tell her. It's almost nine and I'm working my way through the kitchen cabinets, looking for the instant coffee and the Advil.

Any more of those dreams? Those nightmares?

Not this time, I say. It's a wonder what eight or ten bottles of Bud Light can do for your dreams. Sleep was a chalkboard, dusty and blank. The last thing I remember is dropping my pants on the floor and falling face first into the sheets. Though maybe I kissed Fiona.

Good night, I said. Maybe to Fiona, after the kiss. Definitely to Mom, by the time I get to the last cabinet.

You're drinking again. An observation, nothing too judgmental; no kind of tsk-tsk, oh my, please don't do that. Just a friendly reminder. But those reminders tend to get your back up.

Yeah, I tell her, in my head. You want to let that twitch of annoyance ride. You want to hold to the

14

truth of what people say, not to the reason they say it. Or something like that. I heard this on the radio.

I find the freeze-dried but not the Advil. I zap a mug of water in the microwave and stir in the coffee. Then I dry-swallow some Dexedrine.

Mom doesn't blink. She never does.

It's a pretty nice photograph, a snapshot taken by one of my cousins at some family reunion or wedding; maybe it was a funeral, I don't know. I never went to those things when Mom was alive, and I don't go to them now. Maybe I don't want to end up in a photograph on somebody's mantelpiece. A strange kind of shadow hooks down into her cheek, but still, it's nice. She's smiling, and I like that.

The newspaper says VIRGINIA HANDGUN LIMIT LOOKS UNSTOPPABLE. But that's page three. To get there, I've read about the new income tax increase, the new fuel tax increase, the new cigarette tax increase, the new prime interest rate increase, and the new dead bodies over in D.C., thirteen of them in this particular twenty-four-hour go-round. The Reverend Gideon Parks has called for a prayer vigil on the steps of the Lincoln Memorial, but the Mayor doesn't want prayers, he wants more cops. I've finished the first cup of coffee and started on the second by the time Fiona wanders in, dropping a pair of high heels to the floor and mounting up, all the while pulling a brush through that long and curly-kinky hair.

Hi, Mom, she says. Reminding me that it's not really normal to hold conversations with photographs.

Damn if she doesn't look nice this morning. Silk blouse. Those jeans have got her butt up and she's doing that thing with the eyeliner again.

Her name is Ellen. About everyone she knows calls her that, although on occasion one of her girlfriends will call her Elfie.

I call her Fiona. I don't know why. Maybe I just like the name.

She has mud-brown eyes and this little smile that says she knows your number. And she does. She looks good in anything, better without.

I got my period, she says.

What do you say to that? Sorry? Congratulations? I drink my coffee instead.

I said—

Heard you, I tell her.

She tosses the hairbrush down, sweeps her purse and car keys from the Formica counter, gives my forehead an aunt's kiss, and tells me not to forget the dishes and that we're short of milk. Then:

Bye.

It's Tuesday, the last week of April. Fiona works Mondays, Tuesdays, Thursdays, and Fridays at the Vachon Hair Salon in Rosslyn, right across the river from Georgetown. She does manicures, nail designs. Fridays she leaves work at noon and doesn't come home until Sunday, just in time for *60 Minutes*. I don't know what she does when she's away. She's never told me, and I've never asked. Things are easier that way.

I started to follow her one time. I don't know what got into me. Boredom, maybe, or one of those men things: property, territory, mine mine mine. I borrowed a company car, a beat-up station wagon that was less obvious than dirt, and tailed her silver CRX and its JAZZERCISE bumper sticker all the way up the GW Parkway to the Chain Bridge. Right about there I felt like one sorry jerk, and I turned the wagon toward Tysons Corner on Route 123. Drove out to Bloomingdale's and bought her some perfume, little ounce of Cartier Panthère that cost over a hundred bucks. Buying off shame does not come cheap.

I don't tell her my secrets, so why should she tell me hers? Things like that have to work both ways, or they don't work at all.

That Sunday night, while Morley Safer tried to speak wisely with some withered refugee from Afghanistan, I handed her the perfume and she told me that I shouldn't have done it and all that, but she smiled.

Fiona smiles a lot. She's the happiest person I know. Her voice is like whiskey, rough and smooth all at once. So are her kisses.

When I wake up in the night, sometimes she's holding on to me.

little games

You should know right now, if you haven't figured it out yet, that I'm not the good guy.

The name is Burdon: Burdon Lane. Born in St. Louis, Missouri, in Jewish Hospital, though it was the doctors, not the parents, who were Jewish. Grew up somewhere else—in southern Illinois—which pretty much sums up my childhood: It was there but now it's somewhere else. It was the fifties, so that makes me—what? Forty-going-on-old. Brown hair, blue eyes. Six feet and some tall, one hundred eighty pounds. Social Security Number? Yeah, I got one. Actually, I got more than one.

Here's my ad in the PERSONALS section: SWM, mid-40s, divorced, no kids, ISO guns. Big guns, little guns. Handguns, shotguns, rifles, machine guns, and, yeah, okay, grenade launchers and anti-tank weapons here and there along the way. Then again, here's my card: Burdon Lane. Executive Vice President. UniArms, Incorporated.

I'm a businessman, and tucked in the inside

chest pocket of my suit coat, the grey linen three-button off-the-rack job, is the reason I met with Renny Two Hand last night: a key, the kind of key you see on most everyone's key chain, the kind of key that fits the front door or the office door or the mailbox at the apartment.

This particular key fits into a padlock. The padlock hangs on the door of a self-storage rental unit on the third floor of Moving Vault on Eisenhower Avenue in Alexandria. Inside the rental unit is a stack of boxes whose contents, for the most part, are noted on the sides of the cartons in blue Magic Marker. Inside the third box from the bottom, marked DEHUMIDIFIER/BABY CLOTHES/CARRY-ON BAG, are a dehumidifier, baby clothes, and . . . a grey Samsonite carry-on bag.

On Thursday I will visit the storage unit and I will take a grey Samsonite carry-on bag with me. I will open the third cardboard box. I will put my carry-on bag, which is empty, inside the box and I will leave with the carry-on bag from the box. I will drive to the Huntington Metro Station and park in the open-air lot. I will board the Metro, ride the Yellow Line to Gallery Place, where I will change to the Red Line and ride on to Union Station. There I will board Amtrak Train 120, a Metroliner departing at 4:00 p.m., and I will have a cup of coffee and read my book for a couple hours until I reach 30th Street Station in Philadelphia. There I will disembark from the train and I will take a taxicab to a fine seafood restaurant called Bookbinder's, a very busy, hectic place on Walnut between Second and Front, where, still wearing my sunglasses, I will give my raincoat and my carry-on bag to the coat-check girl and I will receive a plastic chit in return, round, with a hole for a hanger and an identifying number embossed in gold. I will meet an old girlfriend of mine, a classified ad supervisor for the *Philadelphia Inquirer* named Lauren Auster, at the bar, and we will have drinks and we will tell stories, some old and some new, and we will laugh, and after a time we will move to a table and we will order shrimp cocktail and Caesar salad and the scrod, with mine blackened and hers grilled in light butter and dill, and at 7:15 p.m. I will put my napkin to my lips and I will announce the need to visit the men's room. There I will enter the second stall, waiting for my turn if I have to, and I will drop my pants and I will have a seat and I will do my business. I will open a package of Wrigley's Juicy Fruit gum and I will chew one piece until the flavor is gone. I will take the plastic chit from my pocket and I will take the gum from my mouth and I will press the gum to the chit and then stick the chit to the wall behind the toilet. I will roll off some paper, dry my hands, flush the toilet, and buckle up. I will walk back to my table, finish the scrod, have a Martell Cordon Bleu, have a cup of coffee, and when the tab arrives I will pay with cash and leave a decent tip, and before eight I will leave with my arm around Lauren and she will finish telling me about her latest boyfriend and we will share a kiss and a hug and then we will find our separate ways home. Which means that I will take a taxicab back to 30th Street Station and catch Amtrak Train 127, the last southbound Metroliner of the day, which departs at 8:14 p.m.

While I ride the rails back to Washington, reading my book, another diner will pay his tab at Bookbinder's and as he leaves he will present his chit to the coat-check girl and he will recover his raincoat and his grey Samsonite carry-on bag, and later, when he finds himself at home, he will open the bag. Inside the bag will be a large swatch of chamois, folded neatly into a bundle and secured by string. Inside the chamois will be a pair of new, nicely customized machine pistols, Heckler & Koch MP-5Ks with clean serial numbers, which he will use or he will sell or he will give away or he will mount proudly upon the wall of his den or his office. I don't much care because we've already been paid.

Yeah, I'm a businessman. That's what Jules Berenger told me, those twelve, thirteen, however many years ago when we sat down to breakfast at the Huddle House on Little River Turnpike and had our long chat over orange juice, pancakes, eggs over easy, and lots of black coffee, before I shook hands with him and signed on, before I became one of the boys. A gunrunner.

Now that wasn't the job description or the title. Actually I became a marketing representative for VisionWorks, an up-and-coming computer software firm. A few years later I became a senior marketing representative for BioInsights, an up-and-coming medical research facility. Then I became a marketing manager for Line One, an up-and-coming telephone services reseller. Jules owns all these companies, or at least a piece of them, and their clients require a great deal of marketing effort and thus a lot of travel, in-country and out.

Sooner or later, like any upwardly mobile young urban professional who knows his job and gets it done, I became a senior marketing manager for the real deal, UniArms of Alexandria, Virginia—the small arms capital of the free world. I never once looked back, and why should I?

I'm living the American Dream: Nice house, nice lawn, nice car; there's no wife, no kids, but what the hell, there's Fiona. I'm drawing down a hundred thousand on the books, with payroll stubs and W-2 forms to prove it. Pay my taxes, too, fucking twenty-eight percent a year and growing with each new smiling Democrat that they put in the White House. Then the state takes . . . what? Five and three-quarters. The city gets half a point, too, not to mention the real estate tax and the personal property tax and now this goddamn recycling tax. Then there's the sales tax. Once you pay the monthly hit for your mortgage, your car loan, your phone bill, electricity, gas, water, insurance, cable TV, and then the credit cards, what have you got? Nothing. Everybody owns a piece of you: the bank, MasterCard and VISA, and most of all the politicians.

Like I said, it's the American Dream.

So I'm a businessman. I buy and sell commodities on the open market, not to mention the occasional closed one. That those commodities have calibers or gauges and muzzle velocities doesn't mean much to the business. Pickups and deliveries can, on occasion, be a bitch. Suppliers, the good ones, the smart ones, do business. They can't afford to screw around. Customers are another story.

Here's how it works:

People need guns. But people can't get guns. At least not all the people, not all the time. Which seems a bit strange, since there is one firearm out there for every man, woman, and child in America.

So let's say you want to buy an AMT Hardballer, a cheap .45 with crappy metallurgy that kicks like a bitch; I'd recommend the long slide auto for better accuracy, probably cost you only twenty-five dollars more. But you have to be able to buy the Hardballer first.

If you live in New York City, forget about it. You can't own a handgun. That's the law. You need a permit, and unless you have big money or big balls, forget even filing an application. But if you live in, let's say, Texas City, well, you can grab hold of one of those babies and snap in the seven-round magazine on the very same day if you want.

Maybe. You do have to fill out this sheet that the Feds call Form 4473, and let them run a background check. And unless you choose to lie, an offense punishable by several years of incarceration, you will have to tell about that arrest and that conviction and that mental problem. Unless you choose to lie.

So here you are, deprived of a necessity of life by the law, the law, the law; here a law, there a law, everywhere a law-law.

Let me try to explain this thing.

These Founding Father guys, Washington, Jefferson, Franklin, whoever, the guys on the dollar bills, they kick the British guys out and they start themselves a new government. Their own government. So what's the first thing they do? They make up rules. The Constitution, for starters. That's a good one: All men are created equal, right? Bullshit then, bullshit now. These guys owned slaves, their women didn't vote, so who were they kidding? Well, nobody. But since they were the guys who wrote the rules, they wrote them just the way they wanted.

So then somebody says: Hey, we fucked up. Wrote this Constitution thing but we forgot a bunch of stuff. We need to write these Amendments to sort of list the stuff we left out. So now there's another set of rules, this thing they call the Bill of Rights, and there in big print is the Second Amendment. Not the first, not the last, and not even in the middle, but second, number two, meaning it's almost at the top of the list. Which is to say, it's important.

This Second Amendment thing says you've got the right to bear arms. Looks clear as window glass to me. But the First Amendment, the one at the very top of that list, says you've got the freedom of speech. Tell that to the teacher who wants to read the Bible in class. Tell that to the video store that wants to rent you some X-rated movies. Tell that to my Aunt Eustacia. She wanted to put this sign that said PRAY FOR PEACE in her front yard during the Gulf War, and the city made her take it down.

In other words, these Founding Father guys, they wrote this Bill of Rights, but they didn't really mean what they said. They just said these things because they sounded like good ideas at the time, but once these guys died, and the next guys were in, the ones who didn't write the rules but sure wished they had—well, they got busy rewriting those rules.

So they tell us that the Founding Father guys didn't really mean we've got the right to bear arms, and they sure didn't mean we've got the right to *buy* arms. What we've got is the right to have some sorry-ass politicians tell us whether we can bear arms, and when and where and what kind of arms we can bear, if we can fill out the right forms and wait long enough. Somebody ought to sit down and rewrite that Amendment to make all that clear.

Meantime, if you want to bear arms, fuck the law: You just need cash. Not a lot. If you've got some green, then there's always somebody like me, somebody who knows somebody else, and they can get you whatever you want. You want a gun—and not just any gun, let's say a clean gun with clean ammo—I can get you one inside an hour. Or take Charlie Hardin out of Roanoke. You want a more exotic weapon, the guy can get it for you, seven-day turnaround max. The weirder the better: One time Charlie pulled a Belgian .223 Minimi belt-fed light squad auto machine gun for me, and it was like going to the catalog counter at Sears. Saw him on a Friday, paid one half down in cash, picked that baby up on Monday. Sold it that night for a two hundred percent markup.

Like I said, it's the American Dream.

stay the same

Ch-ch-ch-changes.

On Wednesday I'm standing in the 7-Eleven, trying to decide between Snapple Mint Tea and a Bud Light, when my pager beeps. Good timing. It's ten-thirty in the morning and I really don't need a drink, not yet. So I go for the Snapple and check the number on the pager while I'm waiting in line to pay.

Bingo.

Sometimes—not often, but every once in a while, before the memory of the last one has faded entirely—the pager gets you at the perfect moment, the one that reminds you that maybe, just maybe, you're working for Domino's Pizza and you're about the best-paid delivery boy on the block.

I trade two bucks for the Snapple, give the change to Jerry's Kids, and wander out front to the pay phone—only a fool would use a cellular for business—and I look over at the dry cleaner that's next to the 7-Eleven while I make the call, not to the number that's showing on the pager, but to this week's number, probably another pay phone, probably in some other parking lot of some other 7-Eleven just down the way from some other dry cleaner, and on the second ring somebody picks up and says:

Hey.

Yeah, I tell him.

Need you, baby.

Somewhere between the *need* and the *you*, I know it's CK; that little nasal twang seeps on through no matter what he has to say. And what CK has to say next is:

Lunch.

Okay, I tell him.

Twelve-thirty.

Yeah, I tell him.

The usual place.

Shit, I tell him.

Click.

Click.

So there goes the afternoon, probably the evening, and maybe even the rest of the week; but what the hell: To make it in this business, you've got to like change. Only dead things stay the same.

The rules to this game are simple: They're our rules. We make them up as we go, and if we don't, somebody else is going to make them up for us.

Sort of like that Constitution thing. And since I like to play by my own set of rules, I like to make them and, every once in a while, to break them.

I drop down Quaker Lane to the Interstate and head south. There's more than an hour to kill and I may as well kill it in style. Today I'm driving the metallic-blue Corsica, about the most forgettable car on the road, and when I find a parking space at the strip mall off Little River Turnpike, I settle in behind the wheel and read my book. Every so often, I lamp the entrance to the Greek Gourmet, which Lukas, the loser who's supposed to be bird-dogging this place, swears to Sunday is on the up-and-up, but Lukas has a bit too much religion. Me, I've never been a believer.

I watch the earnest black couple in front of the CVS Pharmacy, hawking peace and love for the Reverend Gideon Parks, even though everyone ignores them. I watch the bottle-blond gamine who's wearing a dress that fits like a T-shirt and a smile that isn't quite right, leaning into the line of shopping carts at Food Giant. But mostly I watch the Greek Gourmet: Four booths, eight tables, looks like they could sit maybe forty people for a full house, but this place hasn't seen a full house, maybe even half a house, for years.

I spend thirty minutes in front, then I drive around back, find another spot in the shade, and sit for a while and watch the delivery trucks un-load and load. I've got a pair of Nikon binoculars that will let you count the hairs on a ferret's butt, but this excursion doesn't call for much in the way of eyesight. They're moving guns.

Time flies whether you're having fun or not, and soon the great disappearing Corsica winds its way out of the parking lot and back to the Interstate and I'm off for lunch with CK at the usual place. I call Lauren in Philadelphia on the car phone, get her machine, and tell her I'm doubtful for dinner on Thursday, maybe next month, good luck with what's-his-name; and then I call home and leave one of those helpless messages for Fiona:

I don't know, maybe, can't say. Call you later. Maybe.

Then it's time for lunch at the usual place, and sooner or later I'm caught in the corner of a booth at the Red Lobster on Van Dorn, Renny Two Hand on my left, Mackie the Lackey on my right, and I'm listening to CK tell the one about Hillary Clinton's prostate for about the twelfth time and I sure could use a drink. Instead, I ponder the catch of the day or the popcorn shrimp and I decide maybe I should just have the soup and salad and I order clam chowder, Manhattan, which I remember is the red kind because Manhattan means blood, and I can't believe that CK is actually going to have the Shrimp Lover's Feast again.

Like all good sociopaths, CK does things his way, and his way, which is always the same way, includes not talking business until the food has arrived, and the food is the entree, not the drinks, not the bread, not the soup, not the salad. So I suck on an iced tea and listen to a few more old, bad jokes and then Mackie tries to tell us something about this new Tom Hanks movie and sooner or later we get the bread.

Sometimes I try to sit outside this thing. Sometimes in restaurants, or at gas stations, hotel lobbies, I watch the other people, watch them watching us, and I wonder what they think about what they see. Right now two women sit at the table next to us, just five, six feet away, but the noise level is high enough to allow us to discuss their private parts and, even if they were trying to listen, they wouldn't have a clue.

This gun thing isn't like selling cars, all flash and cash; this is about being grey, about hiding in sunlight. I do this thing well. It's not a trick, it's a skill. You have to be plain. Everything about you has to be plain. You shave, you shower, you brush your teeth every day. You wear just a little cologne, and it's not too cheap but it's not expensive, and you wear white shirts with your dark suits, but they're not too dark or you'll look like a lawyer and you can always spot the lawyers, or the people who want to look like lawyers, from a mile away. You want to wear ties, cheap ties, dark cheap ties, and you want to wear a nice Timex with a leather band. You want to wear black shoes that you shine, just barely, about once every three weeks. You want to drive Chevys and Fords. You listen to AM radio, you watch a lot of football and baseball, you eat at McDonald's and Hardee's and Red fucking Lobster, and you rent the top ten videos at Blockbuster. And somewhere along the way, you might get invisible. Though it helps if you're like me:

Born that way.

These women at the next table, thirtywhatever and showing it, should be taking it easy on the french fries, but they're nicely dressed in a JCPenney kind of way. So they're secretaries, right? It's a reasonable guess. Too well dressed, and a little heavy on the makeup, for a friendly get-together, not dressed well enough for the white-collar world. That one of them has a WordPerfect handbook doesn't hurt, but then again, Mackie over there has a nice fat Day-Timer on the table next to him, and he has a white button-down shirt and a suit that's just that right notch above cheap. You can tell by the look of him that he sells insurance, that he worries about those homeowner policies and replacement values and flood exclusion clauses. Just one look, it's all you need. You look at this guy, and you sure wouldn't guess that he's just spent a month in southeast Missouri, moving enough M-16s to arm a battalion of Aryan patriots. Some kind of insurance he's selling.

So: Who knows about those secretaries? Could

be store managers, building inspectors. Lovers. Terrorists. Cops. But not today; today they are secretaries, and when these secretaries turn their not-so-pretty little heads in this direction, we are four men in white shirts and plain ties and plain suits who converse in plain tones.

We are insurance salesmen out for lunch, and since the Shrimp Lover's Feast at long last has arrived, here is what the one of us at the head of the table, the one named Kruikshank, the one we call CK, has to say about the benefits of term versus whole life:

This weekend we have a run. A major delivery, the proverbial wagonload, and what's inside the crates don't really matter. It's top-notch iron and it's very profitable. We take the product north, do a double drop, a wait-and-switch: the goods handed off at one spot, the paper at another. Nothing to it.

So what's the wrinkle? I ask him.

CK stabs at his shrimp. Chews awhile.

New clients. Some niggers. Gangbangers out of the Ville or some other hellhole in NYC. Call themselves the 9 Bravos. Money's good, though, real good. And Sal Maggio gives his word on them, so hey.

Yeah, I tell him. So hey.

CK stabs at another shrimp. Chews. Swallows. Then:

Still, better safe than sorry. So Jules wants a

larger unit and some backup. Which is why—and this is where CK stabs his fork at me instead of the shrimp—Jules wants you along for the ride.

Then, in one of those stutter-step afterthoughts that can only be a putdown, he turns to Renny Two Hand and says: You too.

There's a long silence while CK finishes off his plateload of shrimp, then the baked potato, and then takes a big swallow of coffee. It's over.

This one's mine, he says. Now we got to go see Jules.

So CK actually picks up the tab. A miracle. He hands the waiter a fifty and says, Keep it, kid. And do you and me a favor and get yourself a haircut.

When we're in the lobby, lots of folks still waiting for tables, I pull CK over to this big fish tank full of murky water and lobsters, and I say the obvious:

This is a milk run.

Yeah, he says, parking a toothpick in the corner of his mouth.

You could do this thing in your sleep.

Yeah, he says.

You don't need me, and you sure as hell don't need Two Hand. You need four, maybe five of your own guys. Mackie, Toons, Fryer. What about Dawkins?

Yeah, he says.

So is it so much to ask? I mean, am I missing something or what?

Yeah, he says. Oh, yeah. You're missing something, all right.

Hey, I say to him, and when I put my hand on his shoulder CK gives it a funny stare. You're blowing sunshine up my ass, I tell him. How about a clue, maybe? Why do you want me?

I don't want you, CK says. And I sure don't need you.

He snaps the toothpick and manages to spit it out while giving me a grin.

I don't like that grin, and I don't like the laugh that follows. I'm about to tell him what I don't like when Mackie the Lackey turns toward us and says:

Shit.

Past Mackie the crowd seems unsettled, something, someone, pushing his way through them. Then Mackie says:

It's Doby.

The guy's waltzing into the lobby, heading for a table maybe, who knows. You don't need rear-end collisions, you don't need telegrams telling you about your dead grandmother, and you sure as hell don't need this Doby Mathers guy.

So: Shit is right. I'm wondering about turning around and looking for the back way out. But Doby is so looned, coke probably, that he could be nothing but for real. It's fate, an accident. Still, my right hand is in my coat pocket, and so's my Glock.

Hey, man, he calls to CK, and he gets silence and he looks my way. Say hey, Ray.

Stoned fuck can't even remember my name. Still:

Hey, Doby, I tell him. How's it hanging?

Yokay, Ray. Fine as wine.

CK eyes the lunch crowd and he knows, like I know, that nobody in the lobby, waiting for their name to be called, waiting for a table at the Red Lobster, for Christ's sake, could care less. The guy's weak. He's so weak he can't break wind. CK nods and I give Doby the buck-fifty smile.

Got to go, Dobe.

Cool. He's not moving, and he's standing in my way.

I say, a little louder: Got to go, Dobe.

He's staring right through me, the words burrowing in from his ears to the brain. Must've been taking hits of the white daddy since breakfast. Then: Plink! The light goes on.

Oh, man. Yeah, that's right, Ray. You got to go.

I shrug my way past him and head for the door. But this guy ain't quitting. He's onto CK now.

You don't come round no more, CK. Why don't you come round no more?

CK elbows by him, but the guy won't let it go.

Hey, CK, he says. Hey, man. You don't come round. You got something for me or not?

CK turns on him, jabs a finger into his chest: Get away from me.

Take it easy, man. Doby gives him the palms up. You in some kinda hurry? We oughta talk. Do some business. Have some fun.

And then he says something obscene: Mikey.

He says: Hey, CK. You guys. You know what? You oughta come on down to the lake sometime. No business like show business. Take you to see some of my girls. And hey, man, bring Mikey down too. Whatever happened to that guy? Good guy, real good guy. Bring Mikey down and we'll—

That's when CK takes him through the men's room door. He just hoists the guy by the lapels of his jacket and walks him backward through the door.

Stand by, I say to Mackie and Two Hand, and then I'm in there after them.

Some guy's zipping it up at the pisser and I tell him: Hey, excuse us, our buddy's sick, must have been the crab cakes, and the guy's out the door. By then CK has Doby against the far wall and he measures him with a hard left, kidney punch, doubling him over. He follows with a knee to the gut and I hear this sound like a baby rattle.

Two minutes, I say to CK. Two minutes and then we're out of here.

You don't say nothing about Mikey, CK's saying, like I'm not there, and maybe I'm not. I lean into the door, holding it closed. You hear me, Teflon nose? You hear me, you little fuck?

CK can't quite let him go or he'll fall to the floor. I wonder whether the punk is going to start bawling like a baby. His lips are moving, but there aren't words, aren't even sounds, just this kind of weird windup to a whine.

After a couple more punches the guy starts to vomit and that's when CK lets go, dropping him like a sack of garbage onto the floor. As I shove the door open, heading out, I hear CK tell him these true words of wisdom:

You don't never say nothing about Mikey.

history is of ages past

I didn't do Mikey, but I watched. Good thing, too, because for every night I wake up with nothing in my head but an ache for a straight shot of whiskey and that look in his eyes, I tell myself this is something I need to remember, something I don't ever want to forget.

One time Mikey called me on the phone and said, You want to talk about Jesus? I told him no, but he said, You need to talk about Jesus. I asked him why, and he said, If you have to ask why, then you have to talk about Jesus.

So I said: Okay, Mikey, let's talk about Jesus.

And he said: All right. Yeah. Well, see, I need to know what happens when you die.

Mikey had a wife. Sharon was her name, washed-out redhead with a lot of Irish, liked to wear those dangly earrings. Two kids, too. A boy, Kevin, I think, and this little girl, cute kid. They usually are cute. Then they grow up. Wonder what happened to them.

Mikey worked out of Wilmington, North Carolina, where Jules had a couple auto supply stores, turned a fair profit as I recall. His business card probably read Manager, but what he was managing was the trade out of Camp Lejeune, like this Marine captain with some kind of bad habit and a need to trade ordnance for cash. Risky business, but Mikey could play the angles, and for a time we had some prime goods for yahoo prices, buy low sell high, not just M-16s and M-60 machine guns but some M-203 grenade launchers, plus the grenades to launch.

We don't do much retail, not anymore. Too hairy and too, too dirty. But back then, back when I was coming up, there was never a problem. Even selling on the streets: We'd buy low in Virginia and South Carolina, stuff like those cheapshit Davis pistols or some Third World knockoffs, and we'd sell high, maybe four or five times high, in the inner city. The wise guys were still on top, and whatever else you want to say about them, they kept things clean. You had omertà: the code of honor, the code of silence, whatever. You didn't rat on anyone; you didn't fuck up deals. You played by the rules. You had honor. You did business.

Or someone dug you a ditch.

But that was in the days of the Five Families, before the Cubans and the Jamaicans and the Triads and those fucking Colombians. And then the gangs. Before cocaine became crack. Before things got too gun-crazy and the streets were running red.

Nowadays you just watch your back. But when your insides start turning you out, when you can't trust the guys on your own side of the table, the guys you run with—well, you have to do more than watch.

Somebody was watching Mikey. Somebody didn't like what they saw. Mikey was dirty, probably dirty from the get-go, but hell, no one is hand-picked in this business; it's not the few, the proud, all that bullshit. You want clean hands, clear heads, but like good guns these are scarce commodities. You need stand-up guys, real soldiers, and sometimes you never know. You just never know until it happens.

Take Kruikshank. They call him CK. Two letters, and can you guess what they mean? Clark Kent? Calvin Klein? Captain Kidd? Chung King?

No, no, no, and no.

Word is that the initials stand for Cop Killer. CK doesn't talk about it, won't say a word. Unless he's asked. Then he tells you he won't tell you.

I call him Cuke. He likes that.

Cool, he says. Cool as a cuke.

Now CK is your average certifiable hardcase, the kind of thing you get when you breed a Force Recon NCO with a pit bull terrier. Lives alone in a high-rise apartment, living room, two bedrooms, kitchen, and not one damn piece of furniture, unless you count the television set and I don't. Puts Led Zeppelin posters and pictures of porno stars on the walls. Sleeps on a futon, eats brown rice and Snickers bars. Believes in God and phone sex. Runs seven miles every day but Sunday. He's got three suits, and they're identical, he bought them at the same place, at the same time, these sort of grey plaid nothings.

CK carries a Smith & Wesson Model 29—the Dirty Harry gun, .44 Magnum, chamfered cylinder, full lugged barrel, drilled and tapped for scope mount, with a nine-inch snout that's pure show, the blue steel penis and all that. But like they say in those ads on TV about the knives that cut through beer cans: Wait, there's more. CK names his sidearms. Like they're dogs or kids. So the .44 Magnum is Elvis, and he's got a pair of Browning Hi-Powers called Siegfried and Roy.

One time, waiting out a straw-man scam in Atlanta, this geezer named Smitty told me that the whole CK thing was bullshit. That CK had never squeezed down on anybody, except maybe in his dreams. No way he ever killed a cop.

Have a care, sonny, Smitty told me. He's a talkin dude, not a walkin one.

Of course Smitty was his own piece of work, the kind of guy who would lie just to get away with it. And he didn't see CK that day in Norfolk.

The day that Mikey died. Not right after Mackie the Lackey says to CK:

What time you got?

Same time I had when you asked me ten minutes ago, CK says to Mackie. Plus ten minutes.

Mackie looks up out of picking lint from his crotch and says:

CK, explain this thing to me one more time. You know, about this grand jury thing and about who's been talking to who and why this little a-hole Mikey should shut the fuck up.

And of course there is an explanation but I don't need to hear those words again, because in the end, it's not really what Mikey did that matters. It's the simple fact that it was done. The guy had a job and he was supposed to do it. End of story. I don't want to hear that it was busting his balls or the old familiar refrain about being low on cash. The guy had a job, and the job had some rules. So he had to play by those rules. Which means you don't talk, you don't ever talk, to the cops. I mean, if we don't live by the rules, then we're animals.

So we're sitting there waiting for Mikey, and that's when the radio, one of those oldies stations, the radio starts playing this song, the one the guy sings through his nose about the Hurdy Gurdy Man, and CK reaches over and spins the dial up so the song is playing loud enough to sizzle the little plastic speaker.

Hurdy gurdy he sang, and CK's actually trying to sing along and it's a good thing the volume's topped out because I do not want to hear him sing.

Faggot music, Mackie says, but CK just keeps going.

I said—

Heard you, CK tells Mackie. He rolls down the sound a little and he stares over at me and he says:

You know who's playing lead guitar?

I say: What?

And he says: Do you know who played lead guitar on this song?

I say: No, who played the lead guitar? Which right about now is growling down, real fuzzy, and starting to make me think we're going someplace I don't want to go.

CK drops his boots from the table and looks at me like he's won the lottery.

Jimmy Page, he says.

I decide it's best to look suitably impressed. Huh, I say.

But Mackie leans in. Who the fuck is Jimmy Page?

I don't believe you, CK says. I don't fucking believe you.

Then CK turns right back to me and says, So?

And I say, So?

Which is a mistake, because then he says:

All right, so do you know who's playing drums? On this song? Who put sticks right onto the pads on this song?

CK, I tell him, you got me, you know? This time you really got me, man, because I don't know who played the lead guitar and I don't know the guy who's singing and I sure as hell don't know who's playing the drums.

The airy-fairy guy's singing something about the Roly Poly Man now.

And I tell CK: Okay, was it like Ringo Starr or what?

CK moves his lips nice and slow, like he's the teacher and I'm the retard, and he says: John Bonham.

Mackie burps out the kind of mad laugh at CK that only a guy's partner can make and stay standing. Me, I have to walk the line.

Roly poly roly poly roly poly he sang.

So I say: Uh, CK, help me out with this one, okay? Like, who is John Bonham?

You guys. That's all he says, shaking his head and closing his eyes. You fucking guys. His hand rubs at his temple, *hurdy gurdy he sang,* and sooner or later the song ends, and CK reaches over and spins down the volume on a Pepsi commercial all the way to off.

How many times you heard that song?

CK—

I start to tell him something, but Mackie says: Too many.

Fuck you, man, CK says to Mackie, and then to me: Fuck you too. You just don't get nothing, do you? That song is poetry, man. You know what poetry is? That's these pretty words that mean something. Poetry, man. And not just this I-love-you, will-you-love-me bullshit. The guy is telling us something. The song means something. Poetry.

He pulls the shotgun, a Remington Combat 870, up from its case and sweeps the radio, the filthy ashtray, and a folded newspaper from the tabletop like bread crumbs. His left hand dumps double-ought buckshot shells across the chipped wood surface.

Don't you get it? Don't you ever get it?

He shovels one of the shells into the shotgun and grabs for another one.

The song is about death, he says.

Then he pumps the shotgun, chambers the first shell.

This is when Mikey walks into the room. Or maybe I like to remember it that way. We could have waited twenty minutes more, for all I really know, but that's what I remember: those words, CK loading that shotgun, and then Mikey walking into the room.

Mikey is wearing a suit and a tie. Mikey is carrying one of those dull silver briefcases, the Haliburton hard-shell drug-dealer thing, and he looks

at CK and he looks at Mackie and he looks at me
and he says:

Hey.

That's what else I remember. He said: Hey.

To which he got the greetings all around.

Hey.

Hello, Michael.

Mikey, good to see you.

The last is CK, and right about now I'm almost
convinced that Mikey is going to sit in the folding
chair on the far side of the table and he is going to
open his suitcase and he and CK are going to do
their deal.

Mikey even reaches for CK's hand and the two
of them have a kind of shake across the table, as if
the shotgun isn't there for all to see.

Whatcha got? CK says. Which for some reason
Mikey doesn't like, since he sort of glances at the
Haliburton and yakety-yak goes that smoke alarm
in my head. I know then that whatever he's got is
loaded.

I got what it takes, he says.

Mikey, CK says. His knuckles rap the table,
once. Mr. Berenger wants me to thank you for the
Chapel Hill thing.

Mikey leans back in his chair, takes a look
around at Mackie, me, the rest of the room.

No problem, he says. And he angles forward,
hands out, fingers flipping at the latches of the
briefcase. Just doing my job. Like now—

And I don't know who draws first, Mackie or me, but we're both out of our seats and pointing our pistols down on the guy.

Don't you fucking dare, CK shouts. His hand's on my forearm, no way I can shoot unless it's now. Put down that piece, Mackie. Don't you dare. Don't you even think that you could dare.

CK pushes me away.

You got some talking to do, don't you, Mikey? You got something to say? Am I right? Tell me I'm right. I like to be right. I get angry when I'm not right.

CK bends down and he's almost close enough to kiss Mikey but his front teeth are cutting into his lower lip so that it's white.

Say it, Mikey. Whatever you been saying to the Feds, say it to me. But Mikey just tries to stand, loses his balance, trips on the chair, and falls.

CK slowly shakes his head no. He raises the shotgun from the table and pumps, ejecting the shells one after another, and they spill across the floor with a sound like little muffled bells. Mikey is stumbling away from the table, the overturned chair, and CK is walking toward him and he's taking his time and the shotgun seems to glow in the sunshine and his shadow is streaking across the brick walls and I wonder whether I want to see this. CK jabs the shotgun barrel into Mikey, into his chest, into his stomach, and he tells him: Say it. Say it. Until he's slapping at Mikey's face with the barrel and Mikey starts to cry and CK tells him: Say it. Finally CK slams the barrel into his face, and an arc of blood flies into the wall, wet paint, and then Mikey is down on the floor and CK is standing over him and he tells him: Say it.

I see Mikey start to say something and CK is shaking his head as if he's saying no and then he's bending down toward him, dropping the shotgun to the floor and taking something from his pants pocket, and Mikey just watches as CK cuts him once, then again, and when CK flicks the screwdriver past his face, Mikey doesn't blink, doesn't move, and now the furniture slams and Mackie is walking around the table, across the room, and when he gets there CK shows him the screwdriver, and Mikey is bleeding on his arms and hands and a little on his neck and CK says nothing. Nothing but: Say it.

He stabs the screwdriver into Mikey's stomach and the sound is soft and wet, and there's this push of breath and there isn't much blood at all, so CK slides the screwdriver into Mikey's stomach again, then into his shoulder, and this time Mikey shudders and his back bunches up and he seems to moan and the blood bubbles and then he says: Oh.

Mikey rolls onto his stomach and I think he's starting to die, just a little, and he looks around the room but there's nothing there, an overturned waste can and crumpled papers and burned-out stubs of cigarettes, the scattered wreck of the radio, and blood. Mikey's blood.

They kick him for a while and then he starts to crawl and the blood smears beneath him, and I look at CK and I look at Mackie and I look at Mikey and Mikey is trying to say something through his ruined teeth.

Her, he's saying. No, that's not it. He's saying something else. He's saying: Hurt.

Somewhere along the way, his briefcase got knocked to the floor, his briefcase got kicked open, and I decide to look inside and there's nothing there, no gun, no money, nothing at all but a picture of Mikey and his wife and his kids.

That's when I decide to say no, to tell CK to stop, but the word won't come, the word can't be said, and since I can't say no, I look out the window for a while, watch the sunlight sitting on the grass, and when I turn back around CK is putting his boot to the back of Mikey's head and it presses once, twice, and Mikey's bloody lips widen into a kiss, a full-mouth kiss on the concrete floor, and then CK stomps downward and the sound is like nothing I have ever heard.

The sound is on the radio. I'm listening to the radio and it echoes inside the room and it plays song after song after song and all of them are the same, and Mikey is singing along.

CK wipes off the screwdriver and looks at Mikey. Mackie smokes his cigarette and looks at

Mikey. Me, I'm just looking at Mikey, and when CK sticks the screwdriver into Mikey's ear, there's this scream, a scream that goes on and on and it won't stop, it's like a song, it is a song, the words are loud and the words are clear:

Hurdy gurdy hurdy gurdy hurdy gurdy gurdy he sang.

mr. ex

In the sad old bad old days, and I'm talking about the sixties and the seventies, there weren't any real players in the weapons game: just the good guys and the bad guys. Meaning the Americans and the Russians. Coming in a distant third, hard to believe but it's true, was Mexico, doing its best to suck up to Uncle Sam while keeping those taco-country dictators and revolutionaries alive. Then there were the European wanna-bes, the Germans and the Austrians and the Italians and the fucking French, who would sell munitions to an invading army just east of the Seine if it meant cold cash.

Now we all know that the U S of A doesn't peddle armaments, not our government, no way, just like we all know there's no such thing as cancer. In the Reagan years, we were shipping maybe $100 billion in weaponry a year. Overseas. To our friends. Like Iran and Iraq. For a while there, Interarms, based right across the Potomac River from Our Nation's Capital, snug in a complex of waterfront warehouses in Old Town Alexandria, was the arms dealer for the so-called Free World. They had something like 700,000 shoulder weapons and sidearms in storage, right there in Old Town, and banked annual sales in tens, maybe even hundreds, of millions of dollars. Interarms sold you the guns that Interarms wanted to sell you, which meant that Interarms sold you the guns that the CIA and the State Department wanted them to sell you. But once the Israelis and the Brazilians and, hell, probably even the Polynesians got involved, it was everybody's ball game. The guns were there, the money was there, and all you needed were the people in the middle, the ones who could get the guns for the money, trade the money for the guns.

Enter the Adnan Khashoggis of the world, cutting deals for a hundred helicopters here, fifty jump jets there, assault rifles and machine pistols in the gazillions. Somebody's always got a revolution brewing, a war going on . . . or they're getting ready for one. Talk about a growth industry. This arms thing is even better than drugs.

And where there's a big time, there's always a small time, always somebody who can fill in those little cracks in the apocalyptic pavement. When Gerald Bull is peddling his supergun to the Iraqis, and BNL Atlanta is helping the American taxpayers foot the bill, well, hey, who's really going to care about a backwater sale of a few LAWs to the IRA?

Enter Jules Berenger. That's Mr. Berenger to you. And:

Enter UniArms, Incorporated. My employer. Right across that same Potomac River and right down the street from that same Interarms, Jules Berenger sets up shop. But his outfit, UniArms, is something like the factory outlet, the place for buyers on a budget: Guns R Us.

And it's inspiration: What better cover for an illegal arms operation than a legal one? The man's got good lawyers and even better accountants, must have six different sets of books, but he's also got business sense, not to mention balls the size of Brooklyn.

I follow CK into the waterfront warehouse of UniArms with the usual sense of amusement, wonder, disbelief. There is a Ben & Jerry's Ice Cream Parlor right around the corner, boutiques, bookstores, artists' nooks, and all the other sights for the tourists and shoppers who stroll through this placid and precious place they call Old Town, oblivious to the city block of steel and brick and aluminum siding that wears a street number and a little logo that says nothing. Certainly oblivious to what's inside. The loading docks face the Potomac, and we've parked the cars on that side and entered through the usual frenzy of afternoon activity. Crates are coming in and crates are going

out. Crates line the loading docks and tower
along the walls in bricklike stacks. Crates ride
forklifts out and in, out and in, and the warehouse
floor is a maze of—what else?—crates, the spare
concrete cluttered with folding chairs, tables, and
a few warm bodies wandering around with their
clipboards, checking, filling out forms, checking
again, filling out more forms. The crates are
packed with fashionable firepower: assault rifles,
machine guns, rocket launchers, riot guns, pistols,
ammunition, and more ammunition. Forget about
the UniArms complex farther south, down beyond the Beltway toward Richmond. There are
enough weapons right here on the floor to start an
insurrection, a minor war. This little city, this Old
Town, sleeps without any idea about what kind of
combat machine is sitting in its midst.

The warehouse is always strangely quiet, almost peaceful, and cool. At the far end, an angled
staircase leads to the upper floors, more storage
and then accounting and then the loft that houses
the executive offices. I nod hello to the security
guys and some people on the floor, and then I notice who's sitting over there on the couch, by the
water cooler and the stairs:

Mutt and Jeff with an attitude. And painted
black.

The first one's lounging back, a scraggly little
twerp with a glued-tight smirk, must weigh a
hundred and twenty pounds wet and this is no

lie: He's got the bandanna tied tight to his skull, he's got the sweatshirt, he's got the black sweat-pants, he's got the gold chains, he's got the sleepy eyes and the hand in his crotch, digging away at his nutsack like he's some gangsta rapper—Ice Pick, Ice Dick, whatever. The other one is hidden; he's there but you don't see him. You want to look at the other guy instead and you have to pay attention, you have to notice, you have to lock this one in your sights and hold him. His clothes are dark, nondescript urban camouflage. His ball cap is pulled down hard, the brim right on top of the sunglasses, and he's got those long woolly dread-lock things for hair and a surly sort of smile. The little one's dark like chocolate, but this one's nearly vanilla. He sits dead still. His hands are folded neatly in his lap and I know he's carrying and I also know he won't hesitate to use what he's carrying.

CK nods at them and the little one nods back.

Uh-oh, I say to Renny Two Hand, so soft and so slow. Uh-oh.

Then we're past them and climbing the stairs, where Lukas joins up with us. There's a sweet view of the Potomac and there's a bunch of her-ringbones standing around worrying about in-voices or receivables or their next cup of coffee. They give us this weird glance when we saunter past them. I never understand these accountant guys, but that's okay, since they never understand me.

Jules, that's Mr. Berenger, sits behind the door at the other end of the hall with the pebble-glassed window marked EXECUTIVE OFFICES, and if the window's not enough for you, let me just say the words:

He's an executive. In fact, he's about ex-everything: ex-military, ex-lawyer, ex-con, ex-husband. Took him about twenty years, but he finally found his niche. He's been running UniArms since the late seventies, and life has been treating him well. It should. He found the mother lode.

Like me, Jules is a businessman. And he takes care of business.

The guy's short, built like a brick wall, his features chipped but somehow gentle, like he's somebody's grandfather, even though he's not. At least I hope not. Sometimes only his eyes move: Grey ice, spinning, spinning. A lot of thinking goes on behind those eyes, playing more angles than a bagful of protractors. I tell myself that once we get inside the office, I'm not going to say a thing. Just sit down and watch what happens.

Jules is sixty years old and, like most guys his age, no matter what he does, he still looks his age. Hairpiece, a little tuck beneath the eyes, the chin, but still the guy looks sixty years old. Acts his age, too. Which means he chases anything and everything in a skirt.

Now money may not buy much these days, but it can still get you laid. And Jules gets the bang for the buck. Back when I was coming up, there was this blonde named Megan, didn't have a clue but boy did she have a pumpkin of an ass. Then there was Sherry, only she totaled Jules's BMW and that was that, and then this Japanese piece of work, Yuki or Yoko, who lasted about a month. Then came Connie, she studied massage therapy at the community college, and now there's Sally, she does decorating for hotels or something, but mainly she just does. This Sally isn't built, she's constructed. Body by Fisher, face by Mary Kay. Does she look good? This babe looks like the Indian woman on the fucking butter package.

CK knocks on the glass, and this voice inside says: One minute.

CK looks at me and I look at CK and CK looks at me again and then the door opens and out come the suits, single file, three of them, and they don't look at me and I don't look at them and then we're inside.

Hey, Jules, I say. You're looking good. In fact he looks like he needs a long vacation. Needs to lose about thirty pounds and that hairpiece, which looks like something the cat dragged through the gutter before he dragged it in. But hey, the man's the boss. And like my Uncle Mort used to say, if you can't say something nice about somebody, then shut the fuck up.

CK throws his ass down on one of the uphol-stered chairs and Mackie the Lackey does the same, which means that Lukas and Two Hand and I have to stand. Nobody, and I mean nobody but the girls, ever sits over there on the divan.

For a long time nobody says a word. Jules goes first, that's the law, so sometimes we stand around like waiters while he makes phone calls or shuffles paper or diddles with himself. Nice work if you could get paid by the hour. Finally, and it's a long, long finally, he looks up from the Famous Desk like we just walked in the door and he says:

You don't look so good, Lane. In fact, you look like you need a long vacation.

Thank you, sir.

We got a few little things on the agenda here, then we get down to business. First, accounting says the new numbers add up on this Safari Guns place, the one out in Annandale. Nice work, Lane. But next time a little less drama, okay?

I nod my earnest yes.

Now what about this Kazanian deal. The Greek Gourmet? Pita bread guys?

So it's somebody else's turn to step in the shit.

Lukas puts on his white bucks and steps for-ward: Checked them out like you asked, Mr. Berenger. They're clean.

This Lukas guy is a bad act and a bad actor. He doesn't do his job and then he finds somebody else to take the fall. But that's not going to happen today.

I wait for Jules to begin: Okay, here's what—

Then I give Lukas the burn:

You want them, Lukas? Because, hey, you can have them. I dropped by the place today around lunchtime, third time in the past two weeks, and let me tell you what I did. I sat, that's what I did, I sat and I counted the customers. Half hour's worth. This is at noontime, mind you, and they've got sixteen people in and out of there. Sixteen people, thirty minutes. At best they're serving maybe fifty lunches a day, maybe fifty dinners. So tell me this, Lukas. That kind of business, what are they doing with four, five, six deliveries of meat a week? Why do they need all those trucks coming in and out, in and out?

Lukas is lost. He's deep in a forest and he's lost. Finally he says: I talked to these people, Mr. Berenger. I talked to them. Lukas sounds pissed off, but at me, not them. That's his problem, and he better get it fixed.

I tell him:

They're working outside you, pal. They're fucking your wife and your dog and you don't even know it.

Okay, okay, Jules says. I've heard enough. You get your butt out there, Lukas—

Wait a minute, Jules, I tell him. I can take care of—

He doesn't even look at me.

Lukas, he says, I want you to get your butt out there and I want you to shut them down. And I want it done day before yesterday, you got me?

Jules—

The guy isn't deaf. He just isn't listening.

Okay, he says. One other thing.

Now, at last, he's talking to me.

The Philly drop. Give it to Trey Costa.

Done, I say, and hustle my shoulders inside my suit. It's getting warm. A little too warm. So I ask him, first thing: What've we got here, Jules?

Jules looks at Lukas. Get lost, he says. Lukas tries to smile at him and backsteps quickly and carefully to the door and then he's gone.

Jules looks at CK. You told him, CK. Is that right? You told him?

CK nods.

Jules turns to me and says: He told you.

He told me squat, I say. He told me where, which is to say New York City, which is sort of like saying, oh, Rhode Island. He told me when, which is to say this weekend. Lots of hours in there. He told me who, which is to say twenty or so million people. Though he did say niggers, so maybe that cuts things in half. Didn't know we were dealing with gangs again, Jules. Thought we were out of that trade. Thought that kind of action might get some people locked up for something like the rest of their lives. Might get some people dead.

It might, he says. That's why you're going along for the ride. To make sure those things don't happen.

Who's going with me?

You have Mr. James. Spoken as if Two Hand isn't in the room.

I look at Renny. He isn't going to like what he hears, but it's true: If you really need muscle, the kid's not enough, Jules.

I know that, he says. His eyes squinch tight. A bloated piglet. Will you just listen? It's taken care of. And with that he gives a little jerk of the head toward the door.

The two guys on the couch?

There's nothing else to say. Jules starts this shuffling-around thing, pulling open the drawers of the Famous Desk, pawing inside for the matches he can't light, the cigarettes he can't smoke. After a while, he comes up with his favorite play toy, the Barlow knife, and he says: It's not your problem.

These guys are our backup, and you're telling me it's not my problem?

It's not your problem. This is Mr. Kruikshank's run. Have you got a problem, CK?

All heads turn. The psycho smile, straight from a toothpaste commercial:

No problem.

Anyway, Jules is saying. These guys, they're steady. Rock steady.

Oh, yeah, I tell him. They sure look like Gibraltar to me. Did you check out the pants on the little guy? Were they hanging off his butt or am I just imagining things? Tell me something else, Jules. And I don't want *People* magazine, I want *Consumer Reports*. I want who and how, and what I really want to know is . . . why.

Which brings us to the moment. Jules points the Barlow knife down. He stabs it right into the top of the Famous Desk, one of these antique Chippendale things, must have cost him twenty grand, and he digs awhile and he cuts a big chunk of mahogany right out of it. Looks at what he's done like an artist taking in his canvas. Blows air. Then:

What do you do with the money I give you, Lane? Spend it, right?

I nod.

You ever put any aside?

Like in a bank?

Yeah, he says. Like in a bank. Or the market.

The bank, I tell him. Savings account, checking account. An IRA, too.

What about the market?

Nope.

He gives me that *you asshole* shake of the head. Then he starts back to work on the Famous Desk. This time it's a gouge in the side.

Let me tell you something about investments,

he says. You play the stock market, you do this thing like a dog race, and you lose. Now maybe, every once in a while, you get the long shot, but that's not what the market is all about. Buy low, sell high, sure. But that doesn't happen enough to keep you ahead of the game. It's about the long haul. Meaning that the winners are the ones who know how to ride the fucking tiger.

You have to hang in there, and if you're gonna hang in there, you've got to diversify. That's what it's all about. So I play the market, sure, and I'm playing this bullshit biotech thing at the moment. Who knows, maybe one of these monkey-murdering brain barns is gonna get us a cure for AIDS and get me more bank than a Saudi. But that's the side bet, that's the one for fun.

The one for winning, my friend, is what they call diversification. A diversified portfolio. I've got Paramount. I've got U.S. Steel, Glaxo. I've got Lockheed Martin; shit, they're at fifty-four bucks and in three years I bet they're topping a hundred again. Bell Atlantic. Even some iffy internationals. I have money in gold, in futures, in municipal bonds.

And there is a reason that I'm telling you this, Lane.

Yeah, I tell him. Clear as crystal, Jules. Hedge your bets. Diversify. So you're telling me that this pair of yard monkeys out there is Paramount Pictures?

Okay, so maybe that is going a bit far. Jules yanks the knife out of the Famous Desk and shows me its point.

Sit down and shut your pie hole.

Jules, I—

Sit down, sit right there on the divan, and shut your fucking pie hole.

I do what the man says. Like I have an alternative.

What you have out there, whether you like it or not, he tells me, is cash. Cold cash. Big cash.

Jules, I say. No offense, okay? But what you've got out there are a couple guys rolling in so much cash they buy their clothes at Sunny's Surplus. Who the fuck are these guys?

He doesn't answer, just gives me a blank look that sends me this signal that hits the top of my head like lightning.

No, Jules.

But the look says it all: Yes yes yes.

Oh, shit. I'm up off the divan. U Street?

Renny Two Hand leans in, and the kid's got guts; he actually talks. Not the U Street Crew, Mr. Berenger.

Say it, Jules, I tell him. Say it: No, not, never.

Those tight lips tell all. It's U Street, all right. USC. Then he says the words:

Big money.

The world is starting to turn sideways.

Right, I tell him. Oh, yeah, Jules. Big money, all right. Drug money, gang money, crazy money.

Renny starts to say something: Just how are we supposed—

Then he stops because no one is giving him the time of day. He crosses his arms and leans back into the wall. My turn again.

How many?

The floor is definitely tilting.

How many, Jules?

These two, he says. And a few more, meeting you in the Apple. This is no big thing, Lane. This is a milk run. This is money in the bank. And they're gonna make it happen.

Then—

Listen close now. The little one, the one with the rag on his head? That's DeJuan Wilkes. You call him Juan E. You call him Lil D. Better yet, you call him Mr. Wilkes. He's Doctor D's half brother.

Oh, shit. I'm telling myself as much as him, which is when Jules says:

The other one, though, is trouble.

The other one? When the first one is the half brother of D.C.'s own King of the Streets, Deacon Bailey, Doctor D—and that's D as in Death—it's the *other* one who's trouble?

The yellow one's the real gangster. Remember the First Union pull?

Of course I remember the First Union robbery. So do most folks who live in and around the capital. Bloodbaths are hard to forget. Especially the ones videotaped in color on security cameras and broadcast on CNN for about a week after. Before the First Union gig was history, the body count ran to two guards, a teller, a customer, and some poor guy just walking his dog on the street outside. Two perps in ski masks, one with an MP 40, the other with a Mossberg pump, chewed the living daylights out of a First Union branch office six blocks from the Capitol Building while making an unauthorized withdrawal of around $40,000. In the pursuit, D.C. Police got one of them, about forty-seven times by the look of what was left of his raggedy-ass Impala. The other one got away.

Now Jules is telling me that he's sitting right outside the door.

If he gets loose, gentlemen, make sure you're not in the way. But that's not gonna happen, is it? Right, Lane? CK?

No, sir, CK tells him. Then: I mean, yes, sir, it's not gonna happen.

Jules nods back at him like this is all yesterday's news.

Okay, so you go clue in our new business partners. Otherwise, that's it. Except for you, Lane. We need to talk, so . . . gentlemen?

The party's over. CK and the rest of the guys are dismissed, and Jules decides he's done with his whittling. He glances down the edge of the blade, cutting the world in two. Then he puts the knife away and comes over to me, gives me the arm-around-the-shoulder routine.

Burdon, he says.

You were always a good soldier, he says.

Right now I need a soldier, he says.

A good soldier, he says.

The words are one thing. The way he's saying them is another. They're as phony as a kiss from a whore. But I listen, and I look like I'm listening, and that's when it starts becoming clear.

The U Street Crew, like all good pimps and dealers, is no doubt cash-heavy, and that cash is dirty, and what do they need? Guns.

So Jules does Doctor D a deal: not just for guns, but for guns and a little laundry service . . . more guns and more money. Clean money. He brings some of Doctor D's soldiers along for the ride north to keep the buyers, these New York brothers they call the 9 Bravos, in line. The Bravos don't care, and they don't scare either. But if shit happens, and one of the U Street Crew goes down, they've bought themselves war. Which means that Jules gets protection for free.

A nice plan. A sweet plan.

But a little too much of a plan for something that's supposed to be a milk run.

We're almost to the door when Jules says: I'll see you at the wedding.

That one's so far out of left field that I don't have a word for him. So I just say: Wedding?

Sunday? he tells me.

Then I remember. The invitation. To the wedding. His daughter, his only daughter, Meredith, the one in the photo he keeps on the Famous Desk. She's getting married on Sunday, and Jules has hit the big time: She's marrying a senator's son.

I'll be there, I tell him. Wouldn't miss it for the world.

As Jules shows me the door, he draws me into an awkward hug and says:

Burdon Lane. You're my coonhound, son. You never bark up the wrong tree, do you?

I get the feeling I'm the kid being sent off to his first day of school.

He says: Don't go changing that now.

paint it black

So now we got niggers.

This is the kind of thing that comes along and makes you wonder, late at night, covers to the chin, when maybe all the world but you is sleeping, whether you can walk this walk forever. The kind of thing that tickles you with how you're going to be fifty years old, and soon. How you really might be needing Social Security after all. The kind of thing that worms around inside you and then starts to dig and dig deep and, sooner or later, makes you crazy.

U Street's been walking their walk for five years, maybe more, boiling up out of the days when the gangbangers were a bunch of punk nobodies, loudmouthed kids who carried scrap iron and ponied white daddy for the mob. Until the day came when the mob was gone and mobbing took over. There was a shakeout, there was a body count, and then there was the U Street Crew.

Fact of life: There are the guys you elect and

then there are the guys who really run things. Sometimes, not that often but sometimes, they just happen to be the same guys. Happens a lot over there in Dirty City.

But nobody elected Doctor D, the man behind U Street. Born Deacon Bailey. Fifteen-year-old mother, father unknown, raised by an aunt when his mother sucked too much cock and crack and died at the ripe old age of twenty. Started as a lowlife turf bandit in a jumbled graffiti-marred wasteland they call Montana Terrace and worked his way up, pimping, moving drugs, moving guns, moving money, and pretty soon he's got his posse. These guys are predators, and it's not about the block, not about the hood, it's about lebensraum. They move upstream, getting out of retail and into wholesale. One day the good doctor gets indicted for four homicides, assault, reckless endangerment, use of a firearm in a crime of violence, obstructing justice, everything but a parking ticket. Nobody would talk, so nothing would stick. Newspapers call him the "Teflon Con." He orders killings like they're pizza, mostly rival cocaine lords, gets cuffed, and rides out a couple months in D.C. jail before the prosecutors no-paper him, let him walk. First day out, he puts down the Low Four Crew, personally blows the balls off a renegade dealer in front of about a hundred people, none of them available to testify at trial. Not guilty. Now he's King of the Streets, probably employs as many people as Washington Gas and keeps half the city, the Mayor included, supplied with crack and smack.

Another American Dream come true.

But it does make life a bitch for us businessmen. Dirty City was a major market for us, and this kind of action cuts into the profit margin. Hard to say whether life's better with these guys or without them. I mean, consider what the gangbangers did to the straw-man game.

Round about midnight on the third of April, 1991, somebody took some target practice on the corner of 14th and H Streets Northwest. That's about—what? Two blocks from the White House. It was a classic drive-by. A pimp by the name of Maurice Overby did a swan dive into the gutter with a new zipper cut into his chest and throat. Near his body they found eleven spent casings and an Intratec DC-9 assault pistol.

Decent weapon, the TEC-9. Converted to full auto, it spits twenty rounds in the blink of an eye. Couple years later, some wacko walked one into D.C. Police Headquarters and, can you believe it, took out a cop and two FBI agents. And he still had a round for himself.

The TEC-9 that did Maurice Overby was purchased at the Richmond Police Equipment Company. Bill of sale read Otis Campbell. ATF Form 4473 read Otis Campbell. But this Otis Campbell guy owned the gun for maybe twenty, thirty minutes.

It's called the straw-purchase scam, and here's how it worked. We would camp out in Richmond or Roanoke and recruit the usual suspects—homeless, drug addicts, welfare types—and send them off to the gun shops with a shopping list and a fistful of dollars. One old lady, Aunt Becka they called her, eighty years old if she was a day, bought about sixty handguns for us in three months. She did work, and she got paid: Twenty-five bucks a gun. Probably paid the rent and bought her grandkids some toys and clothes, which is a lot more than George Bush ever did for them.

The straw-purchase scam couldn't last. Especially when the Stanton Terrace Crew and the 1-5 Mob started going at each other. And then along comes U Street. Too much competition.

But once it's over, the Feds, as always, finally wake up and it's an election year, so they come down hard. On who? The gun stores. Plugged Richmond Police Equipment for filing false sales reports. Lennie Skittings owned that store. Nice guy. Single father, couple kids, trying to pay off the mortgage like the rest of us. People come by, show the right kind of ID, fill out the right forms, pay with the right bills, what's he supposed to do? So Lennie Skittings pleads guilty, closes down his store, and then one fine Saturday he takes a long ride into the country and blows his mind out with a .38.

Gangbangers started simple. Back in the days, they would break into houses, usually one of the neighbors, to steal their guns. Then they got on to the straw-man game. Now they got the drugs, so they got the money, and they get volume discounts. They get deals. They get all-expense-paid trips to New York City.

Like CK says, as if it needed saying: You got to remember one thing. You can't trust these guys. They'll kill their brother; shit, they'll kill their mother if she gets in the way. They kill each other all the time. And if they kill each other, where do you think a white guy stands when he comes round the neighborhood?

So: You can eat with these guys, you can drink with these guys, and, if Jules Berenger says it, you can goddamn work with these guys.

But you cannot trust them.

A couple black guys used to run with me. One of them, guy named Abednego Jones, was smart. I'm not talking street-smart, though he had all that stuff too. AJ was *smart*.

Tell you how smart this Abednego Jones guy was: He retired. AJ was putting his money aside, or maybe he skimmed some here and there, and one day he just said: Thanks, but no thanks. Bought himself a little house in Sarasota and moved his wife down there and sits in the sun all day long, feeds the birds, goes fishing when he wants. I wonder if he gets a tan.

Now I wouldn't have called Abednego Jones a nigger, and I might have killed anybody who did. Unless AJ killed the guy first, because AJ sure did have a temper. But these guys, these gangbanging pieces of shit? They like the name. I mean, you listen to that rap crap, these guys are calling each other nigger all the time. It's like any other name when you find yourself at the ass end of life: You get it, then you wear it the best you can.

And speak of the devil, there are the U Street guys when I get back to the warehouse floor. I see CK shaking hands with the little one, Juan E, who's all lit up like it's New Year's Eve, and I realize then that the other one, the Yellow Nigger, isn't paying one bit of attention to his buddy or to CK.

Instead he's staring at the guy at the bottom of the steps. At me.

the best-laid plans

Sunup on a lazy morning, with one day to go. So it's Thursday. There's a Pontiac in a parking lot and a sky that looks like puke. Two Hand and I are backseat to CK and Mackie, laying bets on the Orioles-Mariners game. I'm in for $500, and that dimwit Mackie gave me the Mariners and 3. The Pontiac's outside the Dollar Bill Motel on Route 1, just south of Alexandria on the road to Mount Vernon, where, after we lay those bets, we lock and load. Time to eyeball the troops.

When it's time for crime, you need to know who's running with you. Inside this dump are the six guys who can get us arrested, maybe even get us killed. Our African American brothers.

The place is no flophouse but it makes your average Quality Inn look like the Four Seasons. Two little one-story rectangles. All the rooms—all twenty-five, thirty of them—face in, which means they face each other. A scenic view. We stroll across the parking lot and into this open-air corri-

dor of twenty-bucks-a-night splendor, and Renny
counts down the row of rooms to our right: 17, 16,
15, pow. He leans into the black wrought-iron column outside Room 14; and he's got the oowop, an
Uzi, beneath his raincoat. I stand away from the
window, right at the door to 15 and make like I'm
taking a smoke. CK nods to Mackie, and Mackie
nods back, slips a Smith & Wesson .40 from his
belt. He keeps the pistol nose down, reaches his
left hand across, and knock-knocks the door to 14.

Open sesame.

Mackie's inside, then CK, and I wink at Renny
Two Hand and take the plunge. Renny follows,
pulls the door closed behind him, and hail, hail,
the gang's all here.

It's a tiny room and the double bed doesn't
leave much room for company. The bed's got Juan
E with a blunt, a bottle of brew, and a huddle of
his homeys.

I look around and back and what we've got is a
six-man chunk of the U Street Crew and each one
of them is wearing $300 sneakers and droopy
pants and a surly smile and the one thing I think
is that these guys are kids. Juan E's eighteen if
he's a day; none of the others can be older than
twenty-one, twenty-five tops. Except the Yellow
Nigger. And he's way over in the corner, alone,
hidden behind the same old pair of shades, wearing them inside, at 6:00 a.m., lost in some waking
dream and watching TV, it's on ESPN if he can see

it. He's an old-timer in this crew. Ancient. Maybe even thirty-five. Too many of these guys die, by the trigger or consecutive sentences. These guys have been banging, and once you go banging, you don't ever come back. Come eighteen years, they've shot, been shot at, been to juvenile hall six or seven times, been locked up and locked down; they've seen it all, maybe more than me. Maybe.

Yo, cuz, says the closest kid, the one with the headband. White meat in the house.

Fuck you, says Mackie, ever the diplomat. But he pockets his pistol.

Then we've got the handshakes and jive bullshit all around. The bald one, gangly and grins, is Django, and that's Lil Ace in the USC sweatshirt, and then there's Malik, one of those flash-frozen guys who's most definitely got a body count, and finally the one with the headband, that's . . . Headband.

Hey. Hi. Hey there. How ya doin? I mean, just what do you say to a roomful of gangbangers? Well, leave it to Mackie the Lackey:

Who you guys down with? The Bloods? Crips?

So now we've got silence.

Juan E gives Mackie the Wile E. Coyote stare, but Mackie keeps going.

C'mon, says fucking Henry Kissinger. What colors are you running with?

Juan E elbows this Django guy next to him, and this Django guy makes some kind of funny sign with the fingers of his right hand. The homeys, all but the Yellow Nigger, who looks maybe stoned or asleep in front of that TV, nod and laugh, nod and laugh, and finally Juan E curls his lip and says:

You don't know nothin, man. Bloods, Crips, colors . . . fuck that shit. USC beyond all that, you know what I'm sayin? We ain't just a set, we the whole damn ball of wax. D.C. is ours, mothafucka. Chocolate City, you know what I'm sayin? We own the street. And the war's over, baby, ain't you heard? It's over. Nigga runnin for the White House now. Pretty soon we gonna call it the Black House.

Another elbow. Hands slapping. Laugh, laugh, laugh.

But Mackie says, Wait a minute. You talking about this guy who wants to be Vice President? Shit, man, he's no nigger. He's a Republican.

That gets a good enough laugh, but then out of the chatter comes a low voice, like some deep Hennessy and five-packs-a-day shit, and it's this iceman Malik and he's saying:

It's over, baby. Niggas ain't killin niggas no more. We gots bigger fish to fry. Like cod and cat. You know what I'm talkin bout? White fish.

Yeah, right. It's CK and you can tell he's had enough. You got drugs and you got guns, CK says. Let the revolution begin.

Juan E turns on him. You ain't listenin, mothafucka. These are righteous soldiers, you know what I'm sayin? New Afrika.

Yeah, yeah, yeah, CK tells him. Well, I'm an old-timer, see. Traditionalist. Believe in family values, school prayer, knowing your place. Guess I kind of like Old Africa better.

Hey, cuz, Headband says to Juan E. I ain't down with this jainky shit. And I sure ain't gonna go with no Mzungu.

Mackie leans toward Headband, says: What is that, fuckface, some kind of Zulu bullshit? Muslim talk?

Headband looks at Mackie like he's seeing him for the first time. You on this planet or you just too busy bein white? Ain't no Muslim *language*, man. Ain't no such thing. Ever heard of Arabic? Kiswahili? That's you I'm talkin bout, white boy. You the Mzungu, devil.

Cool, Two Hand whispers to me, and before Mackie can squat and drop another stinking turd on this get-together I step up and say:

Hey. Whoa. Time out. Maybe I walked into the wrong room, but I thought this little chat was about something we could do for you, and that you just might do for us. And if we did this thing together, then all of us would make money. Lots of money. It's a nice thing, money. It's got nothing to do with colors. Except green. So why don't we skip the shitkicking this time and just get the fuck along?

I wave in CK's direction. This here's Mr. Kruikshank. He's running this show. And—

And I've got a little something for you, CK
says, right on cue. Mackie? You want to get the
bag?

Juan E frowns, calls over to the Yellow Nigger:
Yo, G.

Whassup? the Yellow Nigger says, and the guy
slips the sunglasses down his nose and looks at
Juan E like he's asked for the time of day. His eyes
are blurs of blue. The guy is either stoned or he's
about three days short on sleep.

Juan E says: Well?

And the Yellow Nigger just closes those blue
eyes and pushes the sunglasses back over them
and I'll be damned if he doesn't smile and say: Let
Mr. Kruikshank do his thing.

Juan E gives CK the nod and CK says something to Mackie and Mackie heads for the parking
lot. Everybody else stands around staring at each
other while the Yellow Nigger takes in more of the
inside of his shades. Finally Mackie's back with a
bulky suit bag and, when CK nods, he unzips the
bag and upends the contents onto the bed. It's a
lot of gleaming iron.

CK tells them it's a little gift, says: Here's something that'll let you peel a few caps back.

So now we get smiles and maybe even some
juice.

While his homeys are oohing and aahing, the

Yellow Nigger stays bored. That takes him up another rung on my ladder. I wouldn't touch one of those pieces of shit either. But we move them like crazy, especially in the inner city. Gangsters love this weapon. It's the Cobray M-11/9, made by the same solid citizens who built the Street Sweeper. A brick of black steel about the weight of a newborn baby, the M-11/9 is descended from the MAC-10, which is a nice piece of work, God bless Gordon Ingram. But you buy a Cobray for the look: evil. It's the Frankenstein of fullies, the gun that made the eighties roar. Sure they're sold as semiautomatics, one squeeze, one shot, but with a quick fix, a couple minutes if you know the right guy or read the right book, these little monsters can fire thirty-two rounds in less than two seconds. Sucker torques like a bitch when you squeeze down. You got to use both hands, point and shoot as many rounds as you can, and pray you hit something before it jams.

CK says to Juan E: We have to talk. They're out the door, buddies for life, with Mackie and Headband in tow, and I'm in here with a roomful of punks with their new guns, not to mention their old ones.

Which means it's my turn again. So I say to the Yellow Nigger:

Listen, my friend. When we find ourselves in NYC, you're with me.

Yeah? he says, never taking his eyes off the TV. Who says so?

You say so.

Yeah? he says, and this time he pulls down the sunglasses and gives me the stare, the one about coming close to a line. As if psychos have a line. A straight one, I mean. The kind you can read, the kind you can respect.

Yeah, I say, and I decide to save him some breath. There's no need to ask why, because I'm going to tell him why:

See, I tell him, the way I figure it, when you get to NYC and you find yourself sitting in some building, lounging in some truck, worrying about a lot of iron and a lot of money with somebody who's not from your streets and somebody who's not from your crew, and let's make that somebody who's not . . . somebody who's white. Well, you need to have the one white guy in the world who you happen to think knows what the hell he's doing.

Yeah? he says again, and this time he looks back at the TV and tells me:

Fuck you.

That's when I pull down on him, the barrel of the Glock pressed right into his temple. Renny, I call out, and when I glance back damned if Two Hand doesn't slap a magazine into the butt end of one of the Cobrays and point it round the rest of the room.

Stay calm, folks, he says. Or this could hurt big-time.

The Yellow Nigger's eyes don't leave the TV. Finally he says:

You draw that thing, you better use it.

I will, I tell him. Unless you tell your homey in the bathroom to lay down his gun and get out here.

That's when the Yellow Nigger smiles and pulls those black-shaded eyes from the TV to me.

You crazy, he says. Ain't nobody in there.

Yeah, I tell him. And pigs don't shit and you don't have a revolver in the bottom left pocket of your jacket. So why don't we bring those hands up to your lap where I can see them? Nice and slow . . . nice and slow. Good, good. Now . . . about your buddy boy in the bathroom. What's he got? Better be a shotgun for this kind of work. Me, I like the Mossberg. Remington's not bad, but I like the Mossberg. And you know what? I saw your little video, the First Union thing. And come to think of it, you like the Mossberg too.

The Yellow Nigger's lips pinch. Maybe it's a smile. Maybe not.

So, I tell him, let's get on with it.

That's when he calls out: Yo, Hitter. Put that fuckin shottie down and get your ass out here.

The bathroom door opens and Two Hand points the Cobray at the slash of light. Hands up and out, he says. And out comes a wiry and nasty-looking dude. With his hands up.

Thank you, I say to this Hitter guy. Just have a seat over there on the bed with your friends.

When he's done just that, I pull back the Glock, ease my finger off the trigger. I roll it over butt first and hand it to the Yellow Nigger. He doesn't even blink, just takes my pistol and points it right back at me. I hear that sound, that almost inaudible click, something like a camera, as the Yellow Nigger presses the trigger safety of the Glock, my Glock, aiming fifteen sonic booms into the starboard side of my skull.

I say: I don't like people pointing pistols at me. Guess you don't either.

I turn to Renny, tell him: Yank the magazine and put the weapon down.

Then I look at his homeys, say: Your guy here can kill me. But he won't. There's a reason he won't kill me, and it's a good reason. It's the same reason I didn't kill him, and I could have, you saw me, I could have blown his brains to jelly and my friend here could have made you dance the hot lead cha-cha and then we could have gone on down to Denny's and gotten ourselves some pancakes.

So I could have killed him and I didn't. We could have killed you and we didn't. We could have gone to Denny's, damn it, and we didn't.

Why? Because we got no fight with you. We got

no reason to fight with you. We got only one reason even to be with you. And that's cash.

I look down at the bed.

Okay, so there's another reason. Guns.

That guy Kruikshank, the one outside with Juan E, is the man who's gonna get you both of these things. Me, I'm the guy who's gonna make sure nobody gets in the way. Or that, if they do, they get hurt.

There's only one way this is gonna work, and it's the hard way. Meaning we trust each other, we look out for each other's back. This guy, his name's Renny Two Hand, this guy and I are your backup. Which means we're gonna kill any motherfucker who looks sideways at you. And you guys are our backup. Which means we put our lives in your hands. Just like your lives were just in ours. So listen:

You were all just dead men.

I roll my eyes toward the Yellow Nigger.

Now I'm the dead man. But I think we like each other a lot better alive. So—

But it's the Yellow Nigger talking now: So this kinda bullshit ain't gonna happen again, he says. Because right now you a ghost. Least you white as one.

His crew starts laughing as he drops the Glock away from my head and points it toward the floor. Nothing like a little comic relief to make your morning. Then:

Fuck all you all, he says to them. And to me: Fuck you too. Maybe I want to be dead. You ever think of that? Should of pulled the trigger, Snow White. Last chance you ever get.

Only chance I want, I tell him. And: I need my Glock.

Yeah, he says, I s'pose you do. He hands the pistol back to me like it's pocket change.

You know somethin? he says. You one mad agent.

Somehow I doubt that this is a compliment. I check and armpit the gun. Then I breathe out everything that's been inside twisting at my guts for the past few minutes.

The Yellow Nigger slumps back down in his seat and into TV land but there's those words again, spoken louder, to his homeys:

White boy's one mad agent.

So I tell him: You really got an attitude, pal.

I don't got no attitude, he says. I got a Mossberg pump.

friday

And then it's Friday and I'm waiting for Two Hand. We're picking out a sedan for the road, some drab something with a monster of an engine, and then it's down to the warehouse for a look-see at the iron we're moving. We're cooping there tonight—CK's orders—so I'm getting my stuff together, and it's not much but you have to take care. Packed a suit, two shirts, three sets of underwear and socks, shaving kit, six high-cap magazines, and five boxes of nine-millimeter ammunition. That's the leather case. The duffel bag is always ready to go.

Fiona's having another one of those mornings, first it was the espresso maker—why couldn't I have bought her a Braun?—and then it was the contact lens, and there is no feeling more helpless than watching a woman, not just any woman but the woman you love, with her contact lens caught in her eye and she's crying and she can't get it out and she is wanting you to do something but you can't, you have to watch those tears and that eye seeping to pink and then red and you hold her and then you don't hold her and then you hold her again and you tell her to relax but she can't relax so you tell her to relax again and again and after a while there's nothing else she can do but relax, and then she tries again and like magic the lens slips out of her eye and into her hand.

But there goes the time you had, the time you needed to spread her out on the bed, to lick that feral life into her, to taste and touch and try to make it right this time. Right for her.

Instead, you have to say goodbye.

I want to understand her, but she speaks in tongues. Fiery prophecies. Faith. Hope. Love, silent at a distant horizon, waiting to fade in like a made-for-television dawn, so bright it burns.

I met her playing pool at this dive called Spunky's, getting hustled for nickels and dimes by Two Hand when this jerk—I was taking the 8-ball on a soft bank into the left corner pocket, cozy shot, end of story, end of game, and this jerk bumps into the butt end of my cue and makes me scratch and lose, and of course the jerk is her. This girl—yeah, I know, I'm supposed to say something like woman but this was a girl, she's even got her long long hair in these two ponytails, like pigtails only without the braids—she's got these eyes, and though I did, later on, I just couldn't get past those eyes, those wide brown eyes that shone with innocent intensity—I want to know the world, I want to love the world, I want to own the world—and she says to me:

Oops.

She's trying to carry a couple beers and a Coke to her friends, these zoned-out big-haired dinner whores at a table across the way, and she's got these three big mugs sort of wedged together in her hands and she's not paying any attention but she says it's like my cue went back and hit her, not the other way around. And she's got beer on her skirt, this blue-jean thing, and it's short, really short, and that's when I see those legs and so what am I going to tell her? Just:

Let me get you another beer.

That's the last time I played pool with Renny.

Talk to me, she says. And it's now, not then.

I manage to shut the leather case before she comes back down the hall and to the door of our bedroom. I scan the dresser. Nothing on top but my prescription bottle. The top left-hand drawer is closed but not locked.

I am talking to you, I tell her. Though I'd rather say, Let me get you another beer. She smiled when I said that. Her smile.

No, you're not, she says. You're talking to me like you're talking to your mother. You're talking to some goddamn picture. You're talking to something that can't talk back.

One time I saw this guy on *Oprah* who did this

funny thing with his hands. Said he could talk to chimpanzees with hand signals, like that sign language stuff for the deaf. Wish I could do that.

Goddamn it, Burdon, Fiona says. Talk to me.

I'm trying, baby, I really am trying. But I've got about five minutes before Renny shows, and about twenty minutes of stuff I've got to do.

Can I take some money out of the bank?

Use the ATM? Sure.

Hundred okay?

Take two hundred. Buy yourself something nice.

She slinks into the bedroom, pulling her T-shirt down taut over her boobs. No bra. Only day of the week she doesn't wear a bra.

Got any ideas?

Yeah, I say. You could use some new pruning shears.

Ummm, she says. Then she purrs. What a guy.

Her fingers are twisting at the back of my hair, she knows I love that, and I flub the knot on my tie. She notices and she seems almost overjoyed.

So hey, Birdman. Where are you going this time?

Business, baby. It's business.

Yeah, Burdon, I know that. You and Renny. You and Renny. Maybe you two guys ought to get married.

She looks over at the mirror again, checking the tangle of my tie and then her lipstick.

Let's see, she says, and she scrunches up her nose, which means she's thinking. After that she smiles, and it's a melter, the one that makes you want to give her everything, and she starts tap-tapping her fingernails against the top of the dresser.

You're going on the road, she says.

Yeah, I say. After all, here's my leather case and the duffel bag is right out there in the hall.

But not for long, she says.

Yeah yeah, I say. No suitcase, no suit bag, so it can't be for long.

You're gonna be back by Sunday, she says.

Yeah, I say, and that one takes a second. Maybe it's a good guess, the luggage is light, but then I remember the wedding. Meredith Berenger's wedding. On Sunday night. And that I promised Fiona she could buy a new dress.

You're going north, she says.

Which is a tough one, which is why I don't say yeah quite as quickly, because it could be just a really good guess, I mean, one out of three is not exactly the stuff of lotteries, and it's north, south, or west because east means the Atlantic Ocean, and after I finally get the knot together on my tie I decide to say:

North?

Yeah, she says. North. North to Alaska, hurry up, the rush is on. Which is some kind of song from some John Wayne movie, and she just laughs and looks at me and says, You know something, Birdman?

And I say: I know lots of things, babe.

To which she says: I've been thinking about what you said to me last week, you know? About doing some different things? Things just for me? And I was thinking that maybe, well, maybe all work and no play makes Jack—well, Jill—a dull girl and maybe there's like some of those things, those different things, that maybe I should do?

She blows out a breath and that might be the longest run of words I've ever heard Fiona say. To which she adds:

So like Melody, she's the stylist in the third chair from the back? With the lizard tattoo, remember? On her shoulder? Well, Melody was telling me about this like huge exhibit thing with all these mummies and lots of gold and this other stuff. Like from Egypt? So I'm thinking maybe I should go see like all this Pharaoh stuff because it's on loan and maybe I might never get the chance again? You know what I mean?

I do know what you mean, hon.

Anyway, she says, so I've been thinking like maybe I should go to the museum this weekend.

Maybe you should, I tell her.

Well, the museum's in New York City, she says.

That's a long trip, I tell her, not missing a beat. Not one fucking beat.

Well, she says, I thought maybe if you were going—

Honey, I say, and I can't even look at her face because it's when she's asking that she's the most beautiful. Honey, I'm going away this weekend. I'm going away on business. Wherever I'm going, whether it's Wheeling or Philly or Virginia Beach or Raleigh or even New York City—I just say the names of cities because I cannot lie to her—wherever I'm going, wherever that place may be, I'm going there on business. With Renny. On business.

Yeah, she says. And that's all she says. She's gone. I hear her bare feet padding back down the hall and into the kitchen and I hear the sounds of cabinets opening, closing, and I hear the water pouring from the faucet into a glass, and then I hear her drinking the water, and by that time I've opened the top left-hand drawer of the dresser and I've slipped two reload magazines of ball ammo into the pocket of my raincoat and another magazine, the Teflon-coated KTW rounds, into the left-hand side pocket of my suit coat and then I'm ready. No, I'm not. I pull the cellular phone from my belt and bury it in the drawer. I take the new one, whistle clean, out of the drawer and hook it on my belt. I lock the drawer, grab my leather case, and then I'm in the hallway, with the words:

Got to go.

She comes back toward me and we meet halfway, right at the landing, and before I can pick up the duffel bag, her arms are around me and she's pressing into me so tight I can feel both her body and the Glock in my armpit cutting into me, and then she's away from me, eyes hot but with a look that's filled with graveside sadness. From outside comes the sound of an automobile turning into the driveway. She cuts those eyes away from me to the vague haze of light pouring through the window and then she looks back with a sigh:

You got to go.

the iron highway

Used to be that when you wanted to run north, you rented a U-Haul and you drove. These days, we use Federal Express. This is an expensive proposition, since you have to buy off a few guys to borrow a van and some uniforms, but it's one that cannot lose. You see these FedEx vans all the time, they're blue, they're white, they're so fucking everywhere that they're invisible, another part of the background. They're also street legal, and you can do about anything you want with them and nobody's going to care. Double park, take a handicapped space, block some traffic, who cares? It's fucking Federal Express. Plus you can't really speed in those vans, and if you could, the cops would cut you a break because you're doing something other than just cruising down the New Jersey Turnpike with your halfwit wife and children. You got a job, just like them, and you're doing it.

Inside the van you've got a guy, two guys on a

highway run, and they're in uniform. Instant authority, instant respect, not just working guys but working guys in uniform. And in the back of the van you've got these neatly ordered stacks of shipping crates, signed, sealed, and set for delivery to Saudi Arabia, with more paperwork than an Act of Congress.

Anyone can stop this shipment. That's a dare. Stop the van. If you can make a legal search—a big if, about as big as King Kong—what will you find? A FedEx van with the right plates and the right registration and the right emissions inspection, and in the back of the van: Weapons. New weapons. Legal weapons. Maybe they're not legal for the streets of our cities, but they are good to go, thank you very much, for our friends and allies overseas. With an inch of paper to prove it. No matter who you gonna call—FBI, ATF, state troopers, local yokels, even the Ghostbusters— you got jack nothing. Just a squeaky clean shipment from UniArms to the Port of Boston, and th-th-that's all, folks.

Then: Our FedEx van vanishes somewhere into the mighty bowels of NYC while those papers take another ride, this time farther north, where they will cover another truckload, tucked safely in some suburb of Beantown with the proper contents, ready to hit the docks, start clearing Customs and make sail for sun and sand and a shooting surfari in Saudiland.

You want to look hard, really hard, you find some problems. But who's looking? We're working for truth, justice, the American way, right? I mean, the Saudis need this iron so they can powder whoever we need them to powder this time or next time. So:

The law is no problem. Not on the run. It's the jackers, maybe, if some fools find the cojones to try, but the real problem is the clients. Meaning that you go to all this trouble to bring home the bacon for some folks, and then they decide they don't want to pay. What a wonderful world. That's why we play carefully, and even then we run north in a funky motorcade, with a Dodge minivan somewhere up ahead with CK's guys and then the FedEx van and then our Oldsmobile and then another car, something hot, a speedster, with two more of CK's guys, that sort of buzzes around the caravan like an angry bumblebee, looking for trouble.

North is where we're headed, north on Interstate 95, the concrete spine of the eastern seaboard, way too many miles of highway weaseling up from Miami and checking out somewhere high above Derry, Maine. North from Dirty City to Manhattan, I-95 to the New Jersey Turnpike and then the tunnel or the bridge. That two hundred and fifty miles, D.C. to NYC, is called the Iron Highway. Not for the hard road or for the cars and trucks it carries, but for what's inside the vehicles: the guns.

Because New York, in its grim and grimy let's-get-ahead-or-let's-get-dead glory, needs those guns, wants those guns, it's got the jones for those guns. It's the city with the most guns in the world, and maybe the most stringent gun laws in the world. There's a word for that, and it's called irony. The irony of iron.

Once upon a time, those guns came from South Carolina, and then things toughened up, so now the guns come from Virginia, and when things toughen up there, well, maybe we'll move on to Georgia or Indiana. But for now, if you live in New York and you want a gun, you go to that distant suburb called Virginia. The FBI says that more than half the guns used in violent crimes in Manhattan are bought in Virginia. No shit. That's my state. My turf. Those are my guns, CK's guns. Sure, there are a lot of free agents out there, a lot of gang stuff—you know, let's take a ride to Richmond and pull a few straw men—but with UniArms, business is business.

And we never close.

These days we run shipments to New York, no more spot deals, no more going north to find a buyer. The buyers find us. Establish their bona fides. Make their down payments. Then, and only then, we run. Just like any other distributor: Menswear, melons, machine guns.

The U Street Crew is riding this out on their own. We brush shoulders here and there along the way, but there's nothing to connect the dots, us to them. Just a couple cars, a couple guys on the Metroliner, the shuttle to LaGuardia. CK's idea. And you know something? It's a good one. About the only thing that's going to draw more suspicion than a car with four black guys is a car with two black guys and two white guys.

Still, I worry. That's my job, to worry. Right now I worry about three things. The Yellow Nigger is dangerous. And he's got a posse of cold kids who have nothing to lose. He's also fearless, and since he's armed, sooner or later he's going to use his piece. It's my job to see that this happens later, meaning after this job is done and he's back doing drive-bys or drug dusts or contract kills or whatever he does for Doctor D.

And Doctor D's half brother, this Juan E guy, seems kind of long on brotherhood and short on sense. Thinks this is a game, nice way to spend the weekend, go raise a little hell in the Apple, drink some Red Bull and get buck wild and, oh yeah, go shake some hands with the 9 Bravos. But that's the way it works; these are the guys, the young fame, they get their money and their pagers and their Porsches and sooner or later, usually sooner, they get their guns. Streetwise is not the word for these guys. They own the street.

And if somebody has a different idea, they just pull on the ski masks and get even.

Mackie the Lackey is driving, which is fine. I check out the scenery again and keep the rest of the conversation to myself as the miles move on by, losing my thoughts to Fiona and, after a while, to sleep.

When CK wakes me, stiff-arm to my shoulder, we're at the Vince Lombardi Rest Stop and he's holding a half-eaten hamburger.

Hey, sleeping beauty. He calls over his shoulder to Mackie and Renny Two Hand: Look who's awake. His head shakes, and he leans in and whispers:

Shit, man, how do you stay so loose? You take something?

No, I say, shrugging out the ache at the bottom of my neck. I don't take nothing. Especially your shit.

Across the parking lot, the FedEx van huddles with a herd of RVs. Closer, one of America's favorite minivans, a Dodge Caravan, slips into a space next to a Jeep Grand Cherokee with handicap license plates. It's almost too easy.

I nod toward the rest stop. Got to go check the plumbing, I tell CK.

Plumbing's fine, he says. But do check it out.

Inside, tourists are wrestling with kids and road maps and boxes of fried chicken. The two black guys at the yogurt stand don't think I notice them, but they have U Street spray-painted all over them. Then there's the plain-clothes security guard at the newsstand, pretending his way through an *Esquire* magazine, and the pickpocket who's cruising the men's room. All these people acting like nobody's noticing them, when they ought to be acting like me. Acting like everybody and their brother, maybe their half brother, too, is noticing them.

After I pee, I wash my hands and ask this guy I don't know who is suddenly standing next to me, combing his hair, if he has the time. He does.

Quarter to three, this guy I don't know says.

Except I do know him and his name's Rudy Martinez and he's part of CK's crew.

The meet is still on.

one last run

Ain't it a bitch? Mackie the Lackey says. We're gonna be rich.

We're past Exit 15A of the New Jersey Turnpike and making good time. Ahead is the grey pincushion of the Manhattan skyline. I was nearly back in dreamland but this Mackie guy can't stop talking.

How much we gonna do on this deal, CK?

That's the way it works. The way it always works.

We're gonna be rich.

You hear this talk, now and again, about how we're gonna be rich, how at last we're gonna get paid. The big one. The quick score. The last run.

Then you look around and you see the same old guys sitting there, riding the routes, playing the game. About the only ones who get out are the ones who make mistakes. For every Abednego Jones with a condo down in some sunny somewhere, there's five in jail, another five dead, and then there's us. Still riding, still running.

So Mackie's still at the wheel, still gonna get rich. If there's one good thing I can say for him, it's that he can drive. Now if he could only keep his mouth shut.

CK twists the dial on the stereo, cranking up the volume on the Led Zeppelin tape. The same Led Zeppelin tape. The only Led Zeppelin tape. The one we've listened to all the way to New York and the one we've listened to on every other ride with this guy.

Renny Two Hand sits in the back seat, crossways to me, picking through the pages of the *USA Today* he bought at the rest stop. I know this routine. First he checks the Orioles and whether it's win or lose, rainouts, even the days off, he bitches. No one but Cal Ripken is exempt. Then it's on to the weather. Scattered showers today, sunny and clear tomorrow. That's D.C. Then it's on to New York. Then Denver. Then Los Angeles. Then Honolulu. He'll tell you what it's doing in Helsinki if you ask. Sooner or later, usually later, he gets to the news. So it's ten or maybe fifteen minutes before you know whether nuclear war has been declared.

Renny's different. That's one way of putting it. Different. He's not even thirty, just a kid, really, in this business. Like me when I was coming up. So I put up with his shit, and anyway the guy puts up with mine.

They call him Two Hand because of that time,

out on the range, he tried to shoot off two pistols at the same time. Saw the damn thing in some movie. As if shooting one pistol wasn't tough enough—if you wanted to knock something down, anyway. So he's blasting away with a pair of .45s that are just kicking his hands up into the air: I surrender. Finally he gets wise and shoots them one at a time. Right. Left. Right. Left. Damn if he doesn't perf up the target dead center. K-5. So he's the legendary Renny Two Hand.

Burdon, he says, folding over the front page with its headline about some civil rights sit-down led by who else but the Reverend Gideon Parks and fumbling out the Entertainment section. He shows me a little color picture of this Dana Delany girl, the actress from that *M.A.S.H.* rip-off, and the boldface beneath the picture pimps some TV movie, Alzheimer's disease and orphans taken hostage or something.

Renny's looking at the picture of Dana Delany like she's here in the car, in the back seat, with us. Girls could go for Renny, they could like him, it's in their eyes when they look at him, dead giveaway. Problem is that Renny doesn't know how to like girls. He hasn't figured out the mystery, which is to know that it's a mystery and just give up worrying about finding an answer because there isn't one.

Look at that face, Two Hand says. She looks so sweet. Not in some movie way, you know, but—

He doesn't finish, because CK, who cuts down the volume on the tape player and turns back on us like an exasperated parent, finishes for him.

Cute, ain't she? Real cute. Button cute.

He smirks and it's a smirk pulled from way down inside his bag of tricks.

You like her, Two Hand? Bet you like her a lot. Bet you think about her sometimes, right? That way. You know what I mean, right? You think about her that way. Am I right? So tell me, kid, what do you think? Really, now?

CK swivels back around and looks out the front windshield.

I mean, you think she likes it up the ass or what?

Renny looks at the back of CK's head, then at his eyes in the rearview. He starts folding the paper back together. Something about late-night talk shows hides the picture. Renny's hands shake and the paper starts to wrinkle as he squeezes.

CK's laugh sounds like poison. When Mackie the Lackey joins in, CK cuts him off, turning to Renny with more words:

I got only one problem with you, Reynolds James.

A lick and a smile.

And the problem is that I don't fucking like you.

Mackie snorts.

You got a problem with that?

Renny just scrunches the newspaper in his hands until at last he says:

No, Mr. Kruikshank. No problem. I don't have a problem at all. Because you know what? I don't fucking like you either.

CK wants to smile again and it's like he can't, nothing will work until a laugh comes out, a little at first and then a lot, and then Mackie the Lackey is joining in, and then what do I know but Two Hand is laughing too, and I must be the only guy in the car who isn't crazy. I need some more sleep.

nightfall

We take the lead somewhere above the Staten Island exits, and the convoy, scatter-pathed, slithers out of New Jersey and rises from the Lincoln Tunnel and into Manhattan at dusk. This city is like an anthill, never stops being alive with traffic, every third car is a cab, and there's nothing to see but people and lights, people and lights, and grey buildings so thick and tall you can't even see the sky. Mackie turns us north up Tenth Avenue and all I can see are people walking and rectangles of light that are storefronts and bars and hotels. In the rearview I see the endless gridlock of cars and cabs and trucks and the FedEx van is back there somewhere, or it's that one ahead on the left, or the one parked over there at the curb. At the next stoplight two kids argue in Spanish, arms waving, and as they cross the street, one of them shoves the other and both of them curse. Stop and start, stop and start, all along Tenth Avenue, past the bodegas and the peep shows and the delis and the parking lots and the cars and the people, most of all the people.

Sooner or later, we reach the City Centre Garage. Pass it and stop next to a fire hydrant. We wait in the car, wait and watch while the others arrive and one by one descend into the bowels of the garage. On the sidewalk, CK's people check things out. Lots of faces. Looks like CK's brought his whole fucking crew: Rudy Martinez, Crimso, Toons, and Fryer. Too many faces. Dawkins, Quillen, Wood Williams. I start counting and stop when I reach twelve guys. Twelve of our guys, and then me, that's thirteen.

Christ, I tell CK. Is this a money-for-guns deal, or are we gonna hop a C-130 and take another shot at Hué?

CK's talking to Crimso, something about the cars, and after he takes a briefcase from Wood Williams he decides to answer me.

The more the merrier, he says. Then: Look at things my way. Mr. Berenger wants this one done right. Dealing with the 9 Bravos is like dealing with a rabid version of U Street. We got to keep them on the leash. Things could be fine. I think they're gonna be fine. But hey, you want to run with an optimist? I don't know what else to tell you, Burdon. Maybe this isn't your style, but you know what? This isn't your call, either. It's my run. You're a good gun, and it's a double drop, so—

I know, I know, I tell him. The FedEx van rumbles by, twists down the ramp and into the garage. We follow on foot. It's a four-story blockhouse with three levels underground. The air inside is chilly and thick with the stench of exhaust. I take short breaths; the stuff will kill you. Things start shaking as soon as we hit bottom.

Yo, CK yells out, and the garage goes quiet. Quillen, he says. You and your boys go do what you got to do.

Which is probably the job of setting up a perimeter. This drop point is a good one, midtown garage that's closed for construction. One way in, but since we're clever boys, two ways out. CK takes me down to the second level and shows me: In the shadows is a heating duct, a little tunnel, really, in case we have to boogie. So Quillen's going to go to the roof with a few good guns, Crimso's probably working the cars outside, two guys parked at each end of the block, and Wood Williams is going to have a very slow night walking the levels beneath us. Nice work if you can get it.

Back upstairs, CK barks things to order: We're gonna get settled in here, CK says, so y'all can get some sleep. Do what you want, but I'm calling it a night.

The U Streeters, the others, shuffle into vague groups, some black, some white, nothing in between. Sleeping bags get tossed. Card games, war stories, maybe even some sleep will follow. The usual. Meantime, CK gathers the chosen few in a circle: Mackie the Lackey next to him, then me, Juan E, and the Yellow Nigger, plus Toons and Fryer and Dawkins.

Okay, he says. Listen up. Here's what we got. Seven in the morning we go by car and cab to the Excelsior Hotel, up across 110th Street. That's your folks' country, Juan E.

Juan E gives up a smile.

The van stays here. Lane, you're staying with it.

All heads turn to me. I can hear the voice of some little kid saying, Tag, you're it! But what the hell, this is what I'm getting paid for.

Two Hand stays with you, CK says. And Jeffers and Rose for the perimeter.

Before I can say spit about being left short-handed, he's on me.

You got only one entrance to cover here. And you know what, Lane? I got faith in those Glocks of yours. The hotel's another matter. That's where we get paid. This is why we need you there, Juan E. You and your crew. To make sure the 9 Bravos don't want to play *GoodFellas*.

Juan E snorts, says, Yo, man, let em. Don't mean shit to me, you know what I'm sayin? Nobody comin in or out of there without me and my set sayin so.

What I like to hear, CK says. Now my boys are gonna handle the lobby, the roof, the street, it's all gonna be tied up nice and neat but I want your people for the inside stuff. For dealing with the Bravos. Keep the fingers off the triggers, right? This is friendly, and it's gonna stay friendly. You and me, Mackie here, couple of my best shooters, we do the meet. Tenth floor. Two Bravos in the room. Only two, that's the rules. Two of them, two of you. The rest of them, and I been told it's six or seven more, we let them onto the floor and—well, like you say, you're the one who's gonna let them in there and out of there.

Aw'ight, Juan E says.

Now this is gonna be fine, CK says. Fine as wine. Something we're gonna take to the bank for a long, long time. Check this out.

CK unfolds a piece of paper from his shirt pocket and it's a photocopy of some official-looking documents, they look like licenses or diplomas, engraved and fancy-edged certificates that say lots and lots of things but mean: payday.

You're looking at a pair of ones and lots and lots of zeroes, CK says. Two million dollars.

Murmurs all around. Juan E shakes his head like he's hearing an old joke. Then CK says:

That's a picture of what they call bearer bonds. And these bearer bonds are legit, like cold hard cash. Word is these things aren't around much anymore, because they're nonregistered, meaning they're off the books of the company, the city, whoever issued them. Which means nobody knows who owns them. You with me so far? What I'm saying is that if you have the paper, you own the money. And this thing is what they call a negotiable instrument, it's like a big check you don't have to sign. I mean, it's not even like a check, it's like a big piece of cash. They aren't made out to anyone in particular, they're made out to the fucking *bearer*. Meaning the guy who's carrying them around. Can you believe that? So whoever's carrying them around can just . . . cash them. No questions asked.

So here's the story on these bearer bonds. We're getting paid on the installment plan. Four parts, a half million each. We got the first part as down payment. When we sit down with the Bravos, we get payment number two and their lives in our itchy-fingered hands, and they get the location of the iron. They bring Mr. Lane here payment number three. He gives them the keys to the van and we give them their guys back, which is when we get payment number four. Then we all go home and congratulate ourselves on being alive. And rich.

Now, we got the tenth floor of the hotel. Perfection. The building's eighteen, twenty stories tops and nobody lives much over the fifth floor. It's gone to shit, and what's left is a homeless shelter. We'll sweep the place and then my guys are gonna hold all the entrances.

He turns back to Juan E: I want one of your

guys, a shooter, the next strongest after what you got right here—

Juan E glances past the Yellow Nigger. That's Lil Ace, he says.

Okay, well, I want Lil Ace to go with one of my boys—that's Meehan, he says to Mackie—and check all the upper floors, then hang on the roof as lookouts. You with me?

Nods all around.

We'll have eyes on the roof, on the street, in the lobby, and when the 9 Bravos show, we'll know pretty much if it's problems or payday. If it's payday, well, Juan E here is gonna have his brothers break bread—

Juan E snorts back a laugh.

—with the 9 Bravos.

You tell your people they need to keep cool. One of these Bravos disses you, you got to accept the disrespect. You want, you can mess with these people later, on your own time. But not on mine. On my time, this is the fucking *Love Boat*. You got that?

Juan E nods. No problem, he says. You know what I'm sayin? No problem. Unless they want to get themselves dead.

One little thing, boss, the Yellow Nigger says, and whether it's the voice or the hiss of derision inside it, CK's head snaps up in his direction. I'm stayin here, you know. With the guns.

He's not asking, he's telling, and you don't tell

CK what to do. But maybe if you're this guy, well, you do. And maybe you get away with it.

CK looks at me, and I give him a poker face and a shrug; I'm the good soldier, right?

But CK wants to play, because with CK it's always hardball, so he says to the Yellow Nigger: Yeah?

Yeah, he says. That hotel ain't got no monopoly on 9 Bravos. You up there playin bearer bonds, we down here sittin on the real deal. And it ain't over till they come on down here and make it be over. They gonna play games with y'all, well this is the place, not no fuckin hotel. So I stay, and maybe if them 9 Bravos get greedy, they'll learn they picked the wrong nigga to fuck with.

Juan E finishes it: My man's talkin truth. I want my nigga here.

End of story. As if it isn't exactly what we wanted: To keep the baddest of the bad, the Yellow Nigger, out of the face-off at the hotel.

So our little summit meeting starts to break apart and it's time for me to haul CK aside.

One thing, CK, I tell him.

Yeah? he says.

When the Bravos come, how do I know that they're giving me the right paper? I mean, what's to keep them from giving me some engraved something or other that looks official, feels official, but isn't five hundred large of bearer bonds?

CK sighs and says, You know something, Lane? You really need to go a little bit easier on yourself. Sometimes you think too much and it don't do anybody any good. I got a word for you, Lane: Trust. Or how about: Faith. Belief.

Yeah, I say. But you know what Charlie Manson used to say: Total paranoia is total awareness. At least let me take another look at that photocopy. I want to see my pieces of paper. I don't want to go home and hand Jules a bunch of VCR warranties.

CK laughs and says: Sure. Hey, listen, anyway, they got these things they call CUSIP numbers, matches right up and you know you're good to go. See, right there. You got to worry, then write those numbers down. See if they match.

He hands me the photocopy and while I'm looking at these funny pieces of paper, trying to memorize the CUSIP numbers, I ask him: Oh, yeah. One other thing. Maybe I missed something, but where's the alternate rendezvous?

CK looks away and he says: For this run, there's only one stop on the way home, and that's Morristown. But between you and me . . . listen, do you remember the south Jersey warehouses?

I nod, though I don't look up from the photocopy. What I'm staring at is paper, a picture of paper, and the paper has emblems and numbers but it can't possibly be worth two thousand large. Two million dollars.

Well, he says, you didn't remember from me. Just don't go telling the dinges, okay? South Jersey's what you might call the white man's rendezvous. Now give me that thing and take a load off your feet. Time's gonna fly tonight.

the wait

Which brings us, with enough waiting, to the hour before dawn, when CK and I shake the night from our bones and wander the garage floor, waking the guys who aren't standing guard or sleeping in a decent bed at one of the hotels. After a night like this one, nobody ought to wonder why I slept so much on the ride north. I can never sleep the night before a major meet, and even if I could I'd be a fool to try.

Instead I spent the night behind the driver's wheel of the van, watching and waiting and worrying. What a way to lose eight hours: sitting on top of enough contraband to start a civil war or earn about a thousand concurrent felony sentences. It all depends on your point of view. And sitting next to me is the Yellow Nigger, with a spurless Ruger .38 and a bag of pork rinds in his lap.

Through the night, CK's guys have been dropping cars at different locations in the city. Renny and I win the Olds for the return trip. The valet stub says it's parked at the Warwick Hotel.

Soon enough Juan E leads his people out, and they're like a pride of young lions. Lots of flash when they check their weapons, and there is no doubt: They may be kids but they mean business. I do think they might do us some good. Right past them comes Renny Two Hand with doughnuts and more black coffee. I swig down what's left of the last cup and, when no one's looking, I eat some Dexedrine.

Then the troops are gone, and it's just the five of us: Renny, Jeffers, Rose, the Yellow Nigger, and me. And all these guns.

Okay, I tell Renny. Go buy yourself more breakfast in that deli across the street. And take your time. It's gonna be a long morning. Get a seat by the window. Keep your eye on that door. Anybody comes inside, hell, anybody even takes a hard look, call me.

Hey, he says. I've got a good feeling about this one. Just one of those things, feels right. And you know something? I was talking to some of those U Street guys last night.

Yeah, I tell him. I saw you.

Well, he says, these guys are okay. Tough guys. But they've got something going. Sort of like us? They've got each other, you know?

Yeah, I tell him. Just don't make any plans to go visit your new pals in the hood, okay?

Yeah, right, okay, he says. It's like any time you—

He reaches down to his belt, brings up his cellular phone.

Give me your number again. When I do, he punches at the keypad, smiles, and says: Got you speed-dialed. Rose and Jeffers and CK, too. I was thinking about Pizza Hut, but you know something? I don't think they deliver here.

He heads for the stairs. You need more coffee, he says, give me a jingle. Maybe I'll deliver.

I find Jeffers and Rose, and they're checking their rifles, matching CAR-15s with ACOG Reflex sights and laser aimers. Perfect for an urban firefight, which is about the last thing I want. I tell them to take to the roof, and I tell the Yellow Nigger nothing.

After a while, we both sit inside the van again. I'm on the driver's side and he's on the passenger side and that's the way it's going to be.

We wait, and then we wait some more.

He's about thirty-five, though I'm no judge when it comes to age. Could be older. Today the dreadlocks are bundled in a knot at the back. He isn't big and he isn't small, just mid-range with a lot of muscle. Not jailhouse muscle, though, you can spot the stuff, smell it too, from a mile away. Maybe he did time, most of these guys from the streets have been in and out two, three times before they're twenty-one, but nothing major. A real smart man who learned his lesson early: Never get caught. His face, pale as sand, is an endless enigma. He hides the blue eyes behind those spooky sunglasses. Add in the smooth voice, each of his few words spoken with quiet threat, and you got somebody you aren't sure you really want to know. Unless you have to run with him.

So what can I say? The silence is getting to me.

Hey, man, what's up?

I stick out my hand. He doesn't move. I pull it back.

You mind telling me your name? I say. But I get the dark glasses, tight lips.

Hey, I tell him this time. Not a question. I tell him:

Your name.

He blows a long breath at me, like a school kid you've told a story that he doesn't quite believe. Then he says:

Jinx, fool.

Jinx, I say. No shit. Jinx.

I look out the window. Quite a view in a basement garage.

Yeah, he says, so what the fuck about it?

Look, I tell him. Jinx. The guys, sometimes they call me Loose, you know? Because in the old days I told too many people to stay loose. My girlfriend, sometimes she calls me Birdman. But that's not my name either. Those are nicknames, right? The name's Burdon. Burdon Lane. And I'm sitting here, and you're sitting there, and it seems to me that maybe you should be telling me your name.

Another breath out. He speaks like he's just met a foreigner:

My slave name is Michael Sexton.

And then he smiles. At least I think it's a smile.

But you, cracker . . . you call me Jinx.

He shows me too many teeth for a real smile. This guy is a predator, a wolf walking with what he thinks are lambs.

I know then that I'd better not lose sight of him. Not for a minute. He's either next to me or dead on the ground.

So, he says. What're you readin?

I look over at my new pal Jinx. He takes off his sunglasses, polishes at them awhile, then slips them into his jacket pocket. He nods at my lap.

The book, he says. You readin your Bible?

There's something in the way he says those words, something that says the idea of my reading the Bible is the most ridiculous and most important of things.

No. Not the Bible, I tell him. Tried one time but I couldn't get past all those begats. No, this is my book. It's called *Crime and Punishment.*

Then I show him the cover, as if he wouldn't take my word on it.

Yeah, he says. Nice book.

Nice book? I say to him, and catch myself, ease back before I laugh. Did you read it?

Suddenly he's the one who's laughing.

Read it? Hell, man, I wrote it.

And we're both laughing then, and somehow it happens, somehow, before I know what I'm doing, as the morning winds its way out of the dark and into the time when the children wake, when the alarms and clock radios roust the sleeping people from their dreams and into the nightmares of their lives, when CK and Mackie and Juan E and the others climb the stairs to the tenth floor of the Hotel Excelsior, I tell my new pal Jinx the story, the one about the book, the one I've never told to anyone, not Renny Two Hand, not even Fiona.

It's my mother's book, I tell him. One of them. She had lots of books, my mom, shelves and shelves of books, up in the bedroom of the old house. About all she did, the last few years of her life, was read. It was about all she could do, lying in bed and letting the cancer eat at her insides. I was there when the doctors told her about the cancer, told her about the time she had left, and they might as well have been telling her about fall fashions for all the attention she paid them; it was like what they had to tell her wasn't anything she didn't already know. She let them drift away, one by one, and then she got back to reading her books.

One time I asked her, I just flat out asked her about the books. I'd visit her a couple times a week, up in that bedroom, and she'd have a book in her hands, on her lap, at the nightstand, and I had to ask her:

Mom, why do you sit here and read all these books?

And she looked at me with eyes so clear that I could see right into her. She folded over the corner of the page and she closed the book, and it was this book, this *Crime and Punishment* book, and she put it right into my hands. And after a long while, she said to me:

Take this book, Burdon, and you'll see.

Read it, she said. Don't look at it, really read it. When you read a book, she told me, you get to the end of a page, and then, well, you turn to the next page. Another page. You get to the end of a chapter, and then there's another chapter. There's always another page, another chapter, another story, another book. You're never done. Even when the words say THE END.

That was the last time I saw Mom cry, but she was smiling, too.

There's always another page, she said. Another chapter.

You're never done.

I don't know what I've said, I don't know what I have done, until Jinx hands the book back to me and says:

Yeah.

Which is when the Motorola rings and I pull it from my belt.

Hello?

It's CK: Your turn.

I hear you, I tell him.

Click.

Click.

And with enough minutes, the Motorola rings again.

This time it's Renny Two Hand: We got company, he says. Three guys and I don't like them. Not at all. They're—

Stay loose, I tell him. Stay in that deli and stay loose.

I click down on the cellular and I know I don't have to tell Jinx a thing. Because down the steps they come, three suits in rumpled raincoats, looking for all the world like Wall Street bankers seriously lost on their way to lunch. Quiet faces. Tight faces.

White faces.

So this is it: The Connection. The Make. The Meet. I've heard a hundred words for this thing but none of them works, not in the real world. Like shit, this thing just happens. You can make plans, you can figure all the angles, you can get busy and get ready. But then it just happens.

There's this awful feeling every time a major deal goes down. Not a rush, no way, none of this nerves-on-edge adrenaline highball that they serve up to the mall zombies in those caper movies. It's nothing but this cold thing that sleigh-rides up your spine. A gremlin born down some-where in your butt just shoots into the back of your brain and sits there, whispering for you to run like a whippet and not to stop running till to-morrow.

This message has astounding clarity. It hurts your head. Sometimes it hurts your stomach too, makes you want to drop your pants and let go.

You want to listen to this thing. Every once in a while it's right, and you don't know it until you just . . . *know* it. That's when you cut your losses. If you don't feel this thing, you're an idiot or you're dead. Probably both.

Right now it's telling me lies.

White faces. And not just the faces, it's the hair-cuts, the overcoats. It's the way these guys are walking toward the van, the way that not one of them is looking back, looking over his shoulder, worrying about what might be back there behind them.

White faces.

Jinx knows what I'm thinking.

Yeah, he says. Who the fuck are these albinos? But hey, you know what? Somethin look this wrong, it's just got to be right.

He takes the pistol from his lap.

It's cool, he says. Nobody gonna get capped.

Them Bravos may be niggas, but they sure ain't stupid niggas. So they get some white bwanas to do their dirty work. Just like you went and got yourself some natives to do yours. Makes about as much sense as anything else on this ride. Come on. Let's get dancin.

Wait a second, I tell him, and I dial Rose, standing watch on the roof.

Yeah?

What've you got?

Three in, nobody out.

Okay, I tell him. Stand by.

I dial Jeffers.

What?

Got anything?

Got nothing. Just tell me when.

Okay, I tell him. Stand by.

Jinx?

He's halfway out the door to the van when he turns back and says: Yeah?

Keep your mouth shut and your finger off the trigger. Just remember one thing: If you hear me say something original like, oh, kill them, well, that's when you kill them, okay? But for now, I'll take Mr. Branch Manager. You go get chummy with his buttboys.

Jinx blows wind over his upper lip and he's out of the van, right arm curved to hold the Ruger behind his back.

I shove my Glock into the front of my belt, where it can be seen.

Mr. Branch Manager hauls up about ten feet shy of the van, sticks out a pale white hand, and says:

How you doon?

That's how he says it, one syllable, like a big pile of sand: Dune.

I'm doon just fine, I tell him back. But I don't shake his hand. I say to him: You got the paper?

Oh yeah, he says. I got the paper. Pause. You got the keys? He cuts his eyes to the van and then back to me.

Oh yeah, I tell him. I got the keys.

Great, he says. So you give me the keys, and then I give you the paper.

No, sir, I tell him. That's not the way it works.

Look, he says. Maybe there's been some misunderstanding, but my job is to come to this garage. Your job is to give me the keys.

No sir, I tell him. Maybe your job is to come to this garage. But if you want the keys, you're gonna have to take them. Because I'm giving them up only at the point of death. Unless, of course, you want to give me the paper first.

His face drops. He glances back at his friends, who are looking a bit worried now that they've met my new pal Jinx. He shows them the pistol and then he shows them the way back to the stairs. This has got to go down one-on-one.

Hey, I tell Mr. Branch Manager. Hey. This time I

get his attention. Listen, fella, why don't we start this all over again? Pretend you just walked in here, okay, and that you said to me: How you doon? That's when I tell you: Hey, I'm doon just fine. Then here's what you say to me: Here is the paper that I was asked to give you. And you want to emphasize the word give, because this is no trade. This is nothing like that. Okay? So: Ready? Now's when I tell you . . .

Hey, I'm doon just fine.

Mr. Branch Manager glances back at his friends again, and Jinx has them nearly to the stairs, and he looks at me with more impatience than a junkie waiting on a fix.

I tell Mr. Branch Manager: You gonna give me the fucking paper or what?

He's losing it, little beads of sweat at the temple, the whole nervous works, and that's when he says: Look, you got to give me the keys.

I don't got to give you jack, pal. And you know why?

I reach for my belt and the guy flinches, I kid you not, he flinches, but all I do is pull the cellular and punch up Two Hand.

Yeah?

What have you got?

Nothing.

Cool.

I click down and then I have my say with Mr. Branch Manager:

Here's why. You walk in here with these pieces of paper, right? You, him, and him, just the three of you and these pieces of paper. Which are where? Probably in your shirt pocket. So now I've got you and I've got the paper, and my pal over there has got your two dinner dates and my buddy across town has your Bravos and the other pieces of paper, and . . . well, maybe I'm missing something, but tell me, okay, why don't you tell me: Just why am I supposed to give you the keys to this van?

He gulps, and now it's like he doesn't want to turn around to look at his friends for fear of what he might see. At last his voice comes creeping out:

Because we had a deal?

Sorry? I say. I can't hear you.

Because . . . we had a deal?

Bingo, I tell him. Now give me the fucking paper.

I was right, he's got them folded in his shirt pocket, and they look real, and I take the pieces of paper, check them out, the CUSIP numbers match, and I fold them up and put them into my shirt pocket and then I tell him:

The keys are in the van.

Jinx sticks his pistol in his pocket, and he's up the stairs with the two other guys.

Then Mr. Branch Manager says the last thing he says to me. He says:

And?

And I walk back to the van and grab my duffel bag, and then I walk away. I pull the cellular phone from my belt and I call CK and I tell him we're done, and do you know what CK says to me? He says:

Hang on.

There's this long silence, then he's back to me and he says:

Had to get some privacy. You there?

I say yes, and he says:

Get the hell out of New York.

His voice is like a whisper, deep-fried by the airwaves.

Go to the second place or go to Wilmington, the train station, maybe. Get way out, get close to home. Find someplace off road to take a blow. You get there and you hunker down.

A distant voice, so soft and suddenly so very clear:

And as soon as you get the chance, kill the nigger.

the shit goes down

When I click down the Motorola and hook the phone back onto my belt, I remember why it was I hated math:

Two plus two doesn't always mean four.

This I remember in the moment it takes me to realize that Jinx is up the stairs and out. Gone. Shit. Back to the phone. I punch up Two Hand's number. He takes it on the first ring.

Yeah, what?

I'm coming up, I tell him. Have you seen Jinx?

Who? he says.

The Yellow Nigger, I tell him.

No, he says, and then: He's with you.

No, I tell him. He's not with me, and that's a problem. A big problem. Our problem. Keep your eyes open. Call Jeffers and tell him. I'll be right with you.

The van revs up with a tired dog growl, and I stand there staring until I catch the eye of Mr. Branch Manager. I don't like what I see. The guy didn't even check the back of the van. I don't like it at all.

I'm through the door to the stairs and up and back out on the street. No one on the sidewalk, no one in sight. Jinx and Mr. Branch Manager's spear-carriers are gone. Across from the entrance to the garage, through the gauntlet of light Sunday morning traffic, Two Hand is standing at the window of the deli. He shakes his head side to side: No. So I shove my hands into the pockets of my raincoat and make like a New Yorker, head down, jaywalking, intent on cappuccino and a bagel.

Renny meets me at the door, gives me a lost look.

Jeffers and Rose—

Let me guess, I tell him. They took their Chevy and booked.

Yeah, but—

Were they following Jinx? The U Street guy?

No, no, Renny tells me. I didn't see him, but look, Burdon, I couldn't have missed him. No way. I was—

You did fine, kid, I tell him. But we have to move, and I do mean move. Something is squirrelly.

I dig in my pockets: Here.

I hand the valet parking stub to him.

Warwick Hotel. That's 54th and, shit—I can never remember—Sixth Avenue, I think. Cabbie'll know. Take the Olds from the hotel and get your ass to Jersey. But whatever you do, stay away from Morristown. Listen to me. This is important. Don't go to Morristown, okay?

I take the pen out of his shirt pocket and write the directions on a napkin.

This is the other rendezvous, I tell him. South Jersey. Some warehouses. I'll meet you there. By one o'clock. Don't wait any longer than one. If I don't show . . . shit, man, if I don't show, go home and find Trey Costa, okay?

But if I—

I turn my back on him because I know he's a good soldier, just like me, he's a good soldier and he's going to go to the Warwick, he's going to take the car, he's going to drive to the second rendezvous, he's going to stay out of trouble.

Me, on the other hand? I've got business. Jinx is gone, and he's either talking money market accounts with the banker guys or he's heading for Juan E and the rest of his crew. This is a no-brainer. I've got to keep Jinx out of that hotel. And find out what kind of shit is really going down.

I flag a taxi and tell the cabbie, one of those guys with a turban, the destination. His eyes sort of glaze over and he starts digging at a *Frommer's Guide to Manhattan*. By now most of the world knows its name, but at right about 9:30 a.m. on this particular Sunday morning, most of Manhattan had forgotten, if they ever even knew about, the Excelsior Hotel.

Shit, I tell the cabbie, and then I give him the street, the avenue, the intersection. Move it, Gandhi, I tell him.

The Excelsior. Nice enough name for a hotel, though a bit grandiose for a place that hasn't housed a paying guest for twenty or so years. Way up across 110th Street in a DMZ, the edge of Harlem.

The cabbie is still dicking around with his guidebook and his maps.

Move it, I tell him again. I rap once on the Plexi-glas.

He doesn't blink, just puts the maps aside, and we start uptown. He takes the west side of Central Park and I never know whether I'm being had by one of these guys or not and I watch the brown-stones give way to blocks of buildings at the fringe of a fantasy of urban renewal that went down hard in the late sixties. Apartment com-plexes that look like junkyards. Each new cross street offers some pathetic vista, a burned-out building, a burned-out car, and among them burned-out men and women and kids who look out at you like refugees from a war.

As the cab hits the intersection, pulls to the curb, I see a line of police cruisers and nearly say out loud what I'm thinking: Oh, shit. But then I see the people gathering across the street and their faces, smiling faces, black faces on black bodies decked out in their Sunday best, a restless tide of pink and blue and yellow and white that seems to wash against the wide and welcoming mouth of the Free African Methodist Church, and I'm thinking: Leave it to CK to set up a meet in the middle of a Sunday-morning church service.

I give the cabbie a ten, tell him to keep the change, a buck tip, nothing too memorable, and then I'm on the street, moving slowly, huddled up in my New-Yorker-in-a-raincoat pose that sweeps me past more cops than I'm likely to see in a week in Virginia. They look bored, journeyman duty, and the street is blocked off for the service, must be one hell of a popular church, and across the way I see a short line of NYPD wagons, plus a couple limos, even some radio and television vans.

On this side of the street is an apartment building, some kind of subsidized housing, a retirement home, still looking good, and flush against it leans the weary Hotel Excelsior. The weathered hood of an awning offers the ghost of its name. The shattered windows on each side of the entrance are guarded by wrought-iron grates that spin into ornate webs. What's left of the building, the bottom few floors, has been taken over by the Methodists and turned into some kind of fleabag flophouse, what they call a shelter, for the homeless and the helpless and, of course, the crack-heads.

It's a perfect place for a meet. A place of the vague, the anonymous, the unnoticed, the lost. A place where faces, black and white, could mingle. Even on Sunday.

In the lobby of the Excelsior the usual scum are lounging around, most of them with the heroin nod, and the smell is astounding, a wet stew of Lysol and spent semen. Wood Williams pretends he's half asleep behind a newspaper, but he grins when I stroll past. I lamp the bank of elevators and can't believe that the door of one is open, the insides lit, because I'd rather take the ten flights of stairs in a wheelchair than commit my life to that wretched box.

The stairwell says it all: The building is dead and rotting from the inside out. Paint and plaster have peeled back, urban leprosy that exposes decaying wallboard and cinder blocks. Holes gape in the walls. The landing of each floor is a mix of busted concrete, shattered glass, beer cans, crack pipes, used Bic lighters, and empty prescription bottles. The stairs seem to give with each step, and each new floor offers new wounds in the structure. At seven I have to jump over steps lumped with broken plaster and brick that have fallen from the ceiling.

On nine, I take a breather at the landing. One floor to go. I hear a voice but can't make much of it. Someone humming. A cough. So things are okay.

Maybe.

I take the last set of steps with a lot of patience. The door to the tenth floor, like many on the floors below, is gone, wrenched from its hinges to make a table or firewood. Or sold somewhere for dope. I can't see a thing in the hallway beyond. So I wait for a while in the shadows until finally I hear the voice again, and this time the words: Ten a.m.

I look at my watch, and it must be slow, since it reads 9:50.

The voice belongs to Martinez, and Martinez belongs to CK and Mackie. I set my duffel bag on the stairwell, then:

Rudy? I say, and take a deep breath and step out into the hallway.

Martinez is there, in the shadows. Another one of our guys, I think it's Crimso, is down the hall, and he's got something long-barreled and automatic, an AK with a custom wooden stock, held high on his hip.

Lane? Martinez says back, in a half whisper, and what else can I say?

Yeah, Rudy, it's me.

Jeez, he says. You could of got yourself shot. What you doin here? Thought you was downtown with the—

I put my finger to my lips.

I tell him: I need to see CK.

Martinez rolls his eyes. Yeah? he says, and he's loose, and the guy down the hall—yeah, it's Crimso—isn't paying one bit of attention, so I say:

He called. It's important.

So Rudy says:

Why didn't you say so? Come on.

We head down the long hallway, and there's nothing much to see, bare lightbulbs, about half of them lit, and this queasy green wallpaper that hangs in torn strips and wedges. The doors to what once were rooms are either open or gone, and there's nothing inside the rooms until we near the end of the hallway. Then things start to get interesting.

Light's coming from a room on our left, and it's full of the brothers, 9 Bravos and U Streeters lounging around on the floor and the torn-up furniture, chilled out, knocking back forty-ouncers of malt liquor, sucking on joints and booshitting, a real social gathering.

Then, past more empty rooms, there's one with Toons and Fryer and they've got canvas satchels on a couple chairs and they're diddling with whatever they've got in the satchels and when we walk on by Toons gives me a thumbs-up and then gets back to diddling.

Then we're at the end of the hall, and there's a door this time, on the right, and the door is shut, and I don't need to be told who's inside.

Martinez raps at the door and when it angles open he says:

Company. It's Lane.

Mackie the Lackey shows me into a roomful of tight smiles. I take in the room, what must have been a suite, wide and long and empty except for a table and chairs, the remains of a dinette set. CK stands at the far end, before two wide and curtainless windows, like the host of a surreal dinner party. Juan E and his Django guy sit at one side of the table, and some boss nigger from Central Casting sits at the other side with a guy who looks like an NFL linebacker turned thug. The boss man must be Daddy Big, a high-stepper for the 9 Bravos.

On the table in front of them are an open briefcase, thick wads of cash, a lot of handguns, and like twenty baggies of llejo. White daddy. Cocaine.

Fuck. I knew it was drugs. I knew it.

Listen, CK says, not to me but to the guys at the table. He's cool. One of mine. Right, Lane?

I nod as I cross the room with Mackie, pass the table, pass Dawkins. The guy's slumped against the wall like he's waiting on a very slow train.

Hey, says Juan E, and he's talking to me: Yo, hey. You. Wonder Bread. How's my bust-yo-ass nigga Jinx?

I give CK the look he needs, the one that says

nothing and everything, and I say to Juan E: Hey, Jinx is just fine.

Then I find my space, an empty spot on the far wall, between the two big windows, with a clear view of the players and a clear path to the door, and I lean back to enjoy what's left of the show.

The 9 Bravo warlord sits, unmoving, unmoved. An onyx statue with two Desert Eagle .45s for a table setting. The linebacker is counting out dollars, and I haven't seen such angry boredom since the last State of the Union address.

Two things stink: The deal is done. And when the deal is done, you don't stick around to shake hands. Or sell drugs. And then there's Mackie, standing over by the window to my right, looking alternately at his watch and then outside and down, to something on the street. Looking just a little too often.

Until he turns to CK and says, Hey, we got to go.

Which is when CK turns up the high beams for his little audience:

Gentlemen, he says, that seems to conclude things for today. There's only one thing to add. A little something. A little gratuity.

CK nods to Mackie, and Mackie lifts two long cases from the floor, placing them carefully side by side on the table.

Attend, CK says to Juan E and the Bravo warlord. Whatever that means. He acts like one of those prissy French waiters you see on TV comedies.

CK takes a pair of those white latex gloves, the ones doctors use, the ones like rubbers, from his coat, and he slips a glove slowly onto each hand as he tells them: Mint condition. Gems. The finest. For each of you, gentlemen.

He reaches and flicks the locks on each case, then tilts back the lids like he's showing off the Crown Jewels. And now that I can see inside, I know that, in a way, these are jewels.

Compliments of Mr. Berenger.

and god said
to cain

I've read about these rifles, heard the stories, seen
the photos, even seen them in trophy cases, but
I've never seen the real deal in a shooter's hands.
Until now.

The room is silent. A fucking hear-the-pin-drop
cathedral. CK raises the first rifle from the case
gently, with a kind of reverence, and holds it out
toward that Bravo warlord, Daddy Big. An offering. And the guy, at last, is moved. He stands and
takes possession of the Maltese Falcon of modern
gunnery. The stuff that dreams are made of:

The Van Doekken Longbore.

The most sought-after sporting rifle in the
world. One of those things that people will swear
to their dying day is a myth, a fantasy, a fairy tale.
But it's for real.

Only a couple hundred of the Longbores exist,
no one knows the exact number, except maybe
Van Doekken, and he's dead. It's the sort of thing
owned by royalty, whether kings and queens or

movie stars and rock stars. Made in South Africa
in the seventies, hand-tooled, engraved, world-
class accuracy, the favored trigger of millionaires
and well-paid mercenaries. I saw my first Longbore in Central America; it belonged to one of the
CIA flavors of the month down there. The second
was in a silk-lined case at the South African Em-
bassy in D.C. This one, in the steady hands of the
Bravo, is my third, and it looks like Juan E's getting the fourth.

I wonder if he even knows what he's getting,
but his eyes widen as CK hands him the prize.
He's dancing inside his skin like a kid who's
struck it rich on Christmas Day.

The Longbore is huge, well over four feet long,
almost three feet of barrel, and it weighs somewhere near fifteen pounds. It's got a bolt-action
repeating center-fire that supposedly sings.

These numbers have been customized, outfitted
for the savanna. The titanium-blue barrel is
topped off with a Nikon scope and a laser aimer.
Satinwood stock, Bavarian cheek piece, gold-
plated trigger assembly. Hand-crafted stock work,
metal work, inlays. Such a beautiful piece of iron,
and such a fucking shame. This is meant for mu-
seums, not mobsters.

And whether Juan E and the Bravo know what
they're looking at or not, this isn't right. This is
not right at all.

In a room full of crazy men and guns, money,

and drugs, there aren't many options. I keep my mouth shut, but I put my hand to my belt, find the grip of the Glock. When the shit goes down, I'm not going down too.

Take a look, gentlemen, CK is saying. Take a look down that scope.

Juan E's got the Longbore to his shoulder and he's peeking down that sight like Davy Crockett.

The Bravo, Daddy Big, is intense. His hand circles the grip and his finger dances at the trigger guard. Itching.

Mackie is looking out the window again, and when the Bravo swings the Longbore his way, peering through the scope all the way to Albany, the room takes a slight spin to the right.

Boss, Mackie says. He turns away from the window, looks at the Bravo and that big rifle and doesn't even blink.

Boss, he says again. We got to get going.

CK ignores him. You can drop an elephant at a thousand yards with that baby, CK tells his grateful audience. But with that scope, that feel, hell, you can drop an ant if you want to.

Juan E swings the rifle around.

Careful, CK tells him, and laughs.

Mu'fuck, Juan E says. Damn.

The Bravo is still silent. He looks through the scope, then pulls away, squints, looks into the distance with his own eyes. Then he goes to parade rest, feels the heft of the gun.

Want some target practice? CK says. Out of his jacket pocket he pulls a shiny magazine. He waves the magazine at Juan E. Let me show you how it's done.

He presses the magazine into Juan E's right hand. Then he digs into his jacket, pulls free another magazine, and tosses it to the Bravo. I cannot believe this is happening.

Okay, CK says. Three-shot magazine, .557 in Magnum calibers. They're monsters. Winchester FailSafes, crossbreed of the best two bullets on earth, the Nosler Partition and the Barnes X. They'll shoot through a Mercedes to get to what you want. A little tricky to load, though. You can't just stick those babies in there. You go at an angle, notch forward and first, okay?

Juan E works the magazine into the Longbore, slaps the bottom. Très chic, he says, with that golden smile. You know what I'm sayin?

Boss, Mackie says. We really do have to go. Like now.

Okay, okay, CK says. But he's talking to Juan E and the Bravo. Now this is the hard part, he says. You got a three-position safety. Let me show you the drill. Toss that baby over to me a minute.

Juan E pitches the rifle toward CK, and the rifle twists, tumbles, rolls, and the sunlight sprays off its gold and into my eyes and I don't know why, I don't know why, I just don't know why but I cry out:

No.

And then it happens.

Mackie leaves his place at the window, his hand darting up from beneath his jacket to stab the silenced pistol into the back of Juan E's skull, which erupts in a sudden whoosh of red.

Dawkins sweeps past the Bravo warlord with a sickle of a forearm that slams him against the wall and sends him and his rifle to the floor.

Django and the other Bravo jerk and fall as Quillen empties his silenced pistol into their torsos.

And CK moves with righteous certainty toward the far window, the Longbore raised in his gloved hands, while Dawkins slides the second Longbore from the floor, swipes the magazine from the fallen Bravo's hand, and I see that Dawkins's hands are gloved, too, those white latex gloves, and he slams the magazine home and moves with that same righteous certainty toward the other window.

I turn and look out, I turn and look down, across the street, to the Free African Methodist Church, to the place where the tide of pink and blue and yellow and white is parted, circling the mighty staircase to the church's open doors, where the microphones are arranged, where the suits are black and the uniforms are blue, where the red-robed pastor gives way to his white-robed colleague from the south, the white-robed man

I've seen on TV, in magazines, the newspapers, the white-robed man who is named Gideon Parks, the Reverend Gideon Parks, who is leading his people, these people, from their long captivity in this modern Egypt, out of slavery and into salvation.

The sound is brute thunder, and the kick of the Longbore shudders through CK and the glass of the window shatters and sends light in all directions and then comes the distant ring of the shell casing as it hits the wooden floor and then the thunder again, this time from my left, from Dawkins's rifle, and the second window shatters, and then again from my right, and then again from my left, and after six shots, three each, they are done, they are done with their shooting but not with what they have planned.

CK spins around, kneels, drops the Longbore to the floor and stabs its stock into the flat of Juan E's lifeless right hand. Dawkins tosses his rifle into the corner of the room. Like Oswald, I'm thinking, just like Oswald.

Okay, CK says, standing and snapping a peek at his watch. Five minutes. Dawkins, Quillen. Go.

Just as the door opens and Rudy Martinez looks in and whistles, says: Party time. He slaps the butt end of the magazine on his machine pistol and heads on down the hallway. Dawkins and Quillen follow, and I hear Martinez, yelling:

They killed Juan E. Those fuckin Bravos killed Juan E.

I look at CK.

CK looks at me.

What the fuck are you doing? I say to CK.

Not a thing, CK says. Not a goddamn thing. Jeez, Lane, I'm not even here. Mackie, Dawkins, Quillen . . . they aren't here. *You* aren't here.

Wild animals are growling somewhere, a few rooms away. Automatic weapons, bursts of rapid fire. Then voices. Shouts. More gunfire.

Listen to that music, CK says. Niggers do such good work. And it's always the same work. They even got a name for it: Black-on-black crime. They're killing each other.

Oh, yeah, I tell him. Nice. Real nice. Let me guess about tomorrow's headlines. Something about a street gang that killed a civil rights leader.

Close enough, CK says. For government work. Because guns and drugs spells assassins. They're the perfect bad guys. They kill the Reverend Gideon Parks and then they kill each other.

Then he says to Mackie: Go.

CK reaches inside his leather jacket and hauls the .44 Magnum from his shoulder holster.

Thought I told you to get out of Dodge, he says.

His eyes drift to the side of my head and his knuckles flex and I pull to the side as he squeezes down and there's this scream in my left ear, this wide-mouthed scream, and I grab at my ear as I look back behind me and I see that Bravo warlord, Daddy Big, trying to stand and then going down like a kid on a Slip'n'Slide, his feet losing it first, arms flailing, and then—bam!—flat on his back. Only this kid isn't getting up to play anymore.

CK looks down the silver snout of that cannon and says to me:

I just saved your life.

I can barely hear, but I tell him right back:

I don't think so. I think that was temporary. I think I'm dead, and it's not so much a question of when but where. You want to tell me why?

If you did what I told you to do—

If I'd done what you said, then what? What?

You'd be heading south, heading home.

As if I care whether you kill me there . . . as opposed to, let's say, here?

I ain't got time for this, Lane.

No, I tell him. They're coming. If you can get past the Bravos and the U Street guys, then the guys downstairs are coming. Cops. Feds. They're coming, CK. They're coming.

He takes another look at his watch. Seems ready to yawn.

Yeah, he says. All in the line of work.

That's when I pull the Glock, there's nothing else to do, I pull the Glock from my belt and I hold it on him as I scoot past the bodies, and he's smiling, just standing there smiling.

Where you gonna go, Lane? Where you gonna go?

I don't know, CK, I tell him. Maybe to hell.

I fire once, blowing plaster out of the wall beside him.

I just saved your life, I tell him. So now we're even.

Then I'm outside, in the hallway, and to my left I see faces, I see black faces and the faces have guns and they're coming up the hallway and I turn to the right and I see white faces and these faces have guns, and there is nothing left for me to do, I dive across the hall and there's another doorway, but there's Martinez and he's hosing the room next door with his machine pistol and when he runs the magazine, Crimso steps in with his AK, jolting flames from the muzzle, and you know the room's a mess. Things go silent and the two of them start to laugh.

Then a voice down the hall, Mackie maybe: Here we go.

Then it's bang bang bang and it's that voice—yes, it is Mackie—and he's saying: He's down. And then there's more laughter and I've got to get to my duffel bag.

They're hustling in the hallway. Five, somebody says. Five down. No, no, four, says somebody else. Then CK:

Count em, he says. Eleven came in, I want ten staying. Make it happen.

Quillen comes past, and he's dragging the body of Daddy Big.

Watch it! Watch it! And this one I can see, some kid darting from his hiding place, a hall closet, and leaping into the middle of them, sawed-off shotgun at his hip.

Gangsta! he yells and lets go with both barrels, but CK puts him down with a classic Mozambique: Two shots to the body, one to the head. Blows the kid right out of his shoes. Punk lost his life to put a couple holes in the ceiling.

It's no contest. These guys are used to drive-bys or just running up and bopping some joker on the street. CK's crew is ready for World War Three.

I roll out of the doorway and scramble down the hall, shooting high, covering fire, as I go. Fifty feet to the staircase and my duffel bag and maybe freedom.

Come on, I'm saying to no one, everyone, but really to myself: Come on. I can't hear the words, just that ringing in my ear and then the snarl of some kind of machine pistol. Rounds bite into the wall behind me, chewing up fat chunks of plaster and drywall and spitting them out.

I pop off the rest of the magazine as I fall into the stairwell. Blue suit coming up the stairs, handgun pointing my way, and I've got no time to reload. I pull the other Glock from my coat and let go left-handed. I'm off balance and the shots are high, out of the center of mass, but they're good ones. Crimson bursts from his head and shoulder, and he spins back and out of sight before I even realize what I've done. Oh, Christ, a dead cop. So call me CK, too.

I'm ready for the next one, his partner, but there's nothing doing in the stairwell. So the cop's alone. My left ear pulses, this sort of push and pull of pain. More gunfire. Somewhere down the hall, it's party central: maximum rock'n'roll. What's left of the U Street kids shooting up the 9 Bravos and trading fire with CK's little army. A three-ring circus. Insane.

I stay right where I am, because this is no time to move. Either they're coming this way or they're not. I say not, but I'm taking no chances. I shake out the magazine on the Glock in my right hand, pull a fresh one from my suit coat, and snap it in.

Footsteps.

Shadows first, then some guy in an Atlanta Braves sweatshirt and fatigues, and then a kid in an oversize shirt and droopy jeans. A couple Bravos. Probably the only ones still vertical. They're waving Uzis back down the hallway and lighting things up pretty well until the sweatshirt guy gets lifted off his feet and blown back out of sight, his right torso pretty much torn away by what has to be some heavy-duty fire. The droopy jeans guy doesn't seem to notice, just runs the mag, tosses the Uzi to the floor, and tears ass down the hall.

I hear him take five shots in the back and then finish the dead man's dance.

Time, gentlemen.

It's CK, and it's one pissed-off CK.

Time is up. Let's move.

I flatten into the wall of the stairwell and they sweep past me, down the hall, dragging the body of the Bravo warlord and one of our guys who's wounded.

I'm trying to think this through, trying to think what comes next, trying to know, trying to know what CK knows and as I'm trying to know I suddenly wish I didn't know, because I don't want to hear these words, but they come, they come, they come:

Fire in the hole.

I don't hear and I just barely see Mackie, moving doorway to doorway in a crouch, coming right toward me, and fuck if he isn't ready, with a Benelli Black Eagle shotgun.

There's a body at his feet, a gangbanger, and he pushes at the kid with the toe of his shoe and then he pushes again. He sighs and lets his shoulders sag. The Benelli swings down, right into the kid's head, and when the shotgun kicks, a clot of brains blows up off the carpet and onto the far wall.

Yeah! he yells out, like this is some kind of football game. Yeah, yeah, yeah! He waves the shotgun at someone down the hall. Now go! Go!

I probably look like a ghost, rising up off the

stairs, covered in plaster dust, pistol in each hand. But no one is watching; no one can see me but the dead kid, the dead cop. Mackie has his back to me, stepping over the mess that used to be the kid's head.

Mackie.

Just saying his name is enough to get him to turn back into my line of fire.

Mackie.

And when he comes around, not wanting to see what he sees, these are the last words that he hears:

Fuck you.

Because that's when I shoot him in the face.

underworld

One down, ten or more to go. Real nice odds. But I've got one thing in my favor:

Their plan is to get out of here alive.

The simplicity of this knowledge keeps me moving. CK's not the suicidal type. An escape is in progress. There is a plan and there is probably a backup plan and there is quite possibly a backup to the backup plan.

Confusion is king. It's been five, maybe six minutes since the shots from the windows. The assault on the hotel is coming but it's yet to come. The dead cop was a loner, unlucky, maybe a would-be hero. Whatever, he was in the wrong place at the wrong time, without any backup. Guys like that deserve what they get.

Problem is, right now I'm one of those guys.

Footsteps to the back of me, but they're running away. Getting away; but how? Elevators? No way. Stairs? Not these stairs. Fire escape? Too open, too obvious, unless there's something on the alley side. Must be another set of stairs at the hotel's alley side.

I will not bunker down, let them come for me. Because they aren't coming, they're on their way out; and coming in . . . well, coming in we've got the wrath of God.

Still, confusion is king. Ten floors below, on the street, it must be madness, the lid of sanity blown off just like the Reverend's head. A mob scene, a world of screams and sirens, and not enough badges to handle the traffic. Whoever's out there—NYPD for sure, maybe a couple FBI guys, and probably some trigger-happy members of the Reverend's personal security force—they're rushing into the lobby of the hotel. If they can agree that the shots came from here. I can see them ticking off the same old options: elevators, stairs, probably even the fire escapes. All covered. So where is CK going? Where am I going?

There isn't even a choice: I have to go up.

Taking the stairs two and three at a time, breathless before I clear three floors, I hear a commotion and decide to haul in a second and have a listen.

Someone else is making time on the steps. I have to think cops, but the echo is getting to me; the echo's not right. And at last I realize why: The echo's coming down.

Down, for Christ's sake. But that's impossible. No SWAT team on the roof, not yet, so it's one of us. Meaning one of them. And then I remember CK's briefing: Meehan on the roof. Meehan, with the U Street kid, what's-his-name, Lil Ace, on the roof.

The footsteps are coming closer, and there's no doubt it's just one guy. Which means that Lil Ace went horizontal on the roof.

I start back down the stairs, reach the mess coming up from the ninth floor, and keep going, taking a quick peek at the cop I put down and damn if it's not a cop. I mean he looks like a cop, NYPD blue with red roses of blood blooming out of his shoulder, but his name is Ernie Gonsalves and he's one of CK's drivers.

Doors slam open somewhere below and a lot of feet are doing a hustle on the steps. More drama.

It's time to move. Success or six feet.

This time I go slowly, only trusting the muffled sound of things. I holster the Glocks, slip the shotgun from my duffel bag, take a deep breath and then pump. Mossberg Model 500 combat 12 gauge, with a folding stock. A fat kerchunk chambers the first of seven rounds. Heavy shot. Double-ought buck. I'm ready to rumble.

I shrug the duffel onto my shoulder and I turn the corner, don't even look, just fire once, pump, fire again. The shots blow the far wall into pieces but that's about all. Someone's crouched beneath the cloud of plaster dust, and he lets loose with a pistol and I pull in, use the doorframe for cover, and the numbers are still running through my head, ten of them—ten of them, at least ten of them—and then I remember the guy coming down the stairs, the guy coming right down on my back, and that's when I start to think I hear more footsteps. Footsteps from below, a lot of them, running hard.

I lean the muzzle of the shotgun around the doorframe and fire again. It's a 12-bore question, and the answer is a torrent of firepower that sends me right back, almost tripping over Gonsalves's body, as I watch the doorframe and half the surrounding wall ripped into splinters.

My fucking brothers in arms.

Down. It's got to be down. I dance over Gonsalves and down the stairs, push through the door and look up, they're no doubt coming for me now, and I empty the shotgun into the ceiling. Electrical wires flail, sparking, and the lights go out on nine.

I duck into the first of the rooms, as deserted as the rest, and I reload the Mossberg. The barrel is hot, and a little curl of smoke flies in front of my eyes.

It's left or right, and since there are a half-dozen guys with burners coming from the left, I don't really have a choice. A deep breath, and then I run.

Nothing happens.

But only for a moment. I hear someone yell an indecipherable string of words that ends in *now*, and then I hear some pistol shots and I'm thinking I'm okay, I'm thinking I'm going to make it.

Then I hear the Uzi. And I keep on running.

The rounds buzzsaw to the left and over me. Too close. Too, too close.

That's when I realize: I'm at the end of the hall. And there are no doors, no stairs.

No way out.

Fuck that. I'm no rat and this is no maze. I pull a pistol and fire wildly back down the hall, just making noise. Then I kick at the wall, and the plaster and wood fall into shards and sand. Worm-eaten, dry rot, termite damage, ancient, and it's my fucking life.

I tuck the pistol back into my belt and get busy.

I don't even aim, just swing the mouth of the shotgun toward the wall and let go. The first shot blows a triangle of softball-sized holes through the plaster, the second one turns the holes to the size of basketballs, and by the fourth and fifth pump I start to see light, I see something on the other side, and that's when I look back, shadows moving, shadows coming from the doors, the stairs, so it's now or never, and I turn back on what's left of the wall and I fire and I fire and I fire again and when I click on empty I just run, I duck my head and I lead with my right shoulder, and I run straight into that wall and I feel the plaster, the wallboard, the bricks, the whole ripped and rotten thing tear apart, I feel like eight people are hitting me and then none, there's nothing, and I hit the floor, the floor on the other side, in the building next door, and the shotgun goes sliding down the floor.

Ahead is another hallway, this one bright, wallpapered in white and yellow, and as I pull myself up, a door on my right opens, and this old black guy looks out at me like I'm room service and he says:

Did you hear that noise?

Yeah, I say, crawling back to my feet. Yeah, yeah. I heard the noise. Listen, we got a problem.

Dear Jesus, he says, shaking his head. Blessed Jesus.

I'm past him, and when I kneel to get the shotgun I can feel the pain coming on—I just went through a fucking wall—but I pull up and stagger to the next door and I slam the butt of the shotgun into the thing twice. Guy comes to the door, a greyheaded grampa, looking bewildered. He can't take his eyes off the Mossberg. I tell him the first lie that comes to mind:

Police. You got to get out of the building.

What? he says.

I glance back at that tear in the wall and I can see the flames licking away. Fire. No one speaks but I hear the word. Fire. I can hear, tucked in some little place in the back of my head that's reserved for such nightmares, the voice calling:

Fire in the hole.

I said you got to get out of here.

Now this frail little woman, his wife, I guess, is standing next to him, squinting at me through eyes filled with tears and she's saying, John Henry Mason, who is this man? What is going on here?

Fire, I tell them. The building is on fire.

She looks at him. He looks at me. Not a clue. Then she says: They've killed the Reverend Parks. They've killed the Reverend Parks. They've—

Don't you understand? I tell her. There's a *fire*. I'm shouting now, and farther down the corridor, another door opens. Another pair of black faces looks out. They're afraid. So afraid.

Burning, I call to them. On fire. The building is burning, and you've got to get out. You've got to get out now.

And the little lady is pulling a blur of drab fur, some kind of poodle or something, up into her arms and she's saying, John Henry? Do something, John Henry. The building is on fire.

That's when I see the red box, the alarm, by the elevators. I hustle down there and I break the glass and I pull the alarm and there's nothing.

I turn back to the old-timers, six or seven of them by now, and say, Get out of—

There's this fierce whoop-whoop-whoop as the alarm finally kicks in and that really gets things going, whoop-whoop-whoop, and people are out of their apartments and into the hall, people are yelling, and now smoke is wheezing through that black hole from the other building, and people are grabbing things, people are putting on jackets and coats and robes, people are starting for the steps and I stuff the Mossberg back into the duffel bag and I'm ahead of them and all of a sudden there is this spike of pressure like someone slapping at my ears and I trip, I fall, I try to stand, and that's when the sound of the explosion rips into me and I fall again and when I finally find my feet a wave of heat blows over me and then the screams, those awful screams, start echoing all around me, but by now I'm down the hall and I kick through the door beneath the exit sign and I'm running, I'm running down the stairs, and I listen to my feet striking the concrete, a distant sound, hollow and muffled, and when I pull up the number on the door reads 3 and I don't hear a thing and I don't know whether the ringing is in my ears, there's just this whoop-whoop-whoop, but it can't matter now, nothing matters now, nothing but getting out out out, and I take the next flight of stairs slowly, people are moving into the stairwells, people with dull eyes, people with questioning eyes, people hurrying down the stairs, wondering aloud at the whoop-whoop-whoop and the second explosion that suddenly rocks our world, and on the next flight I wait for a moment, everyone is going down, no one coming up, and then I run down that set of stairs, run past the door marked LOBBY and on down the next flight of stairs and then the next and then I'm at the door marked GARAGE and I start to straighten my tie and when I look down at my clothes I know why the guy upstairs was looking so hard at me, I see this kind of ghastly hobo haberdashery stained with plaster dust and blood and I think:

Fuck it.

I pull my pistol. Into the garage, back underground again. I walk out into the fluorescent dinginess like I own the place, looking for my Nissan Sentra or whatever I happened to park down here after I took the grandkids to school, and the light is low and I'm looking for an attendant but I don't see one, I don't see anybody and that's the way I like it.

This is no suburban parking lot but an inner-city boneyard. Cars, left and right, and most of them road-weary and worn. Half of them look like they've been parked here for years. Not many choices. I stand there, dusting off my suit coat, my pants, trying to put myself back together again, and I think maybe the beat-up Vanagon but that won't help me if I have to play stock car, so I decide on an old Buick Regal instead. I switch the plates with a Caddy, looking good, looking real good, and now there's nothing left to do but boost this baby and find my way back home.

I bend down and start to work on the lock of

the door. Jam the blade of my pocketknife into the lock, work it side to side until I hear the metal plate inside go click. And then the footsteps.

That's when some motherfucker shoots me in the back.

And the light shineth in darkness;
and the darkness comprehended it not.

—The Gospel According to St. John 1:5

city of the walking dead

It's no big thing to take a bullet. Especially the ones you don't see coming. The ones from a distance. The ones in the back. In places like Manhattan and Detroit and Dirty City, people do it every day.

The tough thing is getting back up.

I have no idea how long I'm horizontal, eating the filthy concrete of that garage. I have no idea why no one checks me out, why no one kicks me in the ribs. Why no one shoots me in the back of the head. Maybe people are in a hurry and maybe I look very dead.

I don't feel dead. My life doesn't flash before my eyes. I don't float up to the ceiling, look down, and see my body. There's none of this walking toward a bright light, no tunnel with my mother standing at the end, waving me back: It's not your time, it's not your time. No pearly gates, no dancing with angels, and I sure as shit don't get a glimpse of Heaven.

What I see is the weirdest thing:

It's this dog, this tiny dog, and the dog comes limping out of the shadows beneath the Buick Regal. I had this dog when I was a kid. I haven't thought about him for years. I must have been eight, nine years old when I had this dog, and I had him for all of maybe a summer. He was this little, and I do mean little, runt, probably weighed in at all of ten pounds, part Pekingese and part confusion, with what my grandpop called a coat of many colors. He had one eye; that was the way he was born. And not many teeth. Then he got hit by a car or something and his back was twisted up so bad he couldn't walk, so he just sort of hobbled around. The only thing going for him was that somehow, despite it all, he was the best dog a kid could have.

His name was—what else?—Lucky. I loved that little pup, and when he went away it was the worst day of my life. What can I say? I didn't know then how much worse it was going to get.

But now, see, Lucky is back, he's wandering out from under that Buick and since my face is on the pavement, he's looking right at me. With his one eye. At first he limps over and starts licking my nose. Then he sort of sits back and he cocks his head to one side and he says to me, he says:

You left me.

Now it comes as no surprise that my dog, who's been dead for maybe thirty-five years, can talk or that I understand what he has to say. The whole thing makes perfect sense. I even recognize his voice.

It's just that I have trouble talking back.

You left me, he says again.

I try, I really try, but I can't find any words and I can't tell Lucky he's wrong. I try but I can't tell him I was at school that day. The day he went away. That I went to Little League baseball practice and didn't come home until six o'clock. That when I came into the kitchen, my mother was cooking chicken and dumplings and my father was paying bills and after they ignored me long enough my grandpop took his nose out of the newspaper and told me that a chicken hawk had flown down from the sky and taken Lucky away. As if I was going to believe that's what really happened.

Lucky licks my nose again. That eye of his cuts into me. Gospel truth: It's not blinking.

I want to kiss his forehead. Give him a cookie. But I can't. I can't move. I can't speak. That's when he bites into my face and I can feel the skin slice open beneath my eye, I'm crying blood, and he winks at me and runs away, the limp is gone, his back is straight and he's dancing, Lucky's dancing, and then he's scampering back under the Buick, back into the shadows.

That gets me moving. I touch the wound on my cheek, feel something warm and wet. Then I realize I can't feel anything else, and before I can even think I'm paralyzed my hands are pushing me off the floor.

I manage to get onto an elbow when I hear the next voice:

Lookin good, Burdon Lane. Lookin real good.

At least that's what I think he's saying. My left ear hears only a dial tone, thanks to CK's Magnum.

I spit the grit off my tongue, and then I spit the words:

Fuck you.

Whoever shot me made three mistakes:

He used a popgun, probably a .22.

He shot me in the back.

And he only shot me once.

So instead of making a nonrefundable deposit on a six-foot sleep sofa, I've got a good taste of pavement, a left arm so far asleep that it's a pincushion, some kind of flesh wound under my eye, and a place south of my left shoulder blade that feels like it's taken a sharp swing from a ball peen hammer. Whatever took me down will bruise me like Jehu, but it won't kill me. Unless there's internal bleeding. Got to keep thinking those happy kinds of thoughts.

I'm wearing a Kevlar Type IIA ballistic vest. The brand name is Second Chance. Like the big-nosed guy on the TV used to say: Don't leave home without it.

Now there's no such thing as a bulletproof vest. The Du Pont guys invented this Kevlar stuff for tires and didn't know what they had till later. They call it bullet resistant, which means this Kevlar stuff is like that carpet fiber they make; you know, it's stain resistant, which is the smile, the nod, the wink: You live with a kid or a dog or a drunk, you know your carpet's going to get dirty. Well, if you wear a vest, you might still get wet. Good enough shot, good enough round, you'll go down, vest or no vest. Wounds don't always kill you, anyway; it's the shock that counts.

Which is not the kind of shock I'm having now that I see who's talking to me, who's standing there with what looks like one of my Glocks pointed at my head, who else but the Yellow Nigger, my new pal Jinx.

So I say the very first thing that comes to mind:

Where were you?

The wolf smile, just a little teeth, and he says:

You on the floor. I'm askin the questions.

Yeah, yeah, yeah, I tell him. If this guy wanted me dead—well, I'd be dead right now. So I say to him:

Okay. Ask away.

He decides to prove the point and angles the pistol away. His eyes rock upstairs.

They dead, ain't they?

All of your guys, I tell him. I'm trying to figure where this is going. Right about now there's only one safe answer, and that's what I tell him: Maybe all of mine.

Maybe? he says.

Way maybe, I tell him.

And you?

I got lucky.

That's when I see that little dog again. Lucky. *You left me*, Lucky says. *Left me*.

Some kind of luck, Jinx tells me. Out of the fryin pan, Frosty. And into my fire.

He levels the pistol back into my face. Christ, I am getting tired of that shit.

Get yourself off the floor and into the car.

Easier said than done. My left arm is still napping, but that ball peen hammer feeling is gone. Now it's like sharp knives are rooting around in my back and carving me an upper asshole. I take a deep breath and it hurts. I hook the door handle and it hurts. I try to pull myself up and it hurts. Onto my knees, okay. Onto my feet—

Whoa. Somebody's playing games with the concrete, it's tilting left, then right, then left again. A goddamn sea cruise. I get my hands up, but only a little because of the buzzing in my arm and the agony in my back. I stagger toward Jinx. He grabs my left arm, and that's when I lean into him, forcing his pistol hand away with the weight of my body, and put the punch to his gut. I kick up but I miss his crotch, my knee driving hard into his hip instead, and he's got his forearm under my chin and he smashes me back into the car and it doesn't hurt, it's beyond simple things like pain now, and I've got nothing to do but slide right down onto my butt.

Time is tickin, boy. That's what Jinx tells me. Get the fuck up. Get up and get in the trunk.

So now I start over. I find the door handle, use it for leverage, and it takes a while but I get to my feet and try to get my bearings. The waters have calmed. My legs are steadier. But:

I'm not getting in the trunk, I tell him.

The pistol again.

I shake my head. So he knows that I know he isn't going to use it. At least not now, not here.

You want out of here? he says.

Yeah, I tell him.

And then I tell him: Okay. Yeah. So I'm getting in the trunk.

This is not a smart move but I don't think I have a choice. I manage to get one leg up and into the trunk when he gives me a shove.

Hey—

I start to tell him about how he ought to pop a hole in the lid, the side panel, somewhere, give me some fresh air, but it's wham-bam-no-thank-you-ma'am and I'm locked in the trunk of some old Buick Regal that's parked in the basement of a burning building, and I have this sudden feeling that this is where I'm going to stay, and I think to myself, I think: Well, life is what you make it.

This is when I hear the engine fight for life with a cough straight from a throat cancer patient. Everything rattles. The engine turns and turns and after a while it gets going.

My next breath is fumes and my sinuses burn. The Buick is moving, slowly at first, then picking up speed, and I feel an incline and a turn and another incline and the air is getting better but I don't know how long it's going to last.

Then we stop.

I hear sirens and I hear voices and more sirens and I listen and I listen and I don't hear anything for a moment and then I hear Jinx's voice and somebody else. Then Jinx, then somebody else, and the car starts rolling. Stops. Starts. Stops again. Starts, and it's picking up speed and more speed and now I know that somehow, someway, Jinx has driven that old Buick Regal right out of the hurricane, we've made it, we're out, because it's potholes and broken pavement and honking horns, the stink of sewers and sad-faced people.

Hey, New York. Like Old Blue Eyes used to sing: My kind of town.

Except, come to think of it, that's Chicago.

the light of the world

Jesus said: I am the light.

That was before they hung him out to dry on a couple two-by-fours.

I learned that Jesus guy's story a long time ago, right about the time I lost my dog Lucky. They told me that guy's story in Sunday School at the First Baptist Church. I learned that story, and I learned my lesson, too. You keep your mouth shut, and you stay out of the light. Otherwise they'll hang you out to dry, maybe not on a piece of wood but the same sort of thing. And nobody's going to come around on Sundays to worship you.

It's too bright, that light. You see everything. You see so much you get blind. Which is my problem right about now. Too much light. Sunlight. Noon, maybe, who knows? I squint out the ass end of the Buick Regal and into everything, so bright that it's nothing. Light so bright it hurts. Then one big black shadow that hides it all.

The light and the dark, that's what it's all about.
At least that's what they said it was about, and
not just in the Sunday School stories but in the
grade school stories and the television stories and
all the rest of the fucking stories. There's the good
guys and there's the bad guys, the light and the
dark, the white and the black, and nothing no
way nothing in between. No grey. No fucking
way there's grey.

I see those hands, big and black, coming out of
the light, reaching down for me, and I hear that
voice, whispering, whispering at the back of my
head:

Kill the nigger.

Then I hear the other voice, the voice that's in
my face, the dreamy toke voice of Jinx as he reels
my face in close to his and says:

Got me a Chevy.

I start to say something smart and I cough and I
cough and I don't think I'm ever going to stop
coughing. My lungs feel like I've been sucking
five packs a day since the time I learned about
Jesus.

Jinx hauls me up like a sack of garbage and I'm
out of that stinking trunk and onto dry land.
There's nothing like a long hard ride in the trunk
of a Buick Regal to make you love life. Breathing
through a handkerchief, wishing for a taste of
fresh air, feeling your kidneys squirm. Contem-
plating the agony of your bruised back with each

bumpity-bump. Watching the past few hours of your life over and over again, like some bad video you rented and can't get out of the tape deck:

See Burdon Lane. See Burdon Lane fuck up. See Burdon Lane fuck up big time. See Burdon Lane dead in the trunk of a Buick.

Somewhere in there, round about the fourth or fifth time through that sorry adventure through the looking-glass, I did about the only good thing you can do when you're locked in the trunk of a car: I fell asleep. Or the fumes got to me. And somehow I managed to wake up. Now I just got to get out of this sunlight and find me a cold six-pack.

Hey.

I'm still squinting and I still can't make out Jinx's face.

Or the face of the guy next to him. This guy's wearing a bad suit, sort of thing you can pick up at the Goodwill for five bucks, shiny *Soul Train* polyester with a shirt that used to be yellow, and from what I can see of him, he looks like Uncle Ben with about three teeth and a serious hankering for Four Roses.

Hee-hee, the Uncle Ben guy says. Lookee what dropped out the poop chute.

I'm too busy breathing to take much offense. Besides, Jinx is dealing dollars into the Uncle Ben guy's hand and I do think he's the rest of the way out of here, wherever here happens to be.

Where the hell are we? I say to Jinx, and it cramps my throat and I start coughing again.

You in a world of hurt, Jinx says. Then:

Me, though, I'm in Newark. This here's the back of Dooley's Yard. And this here—he tilts his head toward the Uncle Ben guy—this is Arbutus Dooley. And Mr. Dooley, he done bought himself a Buick Regal.

Hee-hee, the Uncle Ben guy says again to nobody special. Then to Jinx:

Better make that another fifty, cool breeze. Didn't know you wanted ole Dooley forgettin somethin white.

Tell you what, old man, Jinx says. He shows the Uncle Ben guy a bill with a pair of zeroes, crushes it into a ball, and adds it to the rumpled stack of green in the guy's right palm. Startin now, you can go and forget every white man in the whole fuckin state.

Hee-hee, the Uncle Ben guy says as he nods a few times and shuffles off to wherever he's got a bottle and a place to put his butt and do his forgetting.

Let's get goin, Jinx says to me. He gestures to this sedan that looks painted with urine, and it's a Chevrolet, but that's all I can say about it. I don't have the faintest clue about the name or the year, just that it's a Chevy something. And its trunk is open like the maw of some hungry metal beast.

Beyond the Chevy something is the first of many gnarled mountains of rusted junk.

Hate to lose that Buick, Jinx says. I love all that metal. Nice smooth ride, too, you know what I'm sayin?

He drills me with those shaded eyes, not showing a smile, not anything. Then he's past me, pulling open the back door of the Buick.

Still, he says. Can't be takin no chances. Somebody gonna be missin these wheels sooner or later. NYPD Blue doin their job today, it's gonna be sooner.

That's as right as rain, I tell him, and I'm feeling better about this already.

Now get in the car.

Uh-uh, I tell him. Just do what you got to do, and do it now. I ain't getting in the trunk of that car.

He reaches into the Buick, slides my duffel bag from the back seat.

Naw, you ain't gettin in the trunk of no car. You ridin with me, bubba. But this—

He lifts the duffel bag.

This motha goes in the trunk.

And in it goes. He tosses my duffel into the trunk of the Chevy something, slams the lid, and says:

Now get in the fuckin car.

So we're in the front seat of that Chevy something, he's driving and I'm riding an empty-handed shotgun, and he's grooving the Chevy something down a ribbon of dirt and rock, past the hand-painted sign for Dooley's Yard and onto a deserted street, the last lap of some industrial park turned into the usual Jersey wasteland.

Just two things, he says to me. I drive. You sit over there, you keep your hands on your lap. And you talk. You got a lotta talkin to do, cracker.

Oh, yeah? I tell him.

Oh yeah, he says. You got somethin to tell me, and the sooner you tell me, the better.

Oh, yeah? I tell him.

Oh yeah, he says. Cause we're almost there.

Oh, yeah? I tell him. Because it's a sign of weakness to ask him where, and I think I have a pretty good idea about this there place, anyway. It's one of those places, been there, done that, and it's probably that rat-trap remains of a gas station up ahead, no, no, come to think of it, that clump of trees behind the station looks more like the place. Yeah, that's it, that's . . . there.

He weaves the Chevy something past the rusted Sunoco sign and through the pumps and around to the back of the station. I don't even wait for him to tell me to get out of the car. I just dismount and head for the trees.

Hey, he says, hustling from behind the driver's seat to catch up with me. He's pulled that Ruger .38.

Let's get it over with, I tell him, and I duck

under some branches, fighting my way deeper
into the trees until I find a nice pocket of grass. It's
a shitty place to have to die, but when you think
about it, there's no good place to die. This looks
like a little bit of peace, though, so I say:

Pull the fucking trigger and let me get some
sleep.

You a bad man, Burdon Lane. A real bad man.
You gonna let me cap you, that it? You gonna step
off right here and now?

Believe it or not, I manage to yawn.

I'm tired and I'm hurting, I tell him. So just . . .
do it.

Tell me why, he says. You gonna go down for
your crew? This some kind of white-boy G thing?

Maybe you don't know nothing about that.

Me? Probly not. I'm just a nigga from Southeast
D.C. But you, devil, you capped the Reverend
Gideon Parks.

I didn't kill—

And here I stop because I started to say nobody,
but I sure did kill somebody and then I killed
somebody else, didn't I? So I just say:

I didn't kill Gideon Parks.

You mean you didn't pull the trigger.

Listen. Believe what you want, pal, but I knew
jack nothing. It was a run. A meet. A deal. Money
for guns, that was it. And that's all I do. That's my
job. Money for guns, guns for money.

That's all you do, then why you wantin to get dead?

Because you want me to tell you something, and I'm not talking.

You gonna go down for them guys? You been played, Burdon Lane.

Could be, I tell him. Could be that you been played, too.

Don't crack wise with me, white boy.

Easy thing to say, I tell him, when you got a gun in your hand.

Ain't that the truth, he says, and it's the funniest truth I've ever heard, sort of sounds like the thing you put on top of a house: troof.

I take another pass at this stand of trees. It really is a shitty place to die and I don't feel like dying yet. And this Jinx guy, he doesn't feel like killing me. Yet. So that means there's another game to play. I tell him:

You think I'm gonna tell you something, pal, then you're wrong. So you got a problem: You can kill me, but then you don't get to find out what you want to know. But if you don't kill me, well, then you got to live with me. And that ain't gonna be easy.

No shit, he says. He armpits the Ruger and stands there for a long, long while before making his move.

So, Mr. Lane, he says. Where we goin?

Funny thing, I tell him. That's what I was about to ask you.

No, he says. That's what you bout to tell me.

I just smile and he shakes his head.

You worse than my old grandmomma. Where we goin, you fuckin ghost, is to find your mothafuckin friends. The meetin place. The rendezvous. The one nobody told me or Juan E about. And it ain't Morristown, neither.

Really? I tell him.

Don't you really me, punk. Maybe I should just dig you a ditch.

Yeah, right. Sticks and stones, pal. Sticks and fucking stones. You know you don't want to kill me, and hey, I know you know. So—

So what?

So tell me about Morristown. Why it ain't Morristown.

I know things too, fool.

Like I told you, pal. I know you know. What I want to know is: How do you know?

I called me that 1-900 number, he says. Dionne Warwick on the Psychic Hotline.

Yeah, well, I hope she told you how you're gonna take down whoever you find wherever it is you're going. With a couple handguns or whatever you got.

Ah, he says. But I ain't gonna be doin it by myself, now am I?

Guess he's got me there.

He checks the horizon, says:

And the sooner we get started, the sooner we get done.

He straightens his sunglasses.

Okay, white boy. I'm drivin, you're ridin. Where we goin?

So I'm back in the front seat of that Chevy something, shaking out the cramps in my arms and legs and wishing I could get the set of steak knives out of my spine. But I'm not telling this Jinx guy where we're going, I'm telling him how we're getting there, which is to say I'm telling him to keep driving south, to stay on the New Jersey Turnpike, to go past the part where the highway divides so the trucks can go one way and the cars can go another way, past the part where it comes back together again, past the part with three lanes and into the part with two lanes, to keep driving and driving and driving. South.

I wonder whether CK was lying about the second rendezvous. I mean, with what was about to go down, would the guy really tell me the rendezvous? CK's not that stupid. But he sure is that arrogant.

Hey, I say to Jinx. Don't suppose you'd let me get into my duffel bag?

Jinx doesn't answer. He makes that Chevy something leap lanes; the guy must be doing eighty and I'm not sure I like the feeling. Just what we need are some Jersey jackboots busting our chops for speeding.

Hey, man, I tell him. Ease back. I only want to get some aspirin.

You hurtin? Shit, man, you shouldn't be hurtin. You a bad man. A big bad man. One of the hitters that did the Reverend Gideon Parks.

I told you. I told you, pal. And I ain't gonna tell you again. I didn't shoot the guy.

Naw, he says to me. Naw, you didn't shoot. You just watched. Is that what you're tellin me? You just watched the parade passin by.

Hey, I say to him. Doesn't much matter what I say, does it?

Wrong, he says, and then he adds: As rain.

I mean, the guy's dead. Does anything else matter?

Fuck, yeah, he says to me. Man was dead already. Don't you think he knew that? Don't you think he knew he was walkin round with the crosshairs on his head? Don't you think he knew the time was gonna come? Shit.

What matters, Jinx says, and here comes that word again, is the truth. What people know, what people remember. The time came for him, maybe sooner than he thought, but who knows, maybe later. So the Reverend Parks gets a memorial service, he gets all sorts of speeches, he gets some schools and streets named after him, maybe he even gets a day named after him. But he's gone, the man is gone, and pretty soon people remember what they been told to remember bout him, and they don't remember what he did and they sure don't remember what he stood for. We got our martyrs, man. We got a few too many of em. What we're missin is the message. We're good at that, rememberin the man and forgettin the message. Forgettin the truth. You know what I'm sayin?

Right about now I don't know anything. I don't want to know anything. I'm just listening and thinking this one through.

Meantime, Jinx says, they got the perfect patsies, don't they? Bunch of no-good gangstas. Guntotin pushermen. Worst kind of niggas. Probly say it was rap music made em do it. So hey, Burdon Lane, what do you say? Was it rap music up there? Is that what it was, made things so crazy?

He reaches over and stabs at the radio, gets static, punches at buttons and gets a Country and Western tune, punches again and gets the voice, that voice, the serious voice of death and disaster, the one they must teach in Newscasting 101, the voice that's saying: Blah blah Gideon Parks blah. Blah blah blah shot blah blah dead. Blah statement blah blah White House blah the President blah blah blah blah blah this tragic blah blah blah civil rights leader blah blah life cut short blah blah blah warring street gangs blah U Street Crew blah blah blah 9 Bravos blah blah methamphetamine blah blah explosion blah blah blah blah still at large—

How do they know all that shit already? Jinx says to me. U Street? The Bravos? And what's with this . . . meth lab?

I know what he's thinking. The Feds tried that one at Waco. I remember passing the hotel room with Toons and Fryer and those satchels. Looked like Semtex to me. And it sure felt like it. The shit just keeps getting deeper. Then:

Still at large? Jinx says to me.

Yeah, I tell him, as the newscast cycles through sound bites of shock and disbelief and sorrow before getting back to the blah blahs.

A little something to keep the boys in blue busy, I tell him. Then I tell him more than I ought to tell him, but I want to remind the guy why he needs to keep me alive. They wasted the Bravo ringleader, I tell him. That Daddy Big guy. They killed him, hell, they killed them all, but they dragged his body out, probably planning to dump him somewhere deep. Nobody's gonna find him, but a lot of folks with badges are gonna waste a lot of time looking. And hey, it's gonna make for a lot of search warrants in Harlem and the Ville, maybe even in D.C.

He's letting that one simmer and the whole thing is a beauty, it's a piece of work, because he's right, they've got the perfect patsies, they're dealers and they're thugs and they're killers and they're black. And best of all, they're dead. Very, very dead. Talk about tidy.

Jinx punches the buttons on the radio again and there's no one talking, there's just music *thrown like a stone in my vast sea* and I look at him but he can't know, he doesn't know, he can't possibly know *I opened my eyes to take a peek* and I reach for the POWER button *to find that I was by the sea* and turn the damn thing off.

Here's what we're gonna do, I tell him. Take the next exit. You decide which way you want to go, west or east. You got even odds; maybe you'll guess right. If you don't, well, maybe I'll tell you, maybe not. Whichever way we go, I'm gonna start telling you to take turns. Maybe they'll take us where we're going, maybe not.

You scared of somethin? he says.

No, I tell him. It's just a good day for a drive. You take care of your business, which is driving the car, and I'll take care of mine.

So we take the next exit and we go right and then we go right again, and I tell him to take a left and we take a left and we go for a while before I tell him to take another left and after enough of this wandering around south Jersey, we get to what looks like the middle of nowhere, which is where it is, and I tell him to stop the car and get it over onto the shoulder of the road.

Time to walk, I tell him, and he's no dummy, he knows we're not going to drive right up to the place. So he's out of the Chevy something and he keys the trunk and takes out my duffel bag and he says:

Lead on.

But I ain't going nowhere, which is what I tell him. Not yet.

I nod to my duffel bag and I tell him: Hey. You know what that Bible guy said about walking through that valley? The one with the shadow of death? The guy who was fearing no evil?

Yeah, Jinx says to me. I know him. Book of Psalms.

Well, that guy, he was carrying a Glock. Two of them, in fact. So what do you say? If you find what you're looking for out there, you're gonna need the help.

Doubt it, he says. And there ain't nothin in the King James version bout Glocks. But maybe in the King Jinx version—

He reaches into the duffel, slips out the first of my pistols, hands it to me, then gives me the second one.

While I'm popping and checking the magazines, he says:

How do I know you ain't gonna find a time to pull one of those things and blast me?

You don't, I tell him. And you know what? That's the sort of thing that makes life so interesting.

rendezvous

So we diddybop through the trees, staying low, and there's my new pal Jinx doing the bob-and-weave and I know for a fact, looking at him move, that he's been in both kinds of jungles: the grey and the green. Moves like a cat. No doubt bites like one, too.

He's got that Ruger revolver, carries it out and down, finger off the trigger and pointing down the barrel. Definitely a professional.

I've got the duffel bag looped over my shoulder and the Glocks parked back in my holsters. Jinx follows my lead but keeps a good interval, about ten yards behind me. Sooner or later he takes my cue and slides behind a tree trunk as the foliage starts to clear. Checks his pistol and brings it up to his shoulder, at the ready.

Stay loose, man, I tell him—and maybe myself. Just stay loose.

I nod ahead to what we can see of the warehouse, the first in a series of low-slung two-story jobs that are owned by Vanegar Chemical Supply, and I know nothing about the company but I know a lot about the line of automobiles parked on the far side of the warehouse next to a concrete viaduct. I've driven a few of those cars in my time.

There's two ways we can do this thing, I say to Jinx: My way or the wrong way. So stay close. And whatever you do, don't shoot until I say to shoot.

Without another word we work the tree line to the cover closest to the warehouse, a swatch of brush that's nearly man height. I look at Jinx and he shrugs, nothing doing, so I take a peek. What I count is about a hundred yards of grass and weeds between us and the building. We've got pistols. Maybe they can do it in the movies—shit, they can do anything in the movies—but there's no way we can use handguns across that kind of distance and have a prayer of hitting anything but empty space.

Check out the windows, I tell him. The backside of the warehouse is dressed in cheap aluminum siding, with a pair of windows and a fire door at its midpoint. If someone's there, we're seen as soon as we break cover; if not, maybe it's a way inside. Sunlight is on the glass, so it's one big guess about whether anyone's at home.

My guess is no, and Jinx's must be the same, because when I step through the brush he steps out from the tree line like he's joining me on a picnic. There's nothing doing, nothing at all but sunshine and blue skies, and I'm thinking we should skirt the right side of the warehouse, use the trash Dumpster there for cover, but I'm also thinking it's quiet. Just like they say in the movies: too quiet.

I'm about to wave Jinx my way when I hear the kiss of tires on blacktop and I make a break for the warehouse but I'm not going to make it so I drop into the grass and hope. Jinx is younger and he's faster and he hustles up and flattens into the aluminum siding of the warehouse just as the car rolls past the Dumpster and into view, and it's a Crown Vic, civilian colors but as obvious as month-old meat: It looks and smells bad. Cops.

I put my finger to my lips for Jinx and he nods and holds, and when I look again, the Crown Vic has cruised past the Dumpster and out of sight.

I make my way to the Dumpster, settle back against the warm metal, and say to Jinx: Coming your way. Check out the tires.

He eases over to the far corner of the warehouse, peeks around, and tells me: Radials.

They got whitewalls?

White as snow, he tells me.

Not the locals, then. State troopers, I tell him. Or Feds. How about the haircuts?

Not too short, not too long, he tells me.

Six'll get you ten they're Feds, I tell him. Then I

tell myself: Which means something's funky as a monkey.

Damn, he says to me.

Damn right, I tell him. You don't need no Psychic Hotline for this one. They're looking for us. Or should I say me. Or—

I don't even want to go down that road. That one is marked with a red sign.

Jinx says: We got to get our asses out of here.

Yeah.

Now.

No, I tell him. Not now. Not yet. Right now we wait. Something is fucked up here.

He's got something to say but he's not saying it, and I lean around the corner of the Dumpster and we both watch the cop car and it's turning away, it's heading north along the access road and it's accelerating and we wait and we wait and then there's just dust and it's gone.

I walk out to the access road, read the tire marks, they run right past the parking lot, and I try to think this one through. We got blues at the rendezvous. So maybe CK and the boys didn't make it out of that building. Maybe somebody got caught. Or killed. Or . . . maybe CK wasn't being stupid or arrogant when he gave me this spot, maybe he told me because it's a setup.

Maybe maybe maybe.

But maybe doesn't explain one car and two cops, or what happens when I follow that access road into the parking lot. When I look around and see nothing, the kind of nothing that is every-thing.

They ain't here, Burdon Lane.

No, I tell him.

What I see is something I haven't seen for a lot of years. Many, many years, but never too many years to make me forget. It's not the kind of thing you're ever likely to forget, unless you were lucky and got yourself a head wound.

I'm standing in the middle of an alien footprint, a place of bent and flattened grass and scattered pebbles, an awkward circle pressed down from the sky, and my gut takes a very bad dip.

They were here, I tell him, and in my mind I see Renny, yeah, I see Renny Two Hand, and he's parking the Oldsmobile in the lot at the side of the warehouse, where a fleet of indiscriminate cars wait for their turn on the road or for scrap. He drove the Oldsmobile down from the Warwick Hotel, he's a good soldier and he's done exactly what I told him, he's parking the Oldsmobile over there in that line of forgotten cars, and that's where I walk. And it's there; Christ, the car is there.

Ain't nobody here, Jinx calls after me, but he's wrong. There's someone, oh, yes, there's someone. Because there's the Oldsmobile, third car in a row of the kinds of cars you see and you don't see, parked next to you at the shopping mall, invisible cars for invisible men, and Renny backs the Oldsmobile into that space and he waits, he waits there for me, and he watches the clock as it winds its way toward one, and he waits there. For me. And that's when it happens, sometime before one, because he's a good soldier, he would not have waited past one, that's when the helicopter floats down from the sky, that's when Renny Two Hand sits up behind the wheel and watches the shadow coming out of the sun, and that smile comes onto his face, that smile, yeah, that's the one. Renny, I want to call to him, just as Jinx sees what I've seen, and that's when little pinks of pebbles and dust start spraying onto the hood and then the windshield of the Oldsmobile, and over the wild whoosh of the rotors comes a cough cough cough and Renny Two Hand jerks back in his seat, I'm looking at it now, I'm fucking seeing it, the driver's door is open and I'm looking at the driver's seat and I can see, through the punctured windshield, the graffiti of blood, the spray-painted alphabet of death, and Renny tries to slide from the car but he falls to his knees; his right palm leaves its print in red, right there, on the blacktop. He looks away from the men with guns closing in on him. No, he says. The color is draining from his face, running onto the blacktop, the dirt. No. His mouth bends and he calls my name, and that's when he stands and that's when—

I push the driver's door closed, and what's left

of the glass of its window shatters. The Oldsmobile's got so many holes it's Swiss metal and the blacktop beside it is still wet and the wet trail leads to a hurricane fence and through a tear in the fence and then down the slope of the concrete viaduct and into a low gully. I follow the blood to the place. That's where he laid down and died.

I stand there for a while looking at him. Renny Two Hand. Reynolds James. Then Jinx says to my back:

Maybe I believe you now. Maybe you didn't kill nobody.

I didn't kill Gideon Parks, I tell him. But I killed two guys. My guys. At least they used to be mine.

He doesn't look surprised. He doesn't look anything but sad. Strangely sad.

I look over my shoulder, toward the east, toward the ocean. There's something out there, isn't there? Something just beyond sight. Something that would show me what this means.

Jinx says what I'm thinking:

We need to get little. We need to get out of here.

Yeah, I tell him. But I can't leave him like that.

Ain't nothin you can do, man. He's dead.

I know he's dead. But I can't leave him like that. They can't find him like . . . that.

Like what? Time is tickin, Burdon Lane.

Time is ticking. But time isn't the only thing in this world. Standing in that gully, the dust or my allergies acting up maybe, stinging my eyes, I remember the funniest of things. I remember Renny talking to me this morning, telling me something about ordering a pizza. And I remember him saying something else, something about—

How'd he get this far? Jinx says.

They let him. Look. And I show him.

The first shots took his shoulders, arms, put him down but not out. No way he could shoot. About the only thing he could do was crawl.

They probably wanted to have a talk, I tell him, all the while wondering what he could have told them.

I point at his chest. When they were done talking, somebody double-tapped him, right in the heart. Looks to me like it was somebody with something heavy. Like a .44 Magnum.

Renny's face is calm. His eyes are closed, not tight but soft. Like he's asleep. But nothing is going to wake Renny up. I try to forget the wounds, the blood. I keep my eyes on that face and I start doing what needs to be done.

I take the cellular phone from his belt, hook it onto mine. Renny's jacket is bunched underneath him and I tug it straight, reach into the hollow of his back. It's a wet mess. He's not wearing a vest, as if that would have mattered. I find the holster and I find that wicked Colt Python. It's cold. He never had the chance to use it. Never fired at another man in his life, so far as I know.

Somebody sure fired at him. Two somebodies,

from the looks of it. Renny must have taken eight hits. And that's before the .44 Magnum.

I take his right hand, bend his fingers back to take the pistol grip, and something falls out of his palm. A bullet. It's a shiny nine-millimeter. I want to wonder what Renny's doing with a nine-millimeter round in his hand at the moment of his dying. His Python's a .357. I mean, the guy's always starting something but never getting it done. But I wonder more about what's going to happen if I don't get busy and haul ass out of here. So I stick the bullet in my suit pocket and get back to getting busy.

I fit the Python into his right hand, put his fingers around the grip. Tuck his index finger into the trigger guard. At least now he's a gunman.

I wipe my hands on his suit coat and I'm trying to leave him when I hear Jinx's voice coming down at me:

Want me to say a few words over him?

No, I tell him. This is not your business.

Bullshit, he says. This is everbody's business.

I look down at Renny Two Hand in that gully. I look down at him for the last time and I bow my head like a preacher man and I say the only words over him that anybody needs to hear:

They're dead, Renny.

Every last one of them is dead.

diner

So they got out of the hotel, got out of the fire, got away from the law, got away from the city, and then they got Renny dead.

This is no surprise. CK had more than a plan. This thing was thought straight through and out the other side. Shoot, shoot, and scoot. Maybe they went down a laundry chute, something as simple as that. Or a service elevator, a set of stairs hidden at the back of the building. Maybe it was something more complicated. Maybe they just sprouted wings and flew out of that hotel like birds.

Maybes don't matter. Not anymore. Not with your best friend dead on the ground and a couple new notches on your gun. Not when you're tired and you're sore and you're hot and you're beating the bush with some badass black dude who's got a hard-on of his own, and when you're almost back to your car, you find a Crown Vic parked next to it and a couple suits and shoes with thick soles worn by guys with ten-dollar haircuts who are writing things in little books, talking into radios, and just generally standing around being cops.

Jinx hauls up short, just like me. Dittoes.

We back off, huddle behind a thicket.

Think we been made? he says to me.

I don't have to think. Just the chance is good enough for me.

Let's book, I tell him, nodding off to my left. Two, three klicks down the road, there's a truck stop, bar and grill, lots of the big rigs and RVs, lots and lots of noise and confusion.

So we're humping through the woods again and it's all some kind of bad Nam flashback, the kind the movie psychos get just before they start revving their power tools. We're beating the boonies, taking a track that parallels the trail, even if the trail is two lanes of concrete and the only Charlie at its end is some potbellied guy who pours you gas or serves you suds.

Sooner or later we ease our way roadside, and there's base camp, something by the name of Tito's Truck Stop, and I remember the place, remember the diner, remember the coffee, remember the greasy home fries, remember the layout, and it's not great but, hey, like the priest told the guy at communion, it's all we got.

I give my pal Jinx the thirty-second tour and then:

You're the suspicious-looking minority, I tell him. So you go first. Find a booth in back and sit facing the front. I'll give you five minutes. You don't come out, I'm coming in. You got a problem, you call me Jake and I go straight out the back door. And if you know what you're doing, you go with me.

Fuck you, he says to me. He takes my duffel bag, shrugs it over his shoulder, sticks his hands in his pockets, and wanders out of the tree line toward the truck stop like he's some kind of boy scout.

He doesn't look back, heads straight into the bar and grill. I check my watch, and give him five. I try to knock the dust off my suit and then I follow him in.

The place is nothing but what you'd expect: burgers and fries, drumsticks and thighs. No cops. Bartender, a bar, a TV bolted to the ceiling at each end of the bar, and lots of thirsty truckers in between, hanging their wide butts off the stools. Down a long row of booths, most of them empty, there's a bleached-out stork of a waitress wandering back and forth with plates and mugs and more mugs. In the last booth, there's my pal Jinx, minding his own business, looking into a menu.

The waitress gives me a smile, I give her a smile right back, shake my head no, and stroll on back to the booth.

I sit. The waitress floats by, and I tell her I want

some coffee. I take my hand off my Glock and out of my pocket. I unfold a paper napkin. I put it in my lap. I look at the menu. I find what I want. I put the menu down. I rearrange the silverware. Check the labels on the catsup, the mustard, the sugar, the Sweet'n Low.

I keep waiting for Jinx to look at me and say: Well? But he doesn't say a goddamn thing, not for a long time. He looks at the menu. He looks at the menu. He looks at the menu.

Then the coffee comes. The waitress does that waitress magic where she pulls a pencil from behind her ear, sticks her tongue into the side of her mouth, and says: Whattyaboyshavintoday?

Gimme a minute, Jinx says. He waits until she retreats into the kitchen, and then he looks up out of the menu, not at me, but at the television set at the far end of the bar, and the bartender, who is twisting up the volume, because CNN is wall-to-wall with murder. Synthesized music swells over this tasteful logo with the silhouette of a guy's head in the crosshairs of a rifle sight, which ushers in a collage of freeze-frame images and computer-generated text and finally some well-permed talking head who announces the up-to-the-minute coverage of the assassination of civil rights leader Gideon Parks. Interviews with a weeping Jesse Jackson and some tight-lipped U.S. senators give way to glimpses of some very pissed-off black folks in front of some government building, which fades into a relentless parade of sound-and-vision bites. There's the usual statement from the President, something about tragedy, something about healing, something about the criminals who will be pursued and captured and punished, and then comes the on-scene footage, a wet dream of a Zapruder film shot with network cameras from three different angles, in color and in close-up, and the replays are coming on like it's the fucking Super Bowl, from the first hit, which tears the Reverend's head apart, to the five other explosions that rive his upper body into a bloody rag of flesh and broken bones.

Some little man at the bar, six feet two, this little man, starts to laugh and clap his hands and the bartender tells him to shut the fuck up.

I look at Jinx but he just looks at that TV, and now a shuddering camera swings around and takes in the Hotel Excelsior, the lens shaking and creeping up the building but seeing only smoke and fire. Then, from a different angle, a steadier lens farther down the street, sweeping like a searchlight over the fronts of the hotel and the apartment building next door and it looks like some foreign country, some foreign war, Baghdad, Beirut, Bosnia, and you can't see a thing but flames and then a huge explosion that tears a couple floors out of the hotel and sends glass and bricks and wood fragments showering down onto the streets.

It's not real, it's someplace else, and I can't even imagine, right now, being inside that place. Or getting out.

But I did, and they did. And I know one thing, damn it, I know one thing more. I take the nine-millimeter bullet from my coat pocket. Hold it until he looks at it, at me.

I know what they asked Renny, I tell Jinx. I know what they wanted to know. They wanted to know if you were dead.

He stirs the spoon around in his coffee, checks the menu again. He doesn't get it. Not yet.

I was supposed to kill you, I tell him.

He sets the menu down and stirs the spoon around some more.

I was supposed to take you south and take you out.

He takes a sip of the coffee like we're talking about tomorrow's weather. Then he says to me:

How's the scrapple?

I say: What?

The scrapple, he says. You been here before, right? So how's the scrapple?

Don't know, I tell him. Never had it.

And that's the rest of that conversation, until the waitress comes around and takes our order. I tell her I want dry toast and more coffee, and Jinx tells her he wants a couple eggs, sunny-side up, and the scrapple.

She goes away, and I try to get things back on track.

We need to get to Wilmington, I tell him. But he just stares through me and says:

I got to go see a man about a dog.

You do that, I tell him, and he gets up and gets gone and I sit there and I try to look at the beer signs. I look at the Bud and I look at the Coors and I look at the Lite and I want more than anything else to drink myself sober.

I give up trying to look at the beer signs and I watch the TV for a while, and after a quick word from our sponsors—looks like this assassination is being brought to you by Infiniti—the news machine starts to recycle, back to Jesse Jackson, the senators, the President, before bringing in more video from the scene, and time slips back and forth, then and now, the yellow and black blossom of an explosion sprouts from the tenth floor of that hotel, and now comes a series of nervous frames shot from a news helicopter hovering over the burning buildings, with police and fire department choppers weaving back and forth beneath it, flames licking up the sides of the hotel and the apartment building next door, all those people, all those poor, poor people, and the angle shifts to the long ladder trucks below and then to the white and unmarked helicopters that dance at the edge of the smoke, fluttering in to land, lots of guts, those guys, setting down on the roof of the

Hotel Excelsior, and there's the FBI Hostage Rescue Team, the Federal SWAT, boarding up and being lifted from the roof, geared out like guys who ought to be wearing swastikas in black uniforms, black helmets, black masks, and damn if the guy in command of that unit, the guy waving the other black-uniformed guys into the chopper, watching them load in a couple body bags, isn't carrying a Smith & Wesson Model 29, a .44 Magnum, in his right hand.

No way that's a service piece. No fucking way.

So now I know how they got out. They didn't walk, oh, no, they flew out of there. In style. Maybe courtesy of somebody Federal.

This is way past two plus two. Now it's like Chinese arithmetic.

So what happens now? If I was them, I'd scatter. Call it Miller time. Take a sea cruise. Shoot back tequila, watch the hula dance, get my knob polished.

Then again, if I was them, I would be worried about one little problem and I'm sitting inside him.

Make that two little problems, because the other one's back from the toilet, which is probably right next to the pay phone, which is probably why he's been gone a lot longer than a flip and a zip.

Have a good talk with your guys? I say, just to remind him who's on first.

Oh yeah, he says.

Well, I tell him. I hope they got some good lawyers. I was them, I'd get the hell out of Dirty City.

Maybe so, he says. But you ain't them. Least not yet. And you ain't there.

Well, hey, I tell him. I got news for you. This is all about getting there from here.

He starts to say something, but I tell him: My way. And there's no room for discussion.

I think for a second, and it's a quick one, because the answer is a quick one.

I get up and go back to the toilets and sure enough, there's a pay phone next to the men's room door. I drop some quarters and call Lauren, my friend in Philadelphia. One ring. Wait and hope the answer is someone real. Two rings. Try to make like I'm calm.

Three rings, then:

Hello?

Hey, Lauren.

Hey, Burdon. What's going on?

Not much. Well, a lot, really.

You coming to Philadelphia? I'm not engaged anymore.

I could of told you that.

Now how—

It's in your voice, Lauren. And you know what? You were too good for that guy anyway.

Oh, Burdon, when you gonna just move on up here and marry me?

I love you too much for that, Lauren.

Yeah, she says. Well, that's a new one. Thought I'd heard them all, but hey, Burdon. That's a new one. So how's your girl?

Fiona is doing fine, Lauren. But—

I know, I know. There's a point to this call and it isn't a social one, is it? So what's up?

I need a favor, Lauren. A big one. A big pain-in-the-ass one.

So that's what it has to be for you to think of me?

That or dinner, Lauren.

She pauses but then she says: So tell me about this favor.

I need you to rent a car. Like right now. I need you to decide that your car needs repairs or something, that you need to rent a car. From somebody solid, like Hertz. Midsize, a Taurus or a Capri maybe, nothing showy. Make sure you get the insurance. I need you to drive the rental car to Wilmington. I need you to park the car at the Amtrak station and I need you to put the keys under the driver's seat. I need you to put the parking stub and the rental agreement in the glove box. I need you to put the Sports section of today's *Inquirer* on top of the dashboard, right up to the windshield, so I know that this car is yours. Then I need you to go do something, have a late lunch, go shopping, I don't care, but leave the car unlocked, and whatever you do, I don't want you to come back until eight p.m. If the car's there, well, hey, it's yours. But if it's not, I need you to call the cops, because that's when you find out your car's been stolen. Then I need you to take the train back home. You got that?

Burdon— She starts, stops, sighs, then starts again. Burdon, she says, are you in some kind of trouble?

Yeah, I tell her, but that's all I'm going to tell her, and it's all I have to tell her, since she says:

Yeah. Same old Burdon. So okay. Sports section of the *Inquirer*, right?

Right. And you're gonna do it right now, okay?

Okay, Burdon. Consider it done. Just remember one thing.

What's that?

You owe me more than dinner.

More than you know, I tell the silent phone, hand down on the hook. More than you know.

I feed in more quarters, try Trey Costa's mobile, get a robot voice that says the number's out of service.

So it's back to the booth, back to the coffee, back to my pal Jinx, and I say to him: Okay, we need to kill some time, not much but maybe an hour. If we get to Wilmington, we're home free. But we got to get to Wilmington and that's, what? Forty-five minutes, tops. You ever steal a car?

Shit, man. I been jackin cars longer than you been jackin off.

So?

So what? he says right back.

So let's do it.

Finish your coffee, he says. It's been done.

His left hand comes up from his lap and he's holding a set of keys.

Pickup truck out back, he says. Got to be the barman's or maybe the cook's. Left his keys in the pocket of his jacket, hangin back there on the hook by the kitchen door. And hey, it's a busy day, lots goin on. Nobody gonna notice for a long time.

After a while his food arrives. He pokes out the eyes of those eggs until they run yellow over the slab of scrapple and he cuts the mess into little squares and starts forking it in.

What is that shit? I ask him.

Ain't what you eat, he says. It's how you chew it.

Okay, I tell him. But you get the fucking bill.

And we take our time and finish our coffee, and after Jinx pays the bill, we walk out the front, then circle around to the back, and we're just a couple guys getting into a pickup truck, he's still driving and I'm still riding and the duffel bag is right between us, and he backs out, then does a beeline for the exit at the west side and takes a right behind a long line of parked semis and then out of Tito's Truck Stop, and he makes the left that is going to take us back to the Turnpike and that's when the siren of the cop car goes bleep bleep,

bleep bleep, and I'm grabbing my Glock and Jinx is saying mothafuck and I tell him to slow down, slow down, and he's telling me to shut up, to shut the fuck up, and to keep the pistol down and to let him do the talking, and now he's braking and he's got the blinker blinking and he's letting the truck float to the side of the road, nice and slow, and he glides that pickup to a gentle stop and he looks in the rearview and he jams the shift stick into park and he turns off the engine and he says to me, Jinx says:

I got it. Keep the gun down. Keep it down.

Then I don't fucking believe what I see. Because he winks at me.

I look out the back window of the truck and watch the cop—it's a state trooper, walking that trooper walk—and I'm thinking my day's been bad enough. I don't want to have to do this thing, take out a state cop, a real cop, but I lift the Glock to the edge of the seatback and I know I will do what it takes.

Jinx is out the door of that pickup, he isn't waiting for the cop, and he's got his hands up and away from his body like some basketball coach who can't believe this blind referee, and he's walking toward the cop and I realize it's a black cop and the black cop's got his hands out in front of him, like slow down, boy, slow down, and Jinx slows down and sort of scratches at his head with his right hand and he's giving the cop some line or the other and he even nods back toward me and the cop looks a little vague and then he snaps to it, gulping some kind of bait as fast as Jinx can throw it and that's when the cop points at something at the back of the truck and Jinx bends down and the cop bends down with him, checking out something on the fender, the taillight maybe, and I feel my fingers relax on the grip and then Jinx is up and the cop is up and Jinx is reaching toward his pocket, nice and slow, and he's pulling out a billfold and he's fumbling around for his driver's license or something and he's handing it to the state cop and the state cop vets it and shakes his head like it's some sorry tale and then he nods once, then again, and he's handing the stuff back to Jinx and I can't believe this guy is about to talk a New Jersey state trooper out of a ticket but that's what he's doing and the trooper looks at me again like I'm some kind of zoo animal in a cage made by General Motors and then he's heading back to his car and Jinx is swaggering back to the truck and he's tossing himself behind the wheel and he's giving me a grin.

Works ever time, he says.

Don't tell me. Some kind of black thing, right?

No, he says. Some kind of green thing. Cost me a hundred bucks.

He yanks the shift back into drive and we're gone.

wilmington

Nobody matters. That's what the train station at Wilmington is saying to me. It's what those artist guys call a study, and it's a study in nothing.

It's a busy nothing, though. Noises all around. Automatic doors shuddering apart and shuddering back together. Broken pieces of conversation, always rushed, sometimes sad, other times angry. Odors. Stale smoke and hot dogs and some kind of cleanser. Movement, constant movement. It's not a train station but a hive of worker bees. People walking, people talking, people standing in lines and lines and more lines. Other people crouched behind barriers, waiting on ticket buyers like they're visitors to a lockup. Dreary people doing dreary things. That's all I see when I lamp the lobby of that terminal, look through the people going places, the people going nowhere at all.

Nobody matters.

No one.

I'm waiting for Jinx. At least that's what I told him, and it better be what he thinks.

What I think is that I'm waiting for a bullet.

After Jinx did his thing with the state trooper, the drive to Wilmington was a piece of cake. Forty minutes flat. Nothing to tighten my balls but my Jockey shorts till we circled the station and checked out the parking lot. The rental car was an easy mark, Hertz must have a million of those red Mercury Capris, but this was the one with the *Philadelphia Inquirer* folded up nice and neat in the window and, if I know my Lauren, it's got a bottle of Jack Daniel's in the glove box.

So our new wheels are not a problem. And losing the truck we borrowed was as easy as finding a parking place.

It's the usual thing that gives me pause: What isn't there. Like I say to my pal Jinx:

Do you see it?

Naw. But somethin's wrong. I can feel it, but I can't see it.

That's right, I tell him. You can't see it. Where are they? Where are the watchers?

The watchers? Jinx snorts in air and shoots back his badass laugh. I mean, it's no big thing to worry, man, but that kind of talk, you might call that crazy talk.

Hey, I tell him. Total paranoia—

But he finishes for me: Is total awareness. Bobby Seale said that.

Bullshit, I tell him. It was Charlie Manson.

Seale, he says.

Manson, I say right back.

Okay, okay, he says. Have it your way. Sounds white, anyway. White and wack. Crazy talk. People watchin you. Give it a rest.

No, no, no. What I'm saying is that something is wrong. Real wrong. Don't you see it?

See what, man? I look round here, I don't see nothin.

Exactly. You look round here, and you don't see nothing. So where are the cops? The five-oh?

There are no cops. No city boys, no transit boys. Hell, I don't even see a security guard. We're standing outside a train station in a not-so-small city, and the closest thing we've got to a blue uniform is over there collecting cash for the parking lot.

Look here, I tell Jinx. The other problem, maybe the real problem, is that they've probably got security cameras in there. The car's gonna be called in stolen at eight, and the first thing they're gonna do is pull the tapes.

And that's a problem? he says. Look at me, man. I'm your basic nigga perp. Got the ball cap, got the shades, got the moves. You stand watch and let me do the dirty deed. Shit, how many guys round this city fit my description? They'll be lookin for weeks. And how hard they gonna look, anyway? It's a stolen car, man. Probly twenty of em a day round this burg.

I like the way this guy thinks. It's the way I want him to think, to buy me the time I need. In the station. Alone.

So okay, I tell him. Do it. Meet me in, say, ten. At the entrance to the station. The front steps. By the cabs.

Then I seal the deal, by telling him I'm not going anywhere without him. I tell him: Just don't forget my duffel bag.

And off he goes and here I stay and I wish I still smoked because I could light one up and make like I had some of my own business to mind. I try looking left, I try looking right, and there is something so wrong with this picture that you know it's got to be right. So I turn around and walk into the station, check out the people waiting in line for tickets, check out the tired old-timer at the shoeshine stand, check out the guy sliding a broom, check out the television monitor and the trains, arriving and departing, and I wonder, for a weak minute, if this is the way to go, forget the car and choo-choo on down to Dirty City.

You get weak like that sometimes. You get impatient, you get distracted, you get dreamy, you let the wrong things make decisions for you. You guess wrong, and you're grease.

Right about now, though, I think I've guessed right. It's coming at me so strong that I know there isn't even a guess to it. This is going to be one of those things like shit, it's going to happen, and I'm here, I'm right here, and I'm the one who's making it happen.

That's when I look at the monitor again, look for the next train to D.C., and I look for the time and it's right and I give them two minutes. Because if CK or somebody else from UniArms wants to see me, this is their last chance: *Go to the second place*, CK told me, *or go to Wilmington, the train station, maybe.*

I'm checking my watch and the second hand is going around the second time when it happens. And it's shit, that's for sure. It's shit on heels: It's Lukas. The guy who couldn't notice guns being run out of a pizzeria.

So here comes Lukas, and the guy looks like he's been folded out of an overnight bag: crisp white shirt, suit pressed as sharp as a K-bar, even his goddamn tie is straight. Some kind of cheap aftershave is wafting my way. He leans in so close you can smell the minty mouthwash.

How's it going? Lukas says to me.

Same old sixes and sevens, I tell him.

The guy's face is flushed, like it's been scrubbed clean, just shaved.

Uh-huh, he says to me.

Uh-huh, I say right back.

Then I stand there in the middle of the station

for about a goddamn minute and watch this guy nod his head, nod his head.

So? I tell him.

So, he says to me. So. You're gonna love this one.

He screws his head around like somebody's trying to listen in on what he has to say, and then he says it:

These three Jews walk into a bar, okay? And the first Jew—stop me if you've heard this one—the first Jew, he says to the bartender, he says, What a day, what a day, gimme some chicken soup and a shot of Absolut. So the bartender, he does what the guy asks, all right? He gets him the soup, he gets him the shot, and everything's just fine. And then the second Jew, okay, the second one, he says to the bartender, What a day, what a day, gimme some chicken soup and a shot of Cuervo Gold. So the bartender, he does what this guy says, too. He gets him the soup, the shot, everything's copacetic, and so now we got the third Jew, right? And the third Jew, he says . . . do you know what the third Jew says to the bartender?

No, Lukas, I tell him. What does the third Jew say to the bartender?

He says: Fuck the soup and fuck the shot, just give me the twenty bucks you owe me.

Lukas laughs out loud, and it's a lousy laugh, it's like the mewl of a sick kitten, and then he rubs his hands together and gives me way too much of a grin. I can smell the soap on his hands, that green gunk you get in public restrooms, smells way too clean.

Ha-ha, I tell him.

I look over his shoulder. Nobody there but civilians.

That's real funny, I tell him.

I look back toward the entrance to the station. Nobody there, either. There's nothing doing in here, nothing but me and Lukas. So:

Lukas, I tell him. You know something? You know what I would of said, like if I was the third Jew and all that?

No, he says. What would you a said?

I would of said, Who the fuck made me the third Jew?

Ha, he says.

Huh, he says.

Then he says: I don't get it.

Yeah, I tell him. You don't get it. What else is new? You got something else to tell me, Lukas? Or are we just gonna stand around in this miserable excuse for a train station and listen to you tell me jokes for the rest of the day?

Oh, yeah, Lukas says. I got something else to tell you. And it ain't no joke, okay? It's something good. CK, he says you oughta come in. There ain't no kind of problem, CK says. Everything's cool.

Really, I tell him.

Yeah, really, Lukas says. That's what CK says.

Just do what you got to do, that's what CK told me to tell you. Do what you got to do.

And there's CK's voice in my ear, cutting through the static of the cell phone: *Kill the nigger.*

Then Lukas is talking again:

And CK told me to tell you something else, but I got no idea what this means, so it's one of those things, you know? CK said to tell you: What you got in your pocket, it's yours. The paper. It's all yours, whatever that means. I figure you know what he means. Just do what you got to do, CK said to tell you, and it's yours.

Really, I tell him again. And what about Renny Two Hand?

Lukas shakes his head. Yeah, well, I heard about that, you know. I liked the kid, it's some kind of shame. But you whacked out Mackie, didn't you? Lukas smiles at that one. Then he says:

CK said to tell you: *Now* we're even.

Yeah, I tell him, and I take one last look around before finishing something that never really started. I say to Lukas:

Well, tell you what, you piece-of-shit errand boy, you go and you tell CK that we aren't even, that we're never even, not until he's six feet deep. You tell him that for me, okay, you fucking retrovirus?

Lukas staggers back a step. I don't even get to push him.

You know something, Lane? CK said you'd tell

me no. He said you were just the kind of stupid fuck that would tell me no.

He looks at his fingernails. I can still smell that soap on his hands. How can shit smell so fucking clean?

So look, Lukas says. You don't want to do the nigger, fine. The nigger's taken care of. So forget CK. This is from Mr. Berenger now, okay? His lips to my ears. Come home, he says to tell you. Just come with me, back to D.C.

Lukas pats his jacket pocket, left breast. I got a ticket for you, club car, first class, there's a Metroliner out of this dump in about five minutes. Mr. Berenger says to come home and get this crap straightened out and—

You aren't listening to me, Lukas. That's your problem, you know it? You never did look, and you never did listen. Well, you better look and you better listen now. Because you see that door over there? I'm walking out that door, and you better hope and you better pray I don't ever see you again.

He shows me his teeth. I don't know what got this guy balls but I'm out of there and I don't look back and when I'm through the station doors and onto the stairs outside there's Jinx maneuvering the Capri past a couple taxis and over to the curb. Just one of Hertz's millions, rental red and spanking clean. Not perfection for the ride we've got to make, but about as good as it gets.

Jinx raises the duffel bag from the seat next to him.

Still got it, he tells me. But it's goin in the trunk.

He ducks down and reaches across the front seat to the glove box. Then:

Shit, he says.

He turns off the ignition and rises up out of the driver's side, duffel in hand, slamming the car door behind him.

Next time you order us up a rental, make it a Caddy or a Lex, he says, jangling the keys in my face. Least somethin that'll let you pop the trunk from the inside.

He fits the key into the tail lock and twists. The trunk lid wings up and open and the smell nearly doubles me over. I stare and I stare and I don't see. It doesn't make sense, not one bit of sense.

It's blood.

Jinx drops the keys to the pavement and dances back from the car like he's been burned.

Blood, and I've never seen so much blood in so little space.

Blood and blood and more blood and there, in the middle of the blood, two legs twisted out of a skirt, bent and broken like twigs.

It's something, the shoes, the legs, the skirt, the blouse, the whole thing adds up into a fist that hits me and hits me:

It's Lauren.

Fuck me, Jinx says.

No. It's not Lauren. Not anymore.

Fuck all, he says. Where is her head, man? *Where is her head?*

I've got an answer but the answer is to another question, and I don't ask the question and I don't say the answer because I'm running, running away, running away from the car, running away from Jinx, running up the steps and into the station. Past the shoeshine guy, who doesn't even notice. Past the broom guy, who does notice but then decides I'm late.

Late. For the train.

I bulldoze through the people and past the ticket agent at the gate, tugging my wallet halfway out of my suit coat and telling him the only thing he wants to hear: Washington. Then I'm through the double door and out onto the empty platform and I'm late, I am too late, the train is pulling out and I run and the wheels are turning and I'm gaining on it but there's nothing I can do but run as the wheels screech and spin harder and the speed picks up and I come nearly to the end of the last car and face to face with Lukas, he's looking out from the rear window of the train like a politician on the stump, and Lukas looks out and he sees me, he sees me and he raises those squeaky clean hands and he smiles and he waves and he says something but I can't read his lips.

I'm at the end of the platform and the train is rolling away from Wilmington, from me.

I push wind from my lungs and go loose.

That's when I swipe the Glock from the holster beneath my suit coat and settle into a Weaver stance. I hear footsteps biting into the concrete behind me and I make them go away and I don't look at anything, just take a deep breath and push the wind from my lungs again as Jinx hauls up next to me, he's got my duffel bag in his hand and a scowl on his face, and he spits out the words between labored gasps:

No way.

I take a deep breath.

No fuckin way.

Loose. I don't say the words, I feel them. Stay loose. Looking with both eyes down the sights of that Glock and into a window, a rectangle of glass that shines back at me, that shines back light, a sun, a fading sun, a faint hope against the night, it's coming, the night is coming, and my father, it's farmland, Illinois farmland, and I see the piece of cardboard with the red crayon circle and it's nailed to the wooden fence and I'm thirteen years old and I look down the sight of my father's Winchester and he says to me, he says:

Stay loose.

You're shining me, Jinx says. You're shining me.

Seventy feet.

Give it up, man, he says.

Eighty feet.

But I'm loose. Down the sights of the Glock I see the fading sun and that cardboard target and I see through that target and I see glass and I see through the glass and I see Lukas and I see death.

Ninety feet.

I blink and look again. I see the flow of distant cornstalks. The starless sky that's grey and calm and grey and calm and grey and grey and grey then black, and I squeeze the trigger, one shot, and a hundred feet away the train window spiderwebs, and the web flares with red, and I have no doubt, not a doubt in the world, that Lukas is dead.

Then the train is gone.

Jesus, Jinx says.

He looks at my gun.

He looks at me.

He looks at my gun.

He looks at me.

Jesus Christ, he says.

No, I tell him: Glock 19.

freefall

I holster the pistol and start walking.

I walk the walk, it's not a shuffle and it's not a hustle and it's not a run, it's a walk, and it's loose, I'm still loose. I'm this travel-weary taxpayer who missed the train or something, and when the police guy comes boiling out of the terminal with a hand in the air, like he forgot to wave goodbye, I ignore what he is and what he says and I keep walking. I walk past the police guy and I walk to the far end of the platform where there's a door that says AUTHORIZED PERSONNEL ONLY. I stop and I sigh and I turn around.

The police guy is wearing a funny uniform, maybe he's a transit cop, and Jinx grabs the funny uniform by the lapels and he hauls the funny uniform out of its shoes and he slams the funny uniform into a post and he yells something into the face beneath the funny uniform's hat and then he slams the funny uniform into the post again and he drops the funny uniform like a bad habit and now it's his turn to walk.

So Jinx walks my way and there's that door that says AUTHORIZED PERSONNEL ONLY and that must mean us, so I push through the door and I walk down a short flight of stairs and I push through another door and now I'm the usual impatient business guy walking through Wilmington Station, through the people inside and through the main doors and through the people outside and what the fuck I hail a cab.

Hey. I'm into the back seat of the cab and Jinx piles in next to me and Jinx slams the door and I say to the cabbie, I say: Hey.

I say: Hotel Du Pont.

Jinx knows enough to zip the lip but he stares at me like I've lost my mind. Maybe I have, but I know exactly what I'm doing. The hotel was going to be our next stop.

We're late for a meeting, I tell the cabbie. Nothing dramatic. I'm the usual impatient business guy. I say nothing to distinguish me from the ordinary asshole in a suit.

So how about it, bud? I tell the cabbie. Hotel Du Pont.

And off we go.

At the Hotel Du Pont, there's a doorman whose red jacket has fringe on the shoulders, yeah, it's a swell place, and the doorman cracks the passenger door of the cab and gestures to me and I take

my time getting out while Jinx passes the cabbie
some bills and the doorman shows us the lobby
and the first thing I want to do is find a pay phone
and call Fiona but I can't call Fiona because she
isn't home yet, it's not time for *60 Minutes*, and I
am not about to leave a message on a piece of
tape. Not yet. So instead I call Trey Costa, I give
his cell phone a jingle and click down on the robot
voice that says: The number you have dialed is
out of service. More good news. So I go to the bell
stand and I tug out my wallet.

Inside my wallet are several luggage tags, and I
find the right one, the one that says Hotel Du
Pont, and I hand the tag and a fiver to the bellman
and he goes away for a minute and he comes back
with a deep blue suitcase and what the hell, I give
him another fiver. I take the deep blue suitcase
around the corner and into the men's room and I
set the deep blue suitcase on the floor and I start
tossing cold water onto my face and after a while
there's Jinx looking over my shoulder in the mirror and I say to him, I say:

What?

He stares at my reflection for a while until he
says:

Nice shot.

I check my face in the mirror while Jinx says:

So now we got ever cop in Wilmington—naw,
let's make that the whole state of Delaware—
lookin for us, not to mention the Jersey cops, the

New York cops, and then there's the Feds, right, let's not be forgettin them. Probly ever fuckin set of initials in the fuckin U S of A is out there beatin the street for you and me. And I ain't doubtin we got more of your buddy boys out there too, am I right?

I nod down at the sink and say to him:

What do you think? Porcelain?

What? he says.

The sink, I tell him. Think it's porcelain?

Fuck all, he says. But he raps the knuckle of his middle finger onto that shining white curve and there's a ring, deep and dull, like a distant cathedral bell.

Yeah, he says.

Of course it's porcelain. Like I said, the Hotel Du Pont, it's a swell place.

I close the drain on the sink and I pull the Glock from the holster at my back, the barrel is still warm, and I yank the magazine and drop the pistol into the sink. I do the same with the Glock in my shoulder holster and then with Renny's cell phone and, what the hell, in goes my cell phone too.

Then I get the juice out of my duffel bag.

I pour the whole bottle over the pistols and the phones and the juice goes to work, melting things into a messy stew. It's acid, something like that, and it's nasty. There go the fingerprints and the sweat, the polymer and the plastic.

I can tell that Jinx has never seen anything like this, and he's never smelled anything like it, either. The FBI can trace the bullets back to the pistol by the barrel groove; the marks are as good as DNA. The fucking FBI can even trace the bullets back to the manufacturer by the acid residue. Which means, if they work hard enough, they're going to learn that the nines in Lukas, Ernie Gonsalves, and Mackie the Lackey were all part of a shipment straight from the factory to the Memphis Police Department. Ha-ha. So without the guns, they got jack nothing.

Unless they've got the firing pins. Which the FBI can match to the shell casings. Which is why I open the drain and let the melted muck seep away, then turn on the tap, washing off what's left. The pins are too large for the drain, so I fold a paper towel and use it to pluck them out and drop them into a commode and flush. Bye-bye. I wrap the barrels and slides in the paper towel, wad more paper towels around them, and bury the wad at the bottom of the trash receptacle.

End of that little game, and time to start another one. So I say to Jinx, I say:

The suitcase.

He's lost, still looking at the sink. I pop the locks and unlatch the deep blue suitcase. First is a new white shirt. Folded and pressed, a bit wrinkled, but nowhere near the dirty and sweaty and bullet-holed one I'm wearing. I take off my suit coat, my shirt, and then I peel off the Kevlar vest.

I wash my chest and pits, check out the fist-sized bruise purpling the left side of my back. Talk about a nice shot: Just below the shoulder blade, just above the kidneys, just left of the spine. Anything higher or lower or to the right could have done some real damage. Guess a certain someone wanted me alive.

I put on the vest and I button up the new shirt. I take a tie out of the suitcase and knot it up. What the hell.

What the fuck you doin? Jinx is finally catching up. You tryin to look good for when they come and snap the cuffs on us?

Nope, I tell him. Look, there's another shirt and tie in that suitcase. And two suits. You take the navy one, let me have the grey. The stuff ought to fit you.

I unfold the grey suit coat, and it's identical to the one I was wearing, although it's clean, pressed, and lacking the bullet hole.

Changed my mind, I tell him. I'll take the navy blue.

I hand him the grey coat and I lose the old pants and pull on the clean blue pair, then check myself in the mirror. Not bad for a guy who's gone through this kind of day. Lost his job. Got his ex-girlfriend killed. Got his best friend killed.

Got a *Time* magazine Man of the Year killed. Got shot in the back. Murdered some guys.

Not bad at all.

I lamp my Timex and I tell Jinx:

Get dressed. I'm taking us home.

Jinx says: And how the hell you doin that?

My way, I tell him. We're getting dressed. Then we're going to the train station.

That's crazy, he says.

They got a train leaving for Dirty City every hour. We got about thirty minutes.

That shit is crazy, he says.

That's right, I tell him. Because it is crazy, and there's a moment when I wonder about him and then his eyes whiten that little bit, just enough, so I know he knows it's crazy and that's exactly why we're going to do it. Maybe the last place in town, the last place on the planet, that anybody will be looking for us right now is that train station.

Jinx reaches a stack of clothes out of the suitcase and heads for the stall. Funny guy. Guess he likes his privacy.

I fold back the other side of the suitcase and remove the taped bricks of foam that are packed there. I tear open the first one and there's a new Glock 19 inside. Another Glock waits in the second brick. The third has four magazines and two boxes of Winchester 9x19 JHPs: nine-millimeter hollow points. I've about finished loading the magazines when Jinx wanders out of the stall, and it's a miracle, the guy went in Hyde and came out Jekyll. The hoodlum is gone, and we've got ourselves a preacher man. I'm shaking my head and hoping not to show a smile and that's when I see the boots. He's still wearing those boots.

You got to lose the boots, man.

Yeah? Jinx tells me. You got another pair of shoes?

I don't and something tells me that, even if I did, he wouldn't be wearing them. So I guess we deal with it.

I nod a final time to the suitcase and I say:

There's a folding-stock Mossberg in there, that long piece of foam. And a dozen boxes of buckshot and slug. All yours. We put the old clothes into the suitcase, and that can be your luggage.

Time to go. I armpit the first of the new Glocks, put the second into the Bianchi at my back. While Jinx wrestles with the suitcase, I slip the bearer bonds from my discarded shirt and into the pages of my mother's book. I fit the book into my hip pocket. But I'm forgetting something. I check my old pants, my old coat, and there it is, in the pocket of the coat, that nine-millimeter bullet, the one from Renny's hand. I slip it into the right outside pocket of my blue suit coat. I don't know why. Maybe it's for luck. Or for not forgetting.

I take a pair of wire-rimmed glasses from inside the blue suit coat and put them on. Look in the mirror. And there he is, staring back at me. That guy. You know . . . him.

The old clothes and the foam packing go into the suitcase and we're almost ready.

Two cabs, he says. I'll be behind you all the way.

Right, I tell him. Next time I talk to you, next time I even look at you, it's gonna be Washington, D.C.

No, he says. Not D.C. Maryland. He says it like it's that wizard guy, the one with King Arthur: Merlin. Then he says:

New Carrollton.

That's a suburb northeast of the District. Best I can remember, it's got an Amtrak station and a Metro station and not much else. He's got his reasons and they'd better be good ones. So:

Okay, I tell him. New Carrollton.

I grab my duffel bag. I'm out of that bathroom and through the lobby and I'm an impatient business guy again. I go to the bell stand and there's the bellman and the bellman doesn't remember me, doesn't have a clue, and I check the duffel and then I'm outside, I push through the revolving doors, and there's the doorman and the doorman doesn't remember me, either, and I tip him a couple bucks and tell him:

Philadelphia Airport.

The cabs are lined up like vultures. The doorman waves the first one in and he tells the cabbie, Philadelphia Airport, and I settle into the back seat and I wait until we reach the end of the block to say to the cabbie:

Guess that guy misheard me. Take me to the train station.

We weave the few blocks to the train station, and there's a detour around the front, there's a red Mercury Capri parked there and the Mercury is surrounded by yellow tape and blue uniforms and I don't want to see that Mercury, I don't want to see any of it.

Five minutes after that I'm standing in line to buy a coach ticket, and ten minutes after that I'm standing in line to board the next Metroliner to Washington, D.C., trying to look interested but not too interested in whatever's happening way south of the platform, more yellow tape and more blue uniforms, and farther along, on a siding, where there's a train car with a broken window and some paramedics who don't have any work to do.

Ten minutes after that I'm riding the rails, and Jinx is sitting a couple rows back like he doesn't know me. I'm sitting with a newspaper folded open on my lap, and yes it's the *Philadelphia Inquirer*, and yes it's the fucking Sports section, and why not, because underneath the newspaper is my right hand and my right hand is holding a pistol and, let's face it, I've only just started pulling the trigger.

I wonder if Jinx knows that.

I wonder if he knows I know he made another

phone call. At the train station. While I was buying the newspaper and fading to grey.

I wonder if he knows how bad I have to make a call of my own. Fiona will be home soon. I check my watch for about the tenth time and I think about that Railfone thing, takes credit cards, but it's a bad idea. If there's a tap, then there's probably a trace, and nobody needs to know I'm riding on a train.

When the conductor guy announces Baltimore in three minutes, Baltimore next, it's like crossing a border, this irrational feeling of safety that I shrug off because Baltimore is the place where shit may happen, and the train slows and the train stops but shit doesn't happen and when the train chugs on out I relax enough to read my book, and Wilmington and the flaring lights, the yellow tape and the blue uniforms and the red, red blood, poor Lauren, it's all gone, it's back there with the other memories and we're getting on with the rest of this story.

Which is getting both easier and harder to figure.

Check this out. They were tapping her line. They were tapping Lauren's line. Or they had a guy on the ground in Philly, watching her, watching her place, waiting for me. Either way, it's shit on crackers. Because the Reverend Gideon Parks went down, what? Five hours before Wilmington. So the tap, the look-see, whatever, it was already in place. Which means—

What? They've been checking up on me, maybe. Or they were planning to take me out too. To let me do Jinx, and then take me out somewhere closer to home. Or—

It means what wiretaps usually mean: Feds. It means they got friends in high places.

The run that's not a run. The buy that's not a buy. The hitters that aren't the hitters. On the television screen, the helicopter boarding an FBI SWAT team that's not an FBI SWAT team.

So I think about this and I think about that and I watch the places and the spaces go by, and after a while I ease my hand off the pistol and I read my book some more and I find myself between afternoon and evening.

And this morning was six hours ago.

And this morning was seven hours ago and the sitting and the waiting start to get on my nerves until:

New Carrollton next, the conductor guy is saying. Next stop, New Carrollton. Three minutes, New Carrollton Station.

Which is where things get interesting again.

Jinx slaps my shoulder on the way up the aisle, and he's leaving the suitcase behind, which is fine. It'll go to Lost and Found, or maybe just get lost.

I tuck the Glock back beneath my suit coat and leave the Sports section on the floor.

Out on the platform, it's New Carrollton, this vague concrete space, one big parking lot with trees in the distance. The sky is dark and cloudy but the air doesn't smell like rain, it smells like autumn, something thick and grey and dying.

Jinx pulls up short. He smells it too.

I read the station and it's clean. Looking good. So I say to Jinx:

I got to get to a phone.

There's a bank of pay phones over there, but I don't think so, I think I ought to walk outside, to the Metro station across the way and I see a telephone kiosk and I find a free phone and I feed it my quarters and I call Fiona. The number's bugged, I don't give a damn, they can hear whatever I say, and it's not what I'm saying that counts, it's what I have to hear.

On the second ring I realize I'm sucking on a breath. On the third ring she answers.

Hey, who's there?

Fiona, I tell her.

Fiona who? she says. Just like I told her to do when I called and spoke her name. Unless there's a problem. So: Everything is cool. Everything's fine.

I'm breathing again.

Then she laughs and she says:

Hey, baby. You coming home?

Wait, wait, wait, I tell her. You okay?

Yeah, she says. What—

Any of the boys come round?

Birdman, she says, what is going on?

Honey, I tell her. Not now, okay? Just tell me—

Trey's here, she says. Been here since . . . I don't know when, baby. He was here when I got home, sitting out front in his car. He won't tell me why, he said to wait for you. So are you going to tell me? What is going on?

Okay, okay, I tell her. Look, just take it easy, okay? I'll be there before you can whistle.

I can't whistle, she says. But hey, Birdman. You got a great horoscope today, did you know that?

No, hon, but—

It's something about . . . wait, here, listen now, it says, um: Bright light shines where previously was dark. Emphasis on direction, motivation, partnership, marital event. Business outing proves fascinating, productive. Isn't that nice, Burdon? Isn't that—

That's nice, hon. Nice, but— Fiona? Put Trey on the phone, okay?

Just a sec, she says. Things start to break up. She's using that damned portable phone. Then: Trey?

Hang on, she says.

I cover the mouthpiece with my hand, say to Jinx: Trey Costa is there.

Jinx says: Who the fuck is Trey Costa?

My other man, I tell him.

How do you know he's still yours? How do you know he ever was?

I don't know, I tell him. But what does anybody

know? I believe in this guy. That's what counts, isn't it?

Another burst of static. Shit, shit, shit, I say. Then: Trey?

He's in the garage, Fiona says. Wants to know where you keep the, the—

Strange sounds. I don't quite realize she's crying.

Burdon? she says. What is he doing here? He's got a shotgun. He keeps looking outside, like, like— What is going on, hon? Where are you?

Fiona, I tell her. Listen. Listen real close, baby. I'm where I should be, and so are you. I'll call you again, inside the hour, okay? Then . . . now listen to me, hon—and I speak a little slower—then I'm coming home.

That's when I pause, and I say for the guys who are listening, those fucks, I say: I'll come in a cab. A Diamond cab. You see anything else, there's a problem, okay? Make sure Trey knows too. A Diamond cab, right? Okay?

Burdon—

Sssh. Everything is fine. Okay? And listen, Fiona. If I'm not there by the time your show's over, you get out of the house. You tell Trey to take you to see the world. You tell him that. He knows what to do. Okay? You tell him that.

Burdon, listen, I—

When your show's over. See the world, hon. Okay? Now I got to go.

Burdon?

I got to hang up the phone and go now, okay? I love you, baby.

I love you too.

And I try not to listen, I just hang up the phone, and I look at Jinx and I tell him what we both know:

I got to go get her.

Right about then we get a screech of tires and somebody's laying on a horn, honk honk honk honk, like it's never going to let up, and Jinx lets a laugh out and across the parking lot is a fucking pimpmobile, a platinum Lexus convertible with a noose of gold chain choking its rearview mirror and these evil black Doublemint Twins in the front seat, straight out of the life, living so large that their license plate ought to read GANG RELATED, in neon lights.

Yo yo yo, Jinx! says the guy on the driver's side. My man! He pops out of the door and does the swing-and-sway, coming our way.

Subtle, I tell Jinx. Why didn't they drive a white Bronco?

Jinx says: You in another world now, Burdon Lane. Startin now, we be doin things my way.

Yo, Jinx, the guy says, cruising in close. Like I'm not there.

Yo, QP, Jinx says. QP Green, my man.

There's some of that hand-slapping jive shit and this QP Green guy doesn't even look at me. After they press enough flesh, the QP Green guy says to Jinx, he says:

Yo, nig. See you got yourself a cracker.

Then, at long last, QP Green slides his eyes toward me. They're dull, tired. He's toking. Or maybe he's had a long day too.

Polly want a cracker? QP Green says. Then: We gonna take a ride now. In my Lex.

Says who? I tell him.

With a grin out of midnight, QP Green says: Mr. MAC. And damned if he doesn't slip one of those fine compact autos, a MAC-10 machine pistol, out from under his sweatshirt. He rocks the action, clickety-clack, clickety-clack. Like it's some kind of toy he's showing me. Right there at the station. In the open. In what's left of daylight. And no one's paying any attention.

I shrug and say: Guess we're going to U Street.

Guess so, says QP Green.

Which is when Jinx says: Yeah. And hey, Burdon Lane . . . welcome home.

He points toward the horizon and I look and I smell and I see.

That's my town, I mean, our town—the nation's capital, Washington, D.C.—in the distance. Smoke curls up from the horizon into storm clouds.

Something's burning.

dirty city

QP Green weaves that Lexus through the high-ways and the byways of the Maryland burbs until everything fades to a grey that's as dirty as the sky. We cross inside the Beltway and wiggle on and off New York Avenue, heading south, I think. The geography around here is all screwed up, but we're into the District of Columbia, that's for sure, what with the ragged pavement and the broken buildings and the abandoned cars and abandoned people and a funnel of smoke that's brewing ever closer, and sooner or later QP Green is saying Hey hey hey hey hey, and my pal Jinx says to me:

Get your fuckin head down.

That sets his homeys to laughing and I see the intersection ahead, and there's a crowd on the street and the windows of a liquor store go smash and fire climbs the side of the brownstone next door and I decide to get my fucking head down. Jinx sort of leans over me and QP Green puts that Lex through a hard turn and does corners and more corners until it crosses a bridge, the Anacostia River maybe, and finally it stops, I don't have a clue where, and Jinx is telling me to get up and get out, and the next thing I know I'm standing on a street corner and Jinx is standing next to me.

QP Green is saying something to Jinx, and it's a number, that's all I catch, a number, and then Jinx is saying it back to him, like it's something he's memorizing, and QP Green is shaking his head up and down, right, right, yes. Then Jinx slaps my arm and says to me, he says:

Okay, plain vanilla. Time for our appointment with the Doctor.

QP Green yells out something, sounds like do or die, while he cranks the volume on that tape deck, and some loudmouth rapper is walkin, walkin in his big black boots, and it's boom boom boom as the Lex speeds on out of sight.

I start to wonder if this makes a lot of sense, the two of us strolling around some lost part of Dirty City, but Jinx catches what's on my mind and sends it right back to me:

People be thinkin bout you and me, they think we five-oh. Police. Ain't that the shits? Tells you somethin bout how many white guys you see walkin round with black ones. Especially down here.

But hey, he says, and he nods on down the street to our left. This is a good place, you know? Good people here.

And he's right. I have no idea where we are, but it's a neighborhood. A nice neighborhood. Detached houses lined close on each other in neat rows. Perfect place for a safe house, a crib, whatever. I was expecting a broken-down crackhouse, some litterbox in the Southeast badlands, but this is so serene it's almost middle class. And it's almost, just almost, any other day. If it wasn't a sad day. There are kids outside, and they're riding bikes and shooting hoops and skipping double dutch. There are mothers and aunts and sisters, looking pained, looking at the sky, looking out for their children. And there are guys, too, fathers watering their lawns and pulling at the weeds and talking in quiet voices. A dog barks, gallops across the street and into the arms of a teenager on his porch. Picket fences, and damned if they aren't white and painted. Garbage trucks making their way down the street. It's hard to believe that, over there, beneath those grey clouds, is that restless and rundown place called Dirty City.

This is it, Jinx says. We stop in front of another nice house on this nice street in this nice neighborhood. He shoves me hard, fingers into my bruised back. Get em up and out. And do you and me a favor and shut that mouth of yours.

I bring my hands wide as I follow the little concrete path and wobble up the little porch to the house. It looks like every other house on the street, except for the desperate face and the barrel of an AK-47 peeking out an upstairs window.

Jinx steps around me, opens the front door, and hustles me into the dim interior.

Fuck all, he announces. Then he kicks the door shut.

The inside of the house is another deception, a foyer and a hallway that are wallpapered and decorated in a prim and feminine way, but then, down the hallway, waits a large room that's straight out of an industrial park, painted dirty white and scrawled with more graffiti than a bus station toilet. The room has been torn apart, furniture dumped over and pushed aside to make way for opened crates. Inside the crates are guns: Kalashnikovs and Uncle Sam's favorite, M-16A2s. War guns. On the walls are posters of Martin Luther King and Malcolm X, looking down on the madness like martyred saints, and who knows if they really are. Now there's a place on that wall for the Reverend Parks, too.

A guy in a Kangol cap waltzes by, a Sig .40 in each hand. Folks are pissed off and wanting to get busy. The fireplace is burning and a lot of paper is going into its throat. There's this scrawny runt sitting behind a school desk; his head is too big for his body, and his fingers are like pencils, and they're doing these frantic jabs into the keyboard of a laptop computer, and the computer is jacked into a phone line and whatever the runt guy's doing, he's doing it for real.

Looks like the U Street Crew is getting out of here and getting out fast.

I know the whole thing in one look, which is all I get, since Jinx pulls me like a bad dog through that room and into the next one, the remains of a bedroom.

Hey, ghetto star.

A guy with a beret high-fives it with Jinx.

Heard you livin, the beret guy tells Jinx. Nobody but you, man. Nobody but you.

The truth, homes. Where's the Doctor?

Counselin, the beret guy says. With Ray-Ban and Cue Ball. You just in time. Lookin like war, man. Lookin like war.

The beret guy decides to notice me. He gives me a sneer. So this is the white meat?

Yeah, Jinx tells him. Then to me:

Wait here. Don't fuckin move.

He follows the beret guy into the next room.

So I'm alone in this empty place. No, no, not alone, it's not empty at all. I hear before I see, tucked in the shadows between a bureau and the far corner, two women, girls, really, holding babies tight to their chests and looking back at me with suspicious eyes, angry eyes. One of the babies swivels her little head and her mouth is open in a sweet laugh that hurts me to see.

Then it's loud voices and heavy footsteps, and

here's the guy wearing the same beret and the same sneer he left with, and a guy wearing shades, and there's Jinx and he's in this other guy's face, and the guy is a black Buddha, a hulking heavyweight whose head is shaved, and he's got to be, just got to be, Cue Ball, and the beret guy is talking the talk with Cue Ball:

The shit was crazy, man. Tag Juan E and my nigga Jinx with killers. Fuckin white devils. Tried to tell you but you wouldn't be listenin. Tried to—

His words disappear into a sudden silence. A shadow walks across the wall, the ceiling, and onto me, and I feel a gremlin whispering in my ear but I stand in, I stand tall, as the shadow walks into the room and solidifies into a man.

There is only one Doctor D, the King of U Street, the King of Southeast, the King of Dirty City for all I know or care. The newspaper photos don't do him justice. The guy gives new meaning to the word ebony. He's beyond black, he's darker than dark, and he's not cold, he's not ice, he's fucking Antarctica.

Jinx says the one thing that no one needs to say:
This is Doctor D.
So what do you do? Just what the fuck do you do?
I stick out my hand and I tell him:
Burdon Lane. Pleased to meet you.
Doctor D looks at my hand and then he looks at me like I'm a fly, no, a fly turd, something so

small he wouldn't spend the time to wipe me off his boot. Then:

If you know me, he says, you owe me.

The guy's voice is absolute power. It could convert the dead.

The guy in the shades wanders over, dances his hands around inside my suit coat, leaves the Glock in the Bianchi holster but yanks the one from my armpit.

Boy, the guy in the shades tells me, you gots to be the only white meat inside a mile, cept for police and fire and EMS. Are you crazy? he says. Then he pushes the Glock into the hollow of my throat. Or are you Jesus?

He lets his finger curl onto the trigger.

Bang, the guy in the shades says, and he starts laughing like a loon. He slides the Glock up to my chin before he drops it away. Then he says:

Cause nobody else this white come to visit the D.

Hey, Ray-Ban. The guy with the beret is tugging at the elbow of the guy in the shades. Hey, Ray-Ban, bro, what you sayin? Jesus was *black*. He was a black man. You know that.

Doctor D gives the beret guy a look that might have wet his Fruit of the Looms. He takes my Glock from Ray-Ban and nods at Cue Ball, who says to me:

You alive, devil. Maybe not for long. But for now, you alive. You want to stay that way, then the Doctor's got a prescription for you: Do what the Doctor say.

Right about now Kareem or whatever they call the beret guy hauls out a pistol of his own, a Walther P5, that's old technology, no ambidextrous controls, shoots only eight, and he starts waving the P5 around.

Lemme smoke him, he says to Doctor D. When you done with this devil, lemme be the one, D. Lemme smoke him. I gots to be the one.

Jinx pushes Kareem's P5 away and says to his playmates:

I got one word for this white piece of shit: Evidence. We been set up. The whole mothafuckin crew. Newspaper tomorrow gonna say that U Street's the one that did Gideon Parks. Hell, CNN's sayin it now. They sayin we pulled the trigger. And this here's the one man who can say it ain't so.

The good Doctor looks at Jinx and he looks at me.

I know that, friend, he says to Jinx.

What I don't know, he says, is why this man would say such a thing.

His arm curls over Jinx's shoulder and he brings him around. What about Daddy Big and those 9 Bravos?

Them fuckin Bravos got dead, Jinx tells him. And Daddy Big? Man here says they capped him, but then they took him out of there, made him go missing on purpose. It'll bring down more heat on the Bravos. Us too.

Figured it. 9 Bravos are too stupid with drugs to work something this large.

Hey, I say to them. That starts the beret guy, the one with the P5, going again, and I get another wave of that pistol. But the Doctor and Jinx are still working their words.

Hey, I say again.

No go, so I say it again:

Hey, I say, and I put some piss into my voice. Hey, Doctor D. Things are looking a little crazy here. What's the problem? Your welfare checks late?

That gets the Doctor's attention, and his eyes flash my way. He's amazed; he's furious. It's now or never.

Listen, I tell him. That was a joke, okay? I mean, I know you guys are busy and all that, but hey. D. Can I call you D? Okay, so D . . . listen, could I ask you a question?

Doctor D's eyes go dull and dire. Not a nice look. Kareem steps between us and that P5 is back at my throat.

Lemme smoke him, D. Another dead cracker don't stop the show.

But the Doctor's going to listen. I know he's going to listen.

You just did ask me a question, he says. Two of

em, matter of fact. And nobody needs permission to ask the Doctor.

There's a pause, and here it comes:

Gettin answers, boy. Now that is another matter.

Doctor D takes a step in my direction.

You know how to pray, boy? Do you know how to pray? Because that's about all you got left to do in this life. The Doctor's gonna give you a minute to pray—he offers a gold-toothed smile—and a second to die.

That lights up Kareem's face and earns me another poke of the P5.

So I tell him:

Maybe so, D. Maybe so. But before I start asking God for things, I want to ask you. Just one question. Call it the condemned man's last request, okay?

That almost gets me a smile. Then:

Yeah. Aw'ight. One question. Ask away, devil.

Well, I tell him. You see, it's a nice neighborhood you got here. Nice houses, nice folks, nice kids. Not the *Cosby Show*, but . . . nice. So what I'm wondering, see, what I keep asking myself, and what I want to ask you, is:

Do they always pick up your garbage on Sunday?

Kareem shoves that fucking Walther into the side of my nose and I can feel the cartilage tear.

I'm gonna smoke him, D. Lemme do him now, lemme—

Doctor D's eyes narrow to slits and I know I don't ever want to see that look again. For a second I think I'll never have the chance.

He pushes Kareem out of the way and goes to the window. He pulls the blinds and looks outside. He looks back at me. He wheels toward me, raising the Glock, my Glock, and he swings that pistol up and . . .

He hands it to me.

Doctor D turns his back on me and my pistol, and he gives the U Street Crew the word, and it's the word of the day:

Fuck.

Then it's all business, a voice that is concrete steady and in command.

Yo. Listen up, he says, and that's all he needs to say to have silence and the rapt attention of his crew. Couple minutes, we gonna have five-oh in the house. Y'all know what to do, dogs. So do it.

Then he says: Yoda. He's talking to the skinny runt with the laptop computer. The kid brings his face out of the computer screen, but it's not a kid, the guy must be pushing thirty.

Do your little thing, the Doctor tells him.

This Yoda guy gives up a squirrelly smile and pulls a metal box of some kind from the junk scattered on the desk. The box is wired and the wires run down the leg of the desk and into a little package taped beneath the near window and then down to the floor and then up again at the other windows, and they're all rigged, it must be plastique explosive, and I'm thinking: Oh . . . shit.

Kareem is rocking back and forth on his heels. He says to me: We gonna make Waco look like *Mister Rogers' Neighborhood*.

I'm still thinking: Oh, shit. I've come all the way from Manhattan to D.C. for a guest role in a weenie roast.

Cept for one thing, Kareem says. We ain't going out like that. We ain't goin out at all.

Cue Ball. That big black Buddha is checking his handgun, a whopper of an Automag V. Get the womenfolks, Doctor D tells him. Then:

Blondie. Jeff.

Two guys in ski masks step up, loading their AKs with long banana clips.

Count to thirty, Doctor D tells them. Then get your asses out front and light things up. Two garbage trucks comin east. It's cops. Shoot to miss, you hear? Just give em noise. And don't get dead. Get your asses back in here and get gone.

Gone?

Jinx, D says, get this devil out of here. And keep him alive. Even if you have to kill him to do it.

The beret guy, Kareem, whoever, tells Jinx: Come on. And Jinx shoves me in Kareem's direction, through a doorway and into the kitchen and toward another doorway and stairs leading to a basement or a cellar, and down and down we go.

I flex my grip on the Glock and keep my head up.

This ain't gonna work, I tell Jinx.

Move, he says to me. Just move. Don't look back. Don't even think about lookin back. Just move.

Those hitters with the AKs must be stone cold, because right about now I can hear them chopping things up outside.

In the basement is this blank darkness, and I can't see a thing. The beret guy catches up with us and he's got a flashlight, he goes on ahead and I can make out something, a sliver of light, and the beret guy pulls at another door, and it's a closet or something, a naked bulb giving off enough light to show rough concrete walls and the outline of the rawhewn corridor ahead. A tunnel. A fucking tunnel.

It's like an old-time Western movie, a mine shaft cut through the dirt and clay and reinforced every few yards with wooden beams. The beret guy shines the flashlight and we go for a hundred feet, maybe more, and there's a right angle and then we stumble into a concrete room, not much of one, eight feet square, with an opening onto what looks like a concrete tunnel at the far side. I'm thinking air raid shelter, I'm thinking sewer, I'm thinking basement of the house next door, I'm thinking who knows and who cares, I'm just moving, and Jinx keeps prodding me with his hand and I see people in the room, a lot of women, some children, a couple more guys with assault rifles.

Whassup? one of the guys says, and the beret guy tells him:

Five-oh.

I say to the guy, he's a kid, really, sixteen, seventeen years old, I say: Not cops. Not just cops. Feds too. FBI, maybe. ATF.

The heat, he says, his eyes burning, and he slaps the bottom of the magazine in his AK and double-times back toward the house.

MJ! says one of the women, and she's dancing up off the floor. MJ! She starts running after him.

Shit, says Jinx.

Let's get, the beret guy says to the rest of the women. C'mon.

Jinx and I head into the concrete tunnel, and the tunnel weaves and wanders, and it seems to go on forever, our footsteps echoing down its walls, joined by the sound of footsteps behind us, lots of footsteps, and voices, and finally a voice that carries over the rest, the voice that says: Move move *move*!

The voice brings Jinx up like a hound hitting a scent. *Move*! he yells at me. He pushes me forward, and I stumble, nearly fall, as the tunnel goes suddenly white and I feel a rush of heat pouring over me from behind and then I see light and the tunnel is gone and there's sunlight and, in the midst of the sunlight, another shadow.

I lamp this guy and it's one of the evil Doublemint Twins from the Lexus. He's got the gold chains, he's got the wide smile, he's got the MAC-10.

Welcome to hell, QP Green tells me.

grave new world

Down the throat and into the belly of the beast. Like that Job guy, that Jonah guy, whoever. The Bible guy who got himself swallowed by the whale. That guy. Right about now, that's me.

This particular belly is carved out of concrete, a grey gut that has sucked in years of muddy water, twigs and branches, broken bottles, castoff cans and needles. It's a waterway of some kind, a drainage ditch or sewer maybe, sunk forty feet into the earth and curving its way to who knows where, probably the Anacostia River. I can't see anything but steep-angled walls of concrete and the burnt sky above. I'm standing on the bottom and so is QP Green.

Move that happy white ass, says QP Green, and he's hustling away, down the waterway, hop-scotching the patches of mud and pools of dirty water, and I move my white ass, though it isn't happy. After we run and we walk and we run some more, QP Green hauls up and starts sucking wind and so do I. He pulls a cell phone from his belt, dials down and says a breathless something, and then we wait.

There's a fork in the waterway, with a jungle gym of pipes and grillwork at the far wall, and after a while I hear footsteps behind us and after that there's Jinx and the beret guy, and by the time I'm breathing easy there's the U Street Crew and a cluster of their women and children, and finally, strolling through the middle of them like it's a Sunday afternoon in the park, not breaking a sweat, there's Doctor D.

The Doctor juts his chin, and Ray-Ban takes the cue.

Who we got? says Ray-Ban.

Cue Ball lumbers out of the pack and barks out names like it's roll call. We got Gemstone, we got Andre, we got Chilly Mac, we got Khalid, we got High Boy, we got Lil Toby, we got Tiny and Hotpoint, we got Levon, we got—

Well, what we got are a lot of very young and very tough black guys who are armed to their pearlies. And pissed off.

And we got their women and we got their kids and then we got the sound of more footsteps and a couple AKs drop to the ready, but it's Blondie and Jeff playing catch-up with the pack. That weird little Yoda guy lopes in their wake like a puppy, the laptop computer clutched to his chest.

He's got bracelets of det cord on each wrist. So we got—

Everbody, says Cue Ball. We got everbody cept MJ. Brotha said he wasn't leavin. He wanted to go out shootin and I guess he done it. And Debbie ain't leavin him. So she's dead too.

Shit, says Ray-Ban, and he looks over to Doctor D. They all look over to Doctor D.

Things go quiet in a bad way. It takes one of those hour-long minutes, but Doctor D locks eyes with every person there, his crew, the women, the children, even me.

The man died for us, says Doctor D. So did his woman. He died for us, and she went and died for him. Don't no one go forgettin that.

He walks over to Gemstone, and his fingers trace the letters that front the USC sweatshirt the guy is wearing. Doctor D looks a long time at those letters before he says:

You listen to me now. You listen good. This ain't about settin, trippin, bangin. Not anymore. This ain't about niggas doin each other over a bunch of concrete nobody owns. This is the real deal here. This is war. And we're gonna fight it now. We're gonna fight it good.

Gemstone, you and Billy take the women here and the little ones; you take em down to Billy's place.

Doctor D calls out names. The choices aren't random; the guy has his reasons and they're the kind you can see: size, firepower, but mostly it's the look, the look that says the guys he calls out are for real.

Rest of you, he says, be goin with Gems and Billy.

There are pained responses from some of the younger guys, the ones he hasn't chosen, but he shushes them and says:

Get on, now. You can do your dyin for us, you just ain't gonna be doin it today.

This Gemstone guy ducks under the pipes at the far side of the concrete valley, tugs the grill-work apart, and shepherds his people inside, into another tunnel that goes somewhere, maybe even somewhere safe.

Throw it up, Gems, somebody says, and this Gemstone guy does something funny with his hand, a sign, a signal, and then he's gone, and then this Billy guy is gone, and the last thing, the only thing, he says sounds like: Do or die.

What's left makes the Dirty Dozen look like debutantes. Bad isn't the word to describe these guys, and worse is a compliment. They're the kind of nightmare that makes the Attorney General wake up screaming. Give me your tired, your poor, your huddled masses yearning to breathe free, and give them assault rifles. That's the U Street Crew.

Yo, Ray-Ban says, and I realize these guys are

like a military unit; I'm listening to the chain of command. Ray-Ban says: Let's get steppin.

But Doctor D speaks and suddenly it's the Ice Age again.

Everbody cept you, High Boy.

This High Boy guy stops so hard he could've walked into a wall. Looks at his homeys. Looks at Ray-Ban. Looks at Doctor D.

What you mean, bro? He tries out a laugh. It's not a good one. He follows up with a smile that doesn't fool me and I'm damn sure it doesn't fool the good Doctor. What you sayin, D?

I'm sayin I only carry you so far, bitch.

Bangers start to back off, leaving High Boy the High and Dry Boy.

You foolin, star. Foolin on High Boy.

Doctor D turns his back on him.

You no-good fuckin stoolie, he says to no one in particular. Then he says to Jinx:

Take my four-nickel and shoot this bitch.

Doctor D hauls a shiny chrome .45 out of his belt and hands it to Jinx. There's something here but it's something I'm missing. The way that Doctor D looks at Jinx, it's all wrong, and there's a moment of near hesitation as Jinx takes the pistol. Nobody notices but Doctor D and me.

Jinx wants to say something, but he cocks the hammer instead. That's when High Boy starts the whine. I hate it when they whine. This is what he whines:

You don't wanna be doin this, D.

The guy can't even beg the right way.

D? Jinx? You don't wanna—

Jinx shuts up High Boy the hard way. He plugs the guy in the left kneecap, knocking him down. High Boy screams, then eats some concrete. After a while he goes quiet, curls into a fetal nerve that just sort of shudders inside a widening pool of blood.

Doctor D shakes his head, looks at Jinx, looks at his set, looks at me, says:

Snitches get stitches. Fuckin FBI must think I'm stupid. That's no nigga.

Nigger or not, this High Boy guy isn't going to walk right again. At least not on this earth.

Doctor D takes the shiny .45 from Jinx and says to his crew: This here my real nigga Jinx. Shoots my chrome-plated four-nickel thing. Shoots it bad. Ain't that right, homes?

Jinx gives him the wolf grin, but it's not all there. Something's missing.

Smart shot, Doctor D says to Jinx, his voice gone soft, just between the two of them—and me. Don't want to be killin us a Fed, now do we? he says. Least not yet.

And there's that something again, and I wonder what it is that Doctor D knows, that Jinx knows, that I don't.

Levon, says Doctor D.

A guy in fatigue pants and a heavy blue sweat-shirt steps up, starts to pull his strap.

No no no, says Doctor D. You and Lil Toby, I want you to drop this bitch out front the Animal Rescue League. Let them sew up what's left. Ever step he take for the rest of his fuckin life he's gonna remember the USC.

Then we're taking steps of our own, down the right fork of that waterway, through more mud and shit, and after a long while there's a pipe, it's almost five feet tall, and we're ducking and scut-tling into that pipe for a hundred yards, maybe more, and then there's another pipe, and then there's a ladder and we're up the ladder and in-side another tunnel, but it's not a tunnel, it's a cor-ridor, we're inside a building, vents and cables running with us to a short flight of stairs and we're up the stairs and into this place of grey brick and dust and rusted metal, some kind of waterworks, part of the old Navy Yard, and the point man pulls up short, then squats, and every-one's down, kneeling, alert, and I see Ray-Ban whispering something into a cell phone and it's cool, it's clear, everyone is up and smiling, tuck-ing their pistols, easing off with their AKs and burners, and that's when I hear the whistle. Some kid is whistling, and he's whistling a song, and I know the song, I know the damn song, but I can't remember its name.

Aw'ight, Ray-Ban says. Do what you got to do, we don't got much time.

The U Streeters fan out across the warehouse floor. Large crates and several cars are stashed beneath netting like forgotten stowage. It's the smell that gets me, though, the sharp smell of fresh paint, and that's when I hear Ray-Ban say:

Yo, Jimmy G.

So the one who's whistling, this Jimmy G, he's all of nine, ten years in the world, dressed like an MTV gangsta with the watch cap and ropes of gold chain, the deep blue sweats and wild thing Nikes, and he's got a can of spray paint in each fist and he's hosing the wall with the left one, some kind of wet red spaghetti that coils its way out of JUAN E LUV and into MOPES before spilling into this strange sort of sideways S, and I'm standing too close to the wall to take in what he's done, so I move deeper into that place and I see he's done it not just today but for days, weeks, months; that Jimmy G or somebody like him has been spinning this intricate web of patterns and pictures in which these words, these names, fade in and out, and that sideways S repeats and repeats, always in this spiral of blue and red, blue and red, blue and red, and it takes me a while but I think I get it, I think I understand, it's infinity broken and it's a U and an S and a C all at once. It's the symbol of the U Street Crew.

And no one needs to tell me about those names.

Not JUAN E or the one he's painting now, the one that spells out MALIK. These are the names of their dead, and there are many of them. Too many to count.

In front of the spray-painted names and symbols is this weird scattering of tennis shoes and boots, forty-ounce malt liquor bottles, lots of chain, a boom box, a rusted pistol, a leather jacket, and all of a sudden I feel like that Neil Armstrong guy, the one who went to the moon, like I'm walking somewhere nobody's gone walking before. At least nobody white.

Get goin now, Jimmy G. It's Ray-Ban talking. You be comin back tomorrow now, okay? Gemstone, maybe Billy, be down to see you. More work to be done, son. MJ's dead, and Debbie too. Maybe more.

There's a certainty to the way he says those last words. He knows there is no maybe. But the kid gives Ray-Ban a look that's long on knowledge and short on surprise.

Your momma's an Arch Deluxe, the kid says, and rattles those cans of paint like he's shaking dice, sprays one last something on the wall, and whistles up that tune again, strolling off to wherever those Nikes take him.

And what I'm thinking is what Jinx says to me.

What you're thinkin, Jinx says to me, is that this kid, he's a nice kid, he's a cute kid, he's a smart kid, he's a talented kid. But you're thinkin, you give the kid another couple years, and what? He's one of these guys here. Well, you think that.

The kid is what you make him, white man. The voice of Doctor D bores into me. He's at my shoulder, and he's looking at that wall and he's saying:

Look around you. This ain't the capital of the USA, this is fuckin Beirut. Woke up here one day, I was twelve years old, listenin to my grammie tell me to go on to school and walkin round the projects and comin home and watchin that TV instead.

That's what did me. The mothafuckin TV. But it wasn't the crime, the violence, all that shootin on the TV that did me. It was the shit between the shootin, man, the pictures of all the stuff, all the toys, all the cars, all the pretty girls, all the shit I didn't have, wasn't never gonna have.

So I'm sittin in front of that TV, smokin weed and listenin to some old funky music, and one day what happens out front of Dunbar High but my cousin Walon goes down. Some nobody's crew potshots at some punk and shoots my cuz instead, so what am I gonna do? What am I gonna do? Well, I'm gonna go over to Virginia and see me a white man, and I come back to the block with a .38 roundhouse and I perf that G and I fuck up two of his homeys but good.

You do that one time, ain't no way you goin back to readin-writin-and-rithmetic. No fuckin way. Because if you gonna do somethin, I say do it good.

Then Doctor D is past me and he's stepping in front of that wall and there's a forty-ouncer in his hand but it's not open, he's holding it by the neck and he spins around like a discus thrower and he slams that bottle into the wall. Malt sprays across the wet paint, and the blues look like tears and the reds look like blood.

Fuck you, Juan E, he says, and he waves the broken neck of that bottle like he's some kind of renegade priest who's blessing the pavement.

Fuck you and you and you and you, he says.

Shards of glass fall from his hand but Doctor D has gone somewhere, someplace I don't want to go.

Rest in peace, Doctor D says, and he comes back from that place with a gleam in his eye and that shiny .45 in his other hand.

And that's what I'm sayin to you, white man: Rest in mothafuckin peace. Ain't nobody livin happily ever after. We don't get out of here but one way, and that's dead. So what the fuck are you doin here? Tell me that, and tell me now.

You want the company? I tell him. You want UniArms? I'll give you the company. I'll give you the guys who killed Juan E and the rest of your people. The guys who killed Gideon Parks. But you got to give me what's mine.

I'm listenin, says Doctor D.

You can do whatever you want with his boys, I tell him. The guys who pulled the trigger. But the old man? Jules Berenger? The man's mine. Him . . . and the one they call CK.

Fool wanna blast me, Ray-Ban says, I'm gonna blast back.

I hear you, I tell him, but it doesn't work that way. And he doesn't work that way. I say it again, straight to the face of Doctor D: The man is mine. We got a deal?

Yeah, Doctor D says. Deal.

It's that simple, and that's what revenge is all about. Something very simple. Getting back what's yours. But you can't bring the dead back, can you? You can't do a goddamn thing about the dead except make more of them.

I say to Doctor D: Who rigged that little surprise back at the house? The kid?

Ain't no kid, the Doctor says. That's my nigga Yoda.

Well, I need to talk to him. Blowing up a house is one thing. How'd you like to light up a whole city block?

I'd like it just fine, he says.

Well, see, I got a place I got to be tonight. I got an invitation. I was thinking you might want to go with me. All of you.

Tell me when and where, he says.

I'm talking about a wedding. The boss's daughter is tying the knot. Seven-thirty tonight. Over in Alexandria. At St. Anne's Cathedral.

Fuck, man, Ray-Ban says. That's whiter than white. That's whiter than Tide can get you. That's the North fuckin Pole.

Yeah, I tell him; then I get back to the Doctor: Which is why, when you and your guys show, you're gonna be invisible.

What you mean? Ray-Ban says.

Jinx cuts him off. Will you shut the fuck up and listen to him?

I say to Doctor D: I mean that you're gonna walk right into that church and no one is gonna blink an eye.

I'm listenin, Doctor D says. This is the part where you tell me why.

You're gonna be what those people think you've been for the past couple hundred years. You're gonna be the help.

Doctor D does something amazing: He smiles. Then he offers me his right hand. Shards of bloody glass shimmer in his palm.

I take his hand and squeeze for what it's worth, let the glass cut me, and like the album cover says: Let it bleed.

Then Doctor D says to his crew:

Let's get strapped.

home

Over the river and through the woods, but there's no grandmother's house at the end of this road, just a two-bedroom bungalow in one of the lesser neighborhoods of Alexandria. We're going home.

Jinx doesn't like the idea, but that's too bad. I've got to do this thing, I've got to get Fiona, and if Doctor D wants what he wants, Jinx is going to have to do it too.

This is about love, I tell Jinx. I don't need to mention it's about bodies getting stuffed into the trunks of cars. Headless bodies. Or the many other fine things that have crossed my mind.

This is bout gettin yourself killed, Jinx tells me. But I don't think so, and anyway, I'm starting to feel like Doctor D: I don't care.

We ride out of Dirty City in one of the Doctor's less conspicuous sedans, a dusty Saturn, and this time I've got the wheel. There's one hell of a traffic jam consuming I-295 but we cross the Wilson Bridge and we exit north on Telegraph Road, and that's about all it takes. The Potomac is like a great divide between chaos and calm. The sky here is clear and blue and you can see the sun, fading away over Alexandria, where this whole thing started and where it damn sure better end.

I drive to my neighborhood, and I drive the cross streets, once down either side. Nothing doing, so I drive to the local 7-Eleven and I call Diamond Cab. Then I drive the cross streets again, and I take a left two streets south of my block and I do a slow cruise of that street. Nothing doing, so I park the car and we start walking between the houses. That happy old sun is setting on another suburban Sunday, and a lot of folks are probably glued to the TV watching the Reverend Gideon Parks die, over and over again.

Across the next street and the next yard, we circle a hurricane fence and I'm looking over a couple garbage cans at the back of my house. Our house. Home.

The shades are down, and so are the lights. Fiona's CRX is parked in the driveway; I can see its silver tail. There's another car parked at the curb, it's a new one to me, and it's blue and it's boring. Maybe it's Trey Costa, though if I was Trey and I was sitting in the middle of this thing, I wouldn't have parked there. So maybe it's no one, a friend of a neighbor. Or then again, maybe it's someone.

Here comes the cab. Yellow and black, with the

red diamond on the door. The cab slows, slows, stops in front of my house.

Nothing doing.

We wait, and the cab waits, a couple minutes. Then the cabbie honks the horn.

Nothing doing.

The cab pulls away, and Jinx starts to move but I tell him: Hang on. So we wait some more, and the cabbie, who's circled the block, pulls up to the house again. It's a little game called ring-around-the-rosy. Like the kid's song. Somebody told me one time that the song was about death, so it fits.

We wait, and the cabbie waits.

Nothing doing.

Then, bless the guy, he gets out of the cab and he goes to the front door.

We can't see what's happening but we hear him knock, then knock again. Then he's walking back to the cab. He shakes his head, climbs in, and after he chews on his radio awhile, he drives away.

So it looks real good or it looks real bad and, as usual, I vote for the bad. Probably we got a couple guys out there on the rooftops with long guns and night vision scopes who are going to pop our heads like balloons the moment we walk out into the yard.

There's only one way to find out, so—

I'm goin.

It's Jinx, whispering in my ear.

I don't even get the chance to tell him no.

Ain't nobody expectin me, he says. I'll check it out, circle round there. He points to the far side of the house, to that Thomas O'Toole guy's place, the house next door. Then, he says, we make our play.

Okay, I tell him. But—

I know, he tells me. Stay loose.

Then he's gone, melting into the shadows of the tall shrubs. I catch sight of him, a glimpse in the faded sunlight, as he breaks cover and dashes past the corner of my house. And then he's gone again. And gone. And gone.

I look at my watch and I look at my watch and after I look enough times at that hand ticking off the minutes I know I can't wait anymore. So I back off to the hurricane fence and I decide, what the hell, I'm going to take a walk down the side-walk, a walk down my street, so I double back two yards over and then I'm out and I'm walking down the street, my street, and there's nothing out of place, nothing but that car at the curb, and I walk until I reach that Thomas O'Toole guy's house, but Jinx isn't there, so I cut through the backyard and into ours, hoping O'Toole's dog isn't out. I pull one of my Glocks and hold it tight to my thigh and I go nice and slow, stepping through the bushes, into the flower bed, easy does it, sorry about the daffodils, Fiona, and pretty soon I'm peeking in the kitchen window.

Nothing doing.

Along the side of the house, to the next window, the one to the dining room, and it's an eerie feeling, skulking in the shadows outside your own house, looking for trouble and fearing what you might find, and all the time hearing the voice of Jinx, hearing that stone-cold killer saying *Where is her head, man? Where is her head?*

Nothing doing. Then something. A shadow leaking out of the living room and into the dining room. Somebody is inside, somebody moving. Barely moving. I look hard at the shadow, read the upside-down contour of that somebody, and it's somebody sitting. Jinx. It's Jinx, sitting.

I duck beneath the dining room window and move to the next window, that's the living room, and I take a quick peek and it's all I need. I ease back out of the flower bed and onto the grass, and I double-time it around to the back door, and I step out of my shoes and I key the lock so slowly, push the door so quietly, and I'm through the kitchen and I'm through the den and I'm behind them.

Cops.

Don't move, I tell them. Don't do nothing. You might even take a pass on breathing for a minute or so here.

Alexandria PD. There's two of them. They're wearing street uniforms, those steel grey shirts, and ain't equal employment opportunity grand. First we got an Asian cop—Chinese, Japanese, Korean, whatever—and then we got a dyke cop, with the chopped boy's haircut and all.

I got a Glock nine-millimeter, I tell them. It's pointed at your backs and it's loaded with AP rounds. It'll blow through your body armor like it's Kleenex, folks. So you stay right there, you don't do a damn thing, and I promise you: Everything will be just fine.

The five-ohs aren't even holding their service pieces on Jinx and how the fuck they got the drop on him I don't know. He's sitting on the couch with this defiant calm, looking at the cops like they're boring relatives who won't go home after Thanksgiving dinner.

Stay loose, now, I say. Just stay loose. I am making you a promise here. Nobody gets hurt. Everything will be just fine. That's a promise, okay? But you have to give my friend there on the couch your guns. Do it left-handed. Do it butt first. And do it slow. You first, fella.

So they're smart cops. They hand over their guns.

Okay. Now give him your radios.

They pass their walkies to Jinx. I give him the nod, and he drops the radios to the ground, grinds each of them to junk under his size twelve boots.

I step in closer, yank the cuffs from the guy cop's belt, drop and do a quick check of their an-

kles. No backup weapons. Then I'm standing and
breathing a bit more easily.

I keep my Glock on them and start making a
wide circle toward Jinx.

Okay. Now here's what we're gonna do. My
friend here, he's gonna take these handcuffs—

I toss them to Jinx.

And he's gonna—

That's when the voice comes sneaking out of
the shadows and taps me on the shoulder:

Well done, Mr. Lane. Very well done.

I knock the lampstand toward the den. Light
flares and the shadows run away, and there's this
guy sitting in the easy chair.

My house. My den. My easy chair.

The guy looks like he stepped down off Mount
Rushmore. Grey hair, grey face, grey suit. A mon-
ument. He might as well have the word FEDERAL
chiseled into his forehead.

Jinx has the bead on the uniforms. I flip the wall
switch and the den goes bright and I get more of
the same. This guy couldn't be more government
if his picture was on a dollar bill.

Hey, I say to the Mount Rushmore guy. Where's
my— And I start to say wife, I do, I really do. I
don't know what I could be thinking. So I say:
Girl? Where's Fiona?

She's here, the Mount Rushmore guy says.

Is she okay? I say.

She's fine, the Mount Rushmore guy says.

So where is she? I want to see her. I need to see her.

Go right ahead, the Mount Rushmore guy says.

I'm out of there and I'm into our bedroom and I'm out of the bedroom and I'm into the other bedroom and I'm out of there, and there's nowhere else, I check the bathroom, and there's nowhere else but the basement, and I'm back to the Mount Rushmore guy and he's got this grin I'd like to slap right off his face and I turn to Jinx and the cops and I look at Jinx and I look at the dink cop and I look at the dyke cop, and that's when I say to Jinx:

Oh, shit.

I look at the dyke cop again. Walk over to her again.

I knock her hat off, take in the cropped hair, the cool eyes, the taut lips, the body squared off by the uniform and the vest, the badge, the fucking badge, and of course the dyke cop is Fiona.

So what do I tell her? I tell her:

Nice haircut, babe. Kind of sassy. Is that what the girls call it, down at the salon where you work but you don't work? Professional, yes, but . . . sassy. Though I got to tell you something, Fiona. I do think I prefer it long.

I start to lean in closer, read the name plate above the badge, but I cannot do that. I cannot do that.

Jesus Christ, Fiona. Jesus fucking Christ.

And before I can think of any other brilliant insights, the Mount Rushmore guy comes out of his dramatic pause and says:

You're compiling quite a résumé, Mr. Lane. We'd heard some fine things about you, but . . . this is impressive, indeed. In addition to violating almost every federal statute involving firearms, ammunition, and export control, not to mention the laws of the several states you've frequented these past few days, we have racketeering and we have conspiracy and we have murder.

And of course, the Mount Rushmore guy says, nodding toward Jinx, there is the matter of your . . . relationship . . . with assassins.

His lips pucker ever so slightly and he tents his hands at his chin, the pose of a contemplative, right-thinking man, and I really don't have time for this shit.

So what's it to you, pal?

No, Mr. Lane. You're asking the wrong question. The question is: What is it to *you*? And the answer, Mr. Lane, is rather apparent, I should think. The answer, if we get you, is life. But if they get you?

. The hands pull apart and he offers what is supposed to be one of those magnanimous gestures.

I think we both understand the situation, Mr. Lane. And in this sort of circumstance—well, I believe there's a television game-show host who said it best: Let's make a deal.

That grey face gives me a grey smile before the punch line:

So what do you say?

What I say is this. I say:

I got two words for you, pal. *Fuck* and *you*.

That puts his hands in his lap and sits him back in the chair.

Burdon?

It's Fiona. The cop with the dyke haircut, I mean. Whatever her name is. I have to keep calling her Fiona or I'm going to go right out of my mind.

Burdon? she says. Why is this so difficult? Trey Costa is safe. We took him in on a two-bit weapons charge, sent him to Richmond, and he's out of the way. Safe. We can do the same thing for you.

I can't even look at her. The Mount Rushmore guy and I are having our own little stare down. Maybe he thinks I'm going to show him something, wide eyes, maybe, or a little sweat. But he'd better think again, because he's going to lose.

Damn it, Burdon, she says. We think we know what happened up there. But you know. You saw it happen. You have to tell us. We want these people.

No, you don't, I tell her. You don't want these people. You want a little law, a little order. You want collars. You want indictments. You want plea bargains. You want jury trials. You want convictions. You want prison terms. You want lots and lots of press conferences. And then you want bigger budgets. That's what you want.

Mr. Lane. It's the Mount Rushmore guy again. At the risk of melodrama, he says, I should tell you that this affair is not going to end quietly. We had a man inside. Sadly, he didn't do us much good. But—

Jinx shouts across the room: That's the problem with you, suit. You always got a man inside, don't you? But what did he know? What did you tell him? What did *you* know? Fuck, he says. Then to me:

Tell em, Jinx says. Go on. Tell em, man.

I tell them nothing.

The Mount Rushmore guy pretends that Jinx isn't in the room. Pretends that this is a meeting with a bunch of suits sitting around a polished oak conference table in some tall building with a picture of the President on the wall and the Stars and Stripes flying outside.

He clears his throat and makes the tent with his hands again.

Mr. Lane. We are prepared to give you prosecutorial immunity. Full immunity. Absolute immunity. Federal and state.

Then Fiona says: And protection.

The Mount Rushmore guy closes his eyes like he's weighing the thought before he says:

And protection. WITSEC. The Federal Witness

Security Program. Relocation, new identity, the whole nine yards.

I look at my pal Jinx. I look at Mount Rushmore. Finally I look at Fiona.

Fuck you, I tell her, but I guess I've done that already. So I tell her: I don't talk. Maybe I'm the one. Maybe I'm the last one. But I don't talk.

Jesus, man. Jinx is halfway to having a fit. We got a way out of here, he says. Not just for you and for me, but for my crew.

You want to shut the fuck up? Do you know who this is?

I'm pointing the pistol at Fiona.

Have you got any idea who this is? Let me tell you, man. Let me tell you. It's the woman who has been living with me for the past four months. It's the woman who's been sleeping with me for the past four months. Do you understand what I'm saying?

There's a wicked smile trying to creep onto my face.

I'm supposed to make a deal . . . with this?

My chest is hurting. I want to pull the trigger. I want to, I need to, I have to.

Finally I tell him: I already made my deal.

I want to show him my deal. I want to show him my home, not my house but my home, three days ago. I want to show him Fiona and me, me and Fiona, I want to show him what was and what never will be, and I can't do anything but say:

I made my deal. And this is what I get. Cops in my house.

Mr. Lane—

It's the Mount Rushmore guy again. I point the pistol back his way. But I don't look at him. I don't ever want to look at this guy again.

I look only at Fiona, and I tell her:

I don't want your immunity. I don't need your immunity. I don't need anything you can give me. Especially protection.

And then I say to the Mount Rushmore guy, I say: You had more than a man inside. You made the deal, didn't you? You made it happen. Didn't you? *Didn't you?*

Because I see it now, not all of it but enough to know that the guys who took delivery, the white guys, Mr. Branch Manager and his two buddies, were Feds. And that the Feds were the ones who made the run happen. Somehow they brokered the deal with the 9 Bravos. To get us to work with U Street, to get us to New York, to get us to sell them guns, to get UniArms and U Street locked down for life. The bearer bonds in my pocket belong to them.

Jesus Christ. Jinx is right: What did they know? What the fuck did they know?

I tell the Mount Rushmore guy:

There's only one way you're gonna get what

you want. And that's if I walk out of here. I'm gonna do that now. And you know what? Whether you like it or you don't like it, you're gonna have to sit there and look at it.

Then I say to Jinx:

Cover these people. I got to get something.

I find my way to the kitchen. I look at the picture of my mother for the last time, and I tell her: Night, Mom.

What? It's Jinx, calling from the living room.

Nothing. I'm doing fine. Just talking to a photo. You worry about those folks, okay? Cuff the old guy and stick him in the closet there. It's a gun closet, locks from the outside. Then cuff the cops to each other.

I take the photo of my mother and I fold it over once, twice. Put it in an ashtray. Strike a match and set it afire. It goes up pretty quick and I like that. It feels like it's time to make things burn.

I walk down the hall and kick open the cheap sheet of drywall beneath the clock, whoops, there goes the Laura Ashley wallpaper, and I pull the leather satchel, my get-out bag, from its cubbyhole. Inside the satchel are clean IDs and credit cards, a counterfeit passport, a cool twenty thou in cash, another Glock 19 with ten mags of ammo, a houndstooth jacket, and the keys to a self-storage shed that no one—and I do mean no one—is wise to, in a place in North Carolina called High Point. I go to the bedroom, open the top drawer of the dresser, and take the wedding invitation. Then it's the closet, I need a new pair of shoes. I reach into the corner and lift out the Remington Home Security shotgun that I gave to Fiona, the one she was scared to shoot, ha-ha. The one I keep loaded just in case. Just in fucking case.

Then I'm back to the den. The Mount Rushmore guy's buried in the closet. Looks like Jinx has done the handcuff thing up right.

And since there's nothing left to say, I say it. Of course I say it.

Hey, Fiona, I say.

She looks up at me, and I want to think that's a tear in her eye but it's the light. It's got to be the light. But I say it anyway:

I love you, I say. Did you know that?

As I say those words, I wonder: What *did* she know? Did she know they were planning to kill Gideon Parks?

There's only one way to find out, which is why I say:

And I wish, I really wish, I could of seen you in that dress.

I show her the wedding invitation and whatever she wants of my eyes.

You did buy that new dress, didn't you? For tonight? For the wedding?

And then we're gone, except for:

Oh, yeah. One other thing. I don't think you're gonna be using the car for a while.

That's when I walk outside, right out the front
door. Look at my lawn for probably the last time.
It needs to be mowed. Look at the tree I climbed
to pull down some neighbor's cat. Look at the
mailbox, the flower bed where the Geary kid
tosses the newspaper every morning. Look at the
sidewalk, look at the street, my street, the place
where I live.

Strike that.

The place I used to live.

You know what? I say to Jinx.

I look at the car in the driveway, the silver CRX
with the JAZZERCISE bumper sticker, the one I followed that time and then gave up on and felt
ashamed. Felt guilty.

I'm pissed, I say to Jinx.

No shit, he says.

No, I say to Jinx. You don't understand.

I heft the Remington.

Stand over there a second, okay? What I'm trying to tell you, see, is that I . . . am . . . *pissed*.

I rack that Remington and I start sending fat
whammies of double-ought buckshot into that
CRX at about five-second intervals. One after
ever-loving one. Blam. Glass and metal sing, fly,
rain in pieces across the concrete, the grass, into
the bushes, the ones I used to trim every Sunday
in the summer. Blam and blam. The front tires
blow and the chassis hits concrete with a dance of
sparks. Blam and blam and blam.

While I'm pumping away, this Thomas O'Toole guy, the guy who lives next door, he comes outside, this Thomas O'Toole guy, and then his little blond wife. They watch me take the car apart with this kind of wait-a-minute expression: Hey, wait, hold on a sec there, would you please? Is this in the bylaws of the homeowners' association?

Jinx says, Let's book. But I don't think so. I turn and spray a round into the car at the curb, flatten its front tires, and the O'Tooles, that happy couple with their happy kid, dance back, wide-eyed, behind their screen door, as if that's some kind of protection, and by then the lights are coming on across the street, and over at the Turner place, and that's when I have to tell them, I have to tell the O'Tooles and the Turners and the Johnsons and everybody else who will listen:

That's right, I tell them. That's absolutely right.

I yell, so everyone, all of them, can hear me:

It's me. The guy with the gun. Your neighbor.

Jinx is insistent. We've got to go. Still, there's time to squeeze off the last round, and I turn and I blow the street number right off the house.

Don't you get it? I tell them. I'm your neighbor.

I am your fucking neighbor.

a cold dish

Night's coming, and it's coming down hard.

There's a way the sky tells you it's tired, that the real light is going out and the pretenders are coming on, and as I look through the window of the Saturn at the houses and the condos and the mini-marts and the strip malls, I decide I'm tired too. I wonder why I used to care, what made me care about Dunkin Donuts or Video City, that Chinese restaurant around the corner, the Exxon station where Tommy Cogan tinkered with my cars, why any of that mattered, why any of it should matter, why I was the guy who could walk into the hardware store every other weekend and buy a couple pieces of brick to work on my little patio and somehow feel good about it.

Especially when it felt so much better to turn that silver CRX into a pile of scrap metal.

After I dropped the empty shotgun and waved goodbye to my neighbors, I let Jinx lead the way back to the Saturn and I knew that if we cleared

the first block without a cop car we were golden.
And golden we were. All the way through the
maze of suburban streets to the turn onto Duke
Street. Which is when I say:

Stop the car.

Jinx drives to the next intersection and takes a
right, pulls the car into a McDonald's, and it's
humming inside, life does go on, whether it's a
dead civil rights leader or riots or war, you got to
keep chewing those Big Macs, and Jinx finds the
Saturn a parking space between two other cars.

Come on, I tell him.

I get out of the Saturn.

Come on, I tell him again.

He shrugs and gets out.

We walk into Mickey D's and I step up to the
counter and I say to the guy at the cash register,
some Pakistani or whatever, one of those turban
guys, I say:

Hey, Sabu. Gimme a vanilla shake.

And Jinx says to me: What the fuck you doin?

I'm buying a vanilla shake, I tell him. You want
something? McNuggets, maybe? When he tells
me no, I tell him:

Well, I want something. I want an answer.

Aw, shit, he says, but I keep talking:

Am I wrong, or was walking in and out of there
a little too easy?

Jinx wants to be annoyed, but he knows, he
knows what I'm saying is right.

I mean, two Alexandria cops and one Fed? The Reverend Gideon Parks is dead, a lot of other folks are dead, and we're suspects, right? They been inside my house, my fucking life, for four months, and we get one man with a plan? That's it? Not the 82nd Airborne? Not even lights and sirens when I take apart that car? Are we supposed to believe there wasn't any backup? Or did they think for some reason it was gonna be easy?

The turban guy gives me my vanilla shake and I give him two bucks.

Have a nice day, I tell him. Then I tell Jinx: Come on.

I don't see what I need in the restaurant, so I take the far exit. Jinx stays with me.

I lamp the parking spaces on that side and I see just the ticket, this guy's sitting with his wife in their little midsized something with one of those metal plates on the back, the fish that says JESUS inside, and I stroll up to these folks slowly, slowly, and I put on a sincere but happy face and I take a little sip of that vanilla shake and I say:

Evening, sir. Ma'am. Sorry to trouble you, but Brother James and I seem to be having a problem with our car. We're ministering tonight over at Good Shepherd? Off of Quaker Lane? The gentleman inside tells me it's up the road. About a mile? I wondered if you'd be so kind—

God bless you, I tell them when they say yes, and again when they drop us at Good Shepherd without giving one thought to the fact that the building is dark or that we could have killed them. And I mean it: God bless them both. There are still some people in the world who have trust. Who have faith in other people, even if it's as desperate and hopeless as their faith in a fish that says JESUS inside.

We wait until they're long gone and we cross the street and stroll through one of those townhouse condo projects and we duck through a hedgerow and down an embankment and we're looking at Dumpsters and loading docks in back of this strip mall called Hechinger Commons, and it's the right place and the right time, and there's an Aerostar van, and the Aerostar van is faded white and painted with red letters that spell out FLOWERS ETC and the Aerostar van is filled with flowers, not to mention a lot of et cetera, because inside the Aerostar van are two of the U Street Crew—no, make that three because there's a driver, and he's not just any driver but that grinning son of a bitch QP Green. Next to the Aerostar van is a pickup truck with more U Streeters in the seats, and next to the pickup truck is what looks like a genuine Virginia Power truck, with that beret guy, Kareem, whoever, at the wheel and that weird Yoda guy peeking out of the cab, and next to the Virginia Power truck is a limousine, a white stretch Lincoln that shines and shines for what seems like half a city block, and I have a fine idea who's riding in the back of that Lincoln.

I walk over to the Lincoln and the driver's window glides down to show me a pair of shades in the driver's seat, and it's not any old pair of shades, it's fucking Ray-Ban, and I take the wedding invitation out of my pocket and I hold that rectangle of gilt-edged parchment in front of those shades and I say to Ray-Ban, I say:

Here's your ticket. You got something for me?

Ray-Ban says: Man, I got nine homeys in the place already. Been there since seven. Delivery boys. Maintenance crew. Even a couple cocktail waiters. Just like you said, man. No problem.

I hand him the invitation. It's a private affair, this wedding. Industry and politics, tying the knot as usual for the closest of friends and family. So this piece of paper, waved out of that fine limo, is going to get the Doctor past security.

Five past eight, I tell him, and then I tell the darkness in the back of that limo: Remember. We do this my way. If I can't end this thing by five past eight, you make your move. And whatever happens, you take out the UniArms warehouse. But you give me the time, the old man, and CK.

Ray-Ban says: U or Die, mothafucka.

The window glides up and that limo cruises away, places to go, people to see.

Now for the rest of the business. Out of the Virginia Power truck pops Kareem, and Kareem sort of does his thing on me and I give him the rest of what I promised: My security card key and the four-digit pass code that works the entrance locks at the UniArms warehouse in Old Town. Just what Kareem needs to get Yoda inside so he can do his little thing.

Kareem looks at me.

Kareem winks at me.

Then he's back in the Virginia Power truck and they're gone.

Then the pickup truck is gone.

Then it's Jinx and me and FLOWERS ETC, and I believe it's about time to make our delivery.

Inside the van, with the doors pulled shut and locked up tight, I say hey to the Doctor's guys, we got Tiny and Hotpoint and a lot of flowers, and I drop my get-out bag behind the flowers and I start running the usual check. I slip the magazines from the Glocks, check the loads, snap them back in. One Glock goes in the Bianchi holster at the flat of my back and the second in my belt, just over the left kidney. I strap a holster on my right ankle and that's for number three. I put two full magazines in the right inside pocket of my suit coat, two more in each outside pocket, and, what the hell, I put a couple in my pants pockets. I don't like the extra weight, but who knows how many rounds you need when you're going to a wedding?

Now I check the troops. Tiny and Hotpoint are

stroking their AKs like kittens. They're nice pieces, and they're from offshore, combat models, ready to fire full auto. Probably bought them from UniArms.

Let me see that, I say to Hotpoint. He passes his AK to me and it's North Korean, clean and oiled and as ready as a 9th Street whore.

He knows what's on my mind. I don't even need to ask him.

Uncle taught us good, Hotpoint says. Taught us in the Storm. Me an Jeff, Tiny an Malik an Lil Ace.

I pass the rifle back to Hotpoint and I want to ask Jinx what Uncle taught him, and when. The guy's too old for Iraq, unless he was senior NCO, and I don't think so. Just like I don't think I really want to know the answer.

Soon enough the van slows, takes a speed bump. We're late, which is the way it happens, but also the way it needs to be. To make the hard part easier, and to make this thing work.

The hard part is getting inside, at least I hope that's the hard part, and when the van slows to a roll and makes the turn onto the long drive that curves up the hill to St. Anne's Cathedral, I feel the kind of calm that tells me it's going to work; we're going to make it just fine.

I raise up, peering through a spray of flowers, and over QP Green's shoulder I take in the spires of the cathedral and what's left of sunset. It's like a picture postcard. And it's better than I remembered. St. Anne's is history: Built in the old days, burned in the Revolutionary War, built again and burned in the Civil War, and built again, third time's the charm, on the long low hill overlooking Old Town Alexandria, where, years later, the Masonic Memorial joined it. The bell tower faces south, toward Richmond, while the doors to the sanctuary open toward D.C. and the heathen north. The east and west walls of the cathedral are a tour guide's wet dream, with glorious stained-glass windows that ascend—and there's no other word for it—they ascend fifty feet into the sky. On this side, the east side, is an expanse of lawn, a gentle slope; to the west, on the shoulder of the hill, is the parking lot and then trees, shrubs, fences, and another one of those cozy Virginia neighborhoods.

There's a rent-a-cop cruiser at the mouth of the driveway and sitting inside with their coffee and doughnuts are two of the finest no-can-dos that Jules Berenger can rent. Up the hill is the trouble. The quarter mile of winding driveway is lined with town cars and limos, each with tinted glass and a guy at the wheel with an earplug receiver who's standard equipment. More luxury liners, including a certain white Lincoln, form a freeze-frame motorcade in the parking lot. More guys with dark glasses and earplugs huddle in the foreground, near a pond with a statue of some lady in robes, St. Anne or the Virgin Mary or maybe even

Gloria Estefan, who the fuck knows. Some other guys with dark glasses are walking a lazy perimeter on grass that's so well kept they ought to be playing golf out there. I see a couple CAR-15s, but mostly it's your typical security: handguns, maybe some machine pistols, but nothing too attention-getting. There could be sniper teams in the distant trees, the backyards of that neighborhood, but that's doubtful. Inside that church is a U.S. senator, but it's a wedding, for Christ's sake. Still, so many fingers, so many triggers.

All yours, I say to QP Green. I hunker back down into the flowers and take a deep breath.

Hotpoint is taping together two banana clips, end to end. Jinx is doing diddly, but he's eyeballing me like he's got something to say.

Smell anything? I ask him.

Yeah, he says. All these pretty flowers. Smells like death.

Maybe, I tell him. Maybe not. Maybe this is going to work.

The van stops.

The driver's window rolls down.

Hi, says QP Green, but I don't recognize his voice, it's suddenly this Bryant Gumbel School of Broadcasting voice, midwest white-bread English, and I don't need to see to know he's talking to somebody big and bad.

What you got? the big and bad guy says.

Hi, QP Green says again. I'm from Flowers Etcetera.

QP Green pauses and I hear papers unfolding and being handed out the window. Then QP Green says:

The, the—um, Berenger-Blaine nuptials?

I look over at Hotpoint and he's laughing into his hand and shaking his head.

The big and bad guy says: You're late.

Yes, sir, says QP Green. But these flowers are for the assembly hall downstairs. After the wedding, they're having a reception there.

The big and bad guy says: Okay. But I want this van out of here in twenty minutes. Think you can handle that?

Yes, sir, says QP Green. The paper gets handed back, the window gets rolled up, and QP Green starts driving us in, all the while saying to the windshield, the rearview mirror, the air all around him:

Yassuh, yassuh, sho nuff, suh. You can suck my mothafuckin dick, suh.

The van slows again. Stops. Through the rear window I can see the cathedral, its spires stabbing into the sky. Then:

Aw'ight, says QP Green.

It's showtime.

Well, I say to Jinx. You know what Gary Gilmore said when they walked him out in front of that firing squad, don't you?

Naw, Jinx says. But I got me a feelin it was somethin real stupid, like: Let's do it.

Yeah, I tell him. Yeah. So what do you say?

He looks at me.

I look at him.

Yeah, he says. Let's do it.

QP Green dismounts and takes his time coming around to the back of the van. He opens the rear doors and leans in to embrace a huge spray of flowers. Hotpoint fits his AK and about a dozen magazines into a long white ornamental vase that holds another arrangement, and then he's out the back, delivering that vase, and me, to the lobby.

U or Die, he says.

It's now or never, and I'm out of the van and between them, hoping for enough cover from the flowers to stroll on up the curved steps to the wide wooden double door of the cathedral. Jinx should be somewhere behind me carrying another arrangement, and stroll is what I do, I do, I do, and we're onto the steps and then we're up the steps and I move away from the flowers, I stroll toward the door, nice and natural, and before I reach the door someone is opening it for me and I look at the someone and the someone is Tully Malone, and Tully Malone looks at me, looks through me, sees just another someone, just another guest, and by the time it all registers on him I'm walking right past him and the best he can do is say:

Hiya, Burdon. I wondered what happened to ya.

There's a smaller double doorway ahead, inset with glass viewing panels, and I can hear an organ piping away and I see a lot of well-dressed people standing, and it's as good a time as any, so I'm through the double door and into the sanctuary while Tully Malone is still doing whatever he's doing out in the lobby and the flowers are being delivered, and Jinx and the rest of his crew get busy. Inside, some kid in a tuxedo and too many pimples gapes at me, nobody told him what to do with really late arrivals, and I just nod and whisper to him, I'm with the bride's family, and he blinks a couple times and waves his hand to the left side of the sanctuary and I take a few steps down the aisle, there must be a hundred rows of heavy wooden pews, and I find an empty pew on the left about ten, twelve rows along, and I ease my way in.

The sanctuary is weighted with a solemn smell, flowers and candles and wood and age, and there's quite a crowd filling out the pews, and all of them are intent on what's happening in front of this wide marble altar—what do they call it? the dais, the something—because that's where we've got the happy couple with the bridesmaids and the groomsmen and the priest, and they're listening to whatever it is the priest is saying into the microphone and whatever it is he's saying ends with the word amen, and that's when everybody says amen.

So I'm there just in time to sit down. The priest drones on in Latin for a while and then there's this reading from the scriptures and this sort of pretty song but I'm not paying much attention to all these words because I'm checking out the big and bad guys standing in the back of the sanctuary and the few toward the front and, yes, the woman over there in the trouser suit, very nice but not quite the fashion for a society wedding, and these other dots and dashes throughout the congregation, the guy with the oversized raincoat, the one with the briefcase, those telltale signs and symbols that they're packing weapons.

And I'm checking out the U.S. senator, all hail-fellow-well-met, like any good father of the groom, and it's the same Senator Anthony Blaine I saw a couple hours ago doing a teary-eyed sound bite on CNN. Guess a dead civil rights leader didn't ruin his day.

And I'm checking out Jules, that's Mr. Berenger to you, and with him there's the latest little trophy blonde and there's the ex, the one that's the mother, and there's the politicians he's got in his pocket, and there's some good-looking suits on my old pals Quillen and Dawkins and Rudy Martinez, and there's another crew chief, McCarty, and then there's a lot of folks I don't know and don't care about, there must be three hundred or so people all gathered here in St. Anne's Cathedral for what the priest just called this joyous occasion.

And finally there's this voice in my ear and it says:

You lose.

Took you long enough, I say to CK, and of course it's CK, it has to be CK, he was going to be here as sure as I was going to be here. He wouldn't have missed it for the world. Because this isn't just a wedding, it's a celebration, isn't it?

Some wrinkled old lady a few rows up turns around to shush me, and when she looks at me, then looks behind me, she thinks better of it and gets back to watching the joyous occasion, and that's when I feel the barrel of CK's Magnum at the back of my neck. But hey, the guy's not going to shoot and ruin everybody's happy day now, is he? So I look at my watch and I ease my head back a little toward him and say:

You got ten minutes.

There's a satisfying silence, and then he bites.

Ten minutes for what?

Ten minutes until it happens.

The barrel of his gun jams into my neck. Shut the fuck up, Lane.

The wrinkled old lady turns around again, no way she can't see that big pistol, and she puts a wrinkled little finger to her wrinkled little lips.

Up in front, at the altar, the priest is saying

something about love, but back here in the cheap seats I'm talking about something more practical.

Doesn't matter what you do, CK. You spray my brains across the guest list, it's still gonna happen. Only right about now you got nine minutes.

Shut up, Lane.

The groom is taking the bride's hand in his own and they're stepping forward, closer to the priest, closer to the microphone, and they're right off the top of the cake, he's this strapping handsome Joe College boy and Meredith Berenger, she's what they always say about brides, only this time it's true, she's radiant, she's gorgeous, and it's nice, it really is nice, and I think I should do like the man says and shut up for a while so that's what I do, I listen to them make their vows, and it takes a couple minutes but it gets to him, you know it gets to him, he wants to know, he has to know, and it doesn't take long till he makes his move.

Here's what we're gonna do, CK tells me. Pretty soon we're all gonna be hauling our asses up to say some more mumbo jumbo or sing some bullshit song, okay? And as soon as we all stand up, you're gonna make like you need to take a piss. You're gonna stand up and you're gonna walk back up that aisle, and I'm gonna be right behind you and so is Elvis.

Cue another jab of the barrel into my neck. Then he says:

And you're gonna walk out into the alcove and

when you get there, you're gonna see this little hall off to the lee side, and you're gonna walk down that hall and there's a little room at the end of that hall, and you're gonna walk into that room and there's some chairs in that room and you're gonna sit down in one of those chairs and then I'm gonna decide whether or not you get to live. What do you say?

I say nothing. I decide to take in those famous stained-glass windows, there are five of them on each side, and the windows are these pretty pictures, they tell the story of the Commandments or the Beatitudes or something else that Jesus guy said or did, and after I look at the windows awhile the priest raises his arms as if he's embracing the bride, the groom, the attendants, the congregation, everybody, and the priest says:

Let us pray with confidence to the Father in the words our Savior gave us.

So we're all standing up and the priest is saying this prayer and I know this prayer and all the people are saying it with him, they're saying:

Our Father, who art in Heaven, hallowed be thy name

And I'm easing my way over to the aisle.

Thy kingdom come, thy will be done on Earth as it is in Heaven

And I'm walking into the aisle.

Give us this day our daily bread, and forgive us our trespasses

And that's when I trespass, and I need forgiveness.

As we forgive those who trespass against us

Because I just can't seem to forgive.

And lead us not into temptation

So I'm not walking away.

But deliver us from evil

I'm walking the other way, the only way that's left to me. I'm walking down the aisle, I'm walking toward the priest, I'm walking toward the altar, and everything seems to go silent but the voice in my head, the voice keeps going, and I think, I really think, it's my mother's voice and I'm almost to the altar, I'm between the groomsmen and the bridesmaids, and that's when I pull the Glock from my belt; I pull the Glock and I turn on CK and I point the Glock at him and he's about twenty feet behind me and he raises the Magnum in his fist and he points the Magnum at me and there's this strange silence, the priest has stopped talking and there's silence, just silence, just silence until I say, along with my mother, I say:

Amen.

Movement, there's movement at the periphery of my vision, the shuffle of feet on heavy carpet, a choked kind of scream or sob or something in the congregation, and the sad sounds of people not knowing what to do, but I know exactly what to do and I'm not losing focus, I'm looking down that Glock at a sight picture I don't ever want to forget and CK knows what I know, that if we shoot we're probably both dead, but that if he misses he might shoot himself a newly married bride or groom.

So it's time to say what I came to say.

I say:

Mr. Berenger.

The shock is passing and the silence is giving way to the white noise of surprise and anger, and there's movement again and it's movement in my direction and I say:

Let's all stay calm. And let's all stay right where we are.

Then I say: Please.

I hear the sounds of hands on grips, some pistols going clickety-clack, and I have a feeling I've got more than CK looking down a barrel at me.

I clear my throat, it's getting dry in here, and I say again, a bit louder:

Mr. Berenger.

To which at long last I hear Mr. Berenger, my employer, my mentor, my friend, dear Jules, say:

Do I know you?

To which I start to say yes, when CK says to me:

Shut the fuck up.

He rocks the trigger back on that hand cannon and he calls out, he calls out loud and clear:

Dawkins.

Then: Quillen.

Then: Kill him.

But Jules says:

Belay that.

To which CK says:

Kill him.

And Jules says:

Clarence!

There are furious noises, and I can't help it, my eyes dart right and I barely make out the wide load of tuxedoed Jules Berenger, an irate penguin, face pinched with rage, shoving his way past a wife and an ex-wife and a bridesmaid and into the aisle next to me and then I'm staring back dead on and down the sight of my pistol at CK. At . . . Clarence?

The guy is named Clarence?

Apparently so, because damn if Jules doesn't yell that word again:

Clarence! He's getting control back into his voice. Stop this, Jules is saying. Clarence, you will stop this *now*.

That's what you call a direct order, but CK doesn't seem to hear him. In his face there's this perverse thing that's pulsing. It's pride. It's arrogance. Or maybe it's just insanity.

CK makes himself grin.

I know where I'm going to shoot him: K-5. Center of mass. Doesn't matter whether they're wearing body armor or not, you always go for the center of mass.

Dawkins, he says.

You kill them or you knock them down, same difference. If you're firing the right piece at the right place with the right ammo, the shock is what you want and the shock is what you get. So it's center of mass: K-5. For as long as my finger keeps twitching.

Quillen, CK says.

I go loose.

Kill him, CK says.

Loose.

CK breathes one in and takes a step closer and I get ready to blow him right out of his shoes and that's when the fun begins. This thing didn't go down according to plan, but right about now the ten minutes are up, at least the right guy's watch says five past eight, and that's when there's a shriek of feedback, the clunk of somebody tapping a microphone, and a voice comes echoing down off the altar but it's not the priest's voice, no it's not, and it's not the bride and it's not the groom, no no no, not at all.

It is the voice of one very bad man, and the voice says:

Dearly fuckin beloved.

I see the eyes of the congregation moving, looking up and locking on the man who stands in place of the priest and the men who stand with him, assault rifles at the ready. I hear the sound of the cellular phone in his hand, a dial tone and the swift melody of a number being speed-dialed.

It's Doctor D. He doesn't speak into the phone, he speaks into the microphone. He speaks to us all.

It's Nigga Day, he says.

Then everything goes boom.

nigga day

The stained-glass windows on the east side of St. Anne's Cathedral implode with a rush of panicked wind.

In that instant, that frozen moment alive with the ring of a thousand tiny bells, before the windows on the other side blow out in a hail of slivered glass, before I hear the actual explosion, the screaming starts.

The roof hitches and the ruined wall to the east crumbles inward, casting down bricks and torn chunks of wallboard and plaster, and through the broken and empty spaces where the stained glass told stories of the saints and the martyrs there's a new picture, a new story; it's the story of a black sky whose bright clouds billow in yellow and red. Angry serpents of flame coil and lash out, vomiting up an entire city block of Old Town Alexandria—the warehouse, the headquarters of UniArms, fractured concrete and wood and plastic and metal and guns and guns and more guns—

and that's when the sound comes, a blast that's like thunder, but a thunder I've never heard, it's the thunder that says what's going to rain now is blood.

And that, of course, is when the shooting starts.

I don't know which idiot rattles off the first shot. It isn't me and it isn't CK, but you'd need a fine-tuned stopwatch to decide that one. Most likely it's some amateur, one of the rent-a-suits in the back of the room, but after the first shot it doesn't matter. This dim bulb back there, he starts rocking off with something full auto, and the U Street Crew gives back some of the same, and the next thing you know we've got a firefight in a Catholic church with a couple hundred civilians in between, on the side, here, there, everywhere.

I see CK's Magnum jerk and as I squeeze the trigger I get punched in the left arm, so I get off a lousy shot but I think I hit him and then I'm staring in a different direction but I didn't turn my head and I know nothing and I'm on the floor and I know something. I know I'm hit but I know I'm okay and I know I'm going to stand up, I don't think about anything else, I'm going to stand up, the thought of where I've been hit doesn't even feature in the act, I just struggle to my feet, leaning into the end of the first pew for balance.

I point my pistol back at CK, trying to get a sight picture, I want to wash the guy, but he's down, he is down in the aisle and he's hit too, and the blur around him becomes motion and the motion becomes people and the people are civilians and the civilians are in flash panic, they're rushing in front of him and behind him and it's a stampede and I hear the roar of gunfire all around me and I can see this swirling rush of humanity, the tuxedos and the suits and the gowns and the dresses, and they all have faces, frightened and astonished and angry faces, and I can't pull, I can't pull the trigger.

CK scuttles away. He's got an entrance wound about the size of a nickel in the meat of his right thigh. Not much blood. Yet. He yanks his belt from the waistband of his suit pants and starts knotting it around his leg, and all the time he's looking at me, and it's that look, you know, the one that would kill, but he's going to need at least one more shot at me for that.

I kneel behind the cover of the first pew and that's when I notice my old pal Jinx and he's kneeling next to me, which is also when I hear him sum things up:

Shit.

This is not what I wanted. This is not, was not, supposed to happen. This was going to end with words. Jules was going to confess his sins, CK's sins, in front of these people, and afterward Doctor D would blow up the warehouse, have his payback, then light out and watch the guys who made this mess try to clean it up. No shooting. No more shooting. Not here. But everything I touch turns to blood.

People are surging in all directions, trying to get away from the altar, but there's no way out. Hotpoint and Tiny should have taken the narthex and they've got the wide double door locked or blocked, and they're keeping the big and bad guys out while they're keeping all these good folks in. Some pistolero in a tuxedo learns that one the hard way when he tries to shoot his way out of the sanctuary and into the narthex and does a backward jig with about a dozen rounds for a partner.

The columns behind the altar disappear, shredded into a confetti of chewed timber and wallboard and brick. One of Doctor D's homeys, it's Khalid, pops up out of the smoke and rocks back with his AK. He dives down before they can rattle back at him and then he's up again with a new magazine.

Flowers blossom around us, pink and red, as the bullets tear across the sanctuary, chew through the wooden pews, chew through anyone who is standing between us and them, chew through these poor people and spit out pieces and gobs and geysers of blood. I see flowers of flesh, flowers of blood, and in the distance I hear the faint shriek of angels, dying.

My God! It's Jules Berenger, and he's saying: My God, stop this! Somebody, somebody, stop this!

But God's not at home.

I get myself partway around and I see Ray-Ban make some kind of hand signal and some of his guys go for the right aisle, AKs up and pointed, but they're not firing, they're yelling at the crowd: Get down! Get the fuck down! Another hand signal and two of the gangbangers stand and unload their AKs on the back of the room, firing over the crowd and ripping the shit out of the wall and a couple of CK's shooters. Like a fucking fire team.

QP Green vaults onto the first pew, a couple feet from me, standing there like John Wayne at the Alamo. He rides his AK on his hip and runs the magazine over the heads of the boiling crowd.

Get down! QP Green yells. Get the fuck on the floor!

No one seems to hear him. More screams, more animal confusion, and finally more gunfire. QP Green takes a hit for his trouble, the top part of his shoulder disintegrates in a cloud of red, and the hit spins him around to meet more bullets. Jinx keeps his head down and scrambles over to the body that plummets to the floor, but it's a gesture. We've got another dead man.

McCarty! It's CK. He's trying to get his people together but there's too much of everything: too much noise, too many people, too many guns.

CK is up, and his men are up, and they're pushing guests out of the way and down, fighting their way through the crowd, some of them firing back at the U Street Crew. CK is shouting, trying to take charge, but things keep spinning right out of control, until the voice comes, the voice comes again:

No more.

It's Doctor D, his amplified voice engulfing the mayhem. No more, he's saying, and the U Street guns go silent, and I see Jules Berenger and he's got his hands in the air, stumbling up the center aisle toward CK, toward his men, stepping over the frightened people pressed to each other, to the floor, and Jules is saying something, and his arms are alive with frantic motion and I hear him shouting:

Stop stop *stop.*

Dear God! he cries out. His voice is hoarse and anguished. *Stop!*

That's when CK lets the barrel of his Magnum tilt into the air. He squints through the smoke and through Jules Berenger, squints at the ruined altar, and barks: Cease fire!

Other voices echo the command and that's all it takes. It's over and done, except for the amateurs. Behind CK, one clown keeps firing his bullshit machine pistol, and when he finally clicks dry, CK strolls over to him, hefts his Magnum and blows the guy's excuse for brains out the side of his head.

Cease fire, he says to the guy's corpse. That

ends it, except for the torn voice of Jules Berenger, calling:

My God—

The silence answers him, and his arms fall back to his sides in a kind of palsied collapse. He circles around to face the altar, where a crucifix, torn from its cables, swings like a scythe through the smoke-filled air and crashes to the floor, angling into the first of the pews. Where the priest crouches at the edge of that marble altar, safer there than in the arms of his Lord. Where one of the bridesmaids, the pink of her gown blotted into deep red, cradles a kid in a tuxedo whose legs are slivered ribbons of fabric and flesh and bone . . .

And where Doctor D stands, High Priest of the Order of Death, his left arm curved around his white-veiled offering. It's Meredith Berenger. His chrome four-nickel, that bright and shiny .45, is pressed to her pretty blond skull. Ray-Ban stands to the other side of her like an unholy best man. Most of the U Street Crew stands with them, pointing their AKs down and dirty.

Please, Jules says, suddenly old and shaking right down to his overpriced shoes.

He reels toward the altar. Toward us. I've got my Glock pointed at him. Jinx stands next to me. The guy still hasn't pulled his piece.

Please, Jules says. To me, to Doctor D, to anyone who will listen.

I let him pass, hold my piece on CK and the rest

of them. The civilians look on like the survivors of an air disaster, their eyes dull and doubting that this could be real.

Please, Jules says, and this time there's an answer.

I don't know that word, Doctor D says. His hand flexes on the grip of that four-five and he says:

You fucked with me, Boss Man, and you lost.

Doctor D cocks the hammer.

And when you lose, he says, you got to pay the dues.

The word is there, right there in my throat, and it's about the shortest word around. Just two letters in it. The word no one seems to be able to say anymore. But I say it, I say it.

No, I say. *No.*

And I've finally said that word in time to stop something.

I turn around and I put my Glock on Doctor D.

No, I tell him again.

Ray-Ban turns his piece on me and right about now I decide that no one is ever going to do that to me again. That I'm going to kill the next guy who even thinks about pointing a gun at me.

Thank God, Jules says, and it's like a whispered prayer. Thank God, Lane.

I say to Doctor D:

You got what you wanted. You killed the thing

Douglas E. Winter

he loved most. You think that's the love of his life you've got there?

No way, I tell him.

I point out the broken east wall to the burning sky over Alexandria.

That's his flesh. His blood. And it's finished. It's dead and gone.

It's only a heartbeat, but it's like that eternity before the dentist touches down with the drill. Until Doctor D says:

Yeah.

He rocks the hammer back and lets his four-five down gently. Meredith Berenger doesn't even notice. She's a teary white-eyed deer caught in the headlamps of reality.

But— Doctor D says, turning his pistol on Jules. Somebody's got to pay.

And he's right, somebody's got to pay and somebody's going to pay, but that wasn't the deal. That was not the fucking deal.

The voice beside me says:

No.

It's Jinx, and Jinx has pulled down at last, and he's aiming his pistol, that spurless Ruger .38, at Doctor D.

This is over, Jinx says. This is where it ends.

I hear the creep of footsteps at our backs and I turn around, and who's coming our way but CK and a couple other zealots, and my Glock brings them right to a halt.

CK starts to raise his Magnum but maybe it's in my eyes. He thinks better and then he knows better.

Way I see it, Jinx says, the dead are dead. But so's this man. Look at him, D. He's white and he's old and there ain't nothin inside him but rot. It's not even a matter of time. He's dead already.

Jinx opens his arms. Like the priest. Like he's hugging the air.

We got a choice, he says. We can be like him. We can kill and kill and we don't have to care. Innocent folks, guilty ones, it don't have to matter. We can just kill and kill and keep on killin. Like him. Like them.

Or, Jinx says, we can be what Reverend Parks said we could be: We can be us. We can say we're not afraid to stop. To put down the gun. To be better than him. Better than them. We don't have to live their way. We don't have to kill to get what we want.

Doctor D isn't looking at Jinx, but he's hearing him. With that shiny four-five still leveled at Jules Berenger, Doctor D says:

The man's right, you know. This shit ought to stop, and it ought to stop here. I ain't killin your daughter, mothafucka. And I ain't killin you. I didn't come here for that.

He lowers his hand, brings the four-five down to his hip.

I ought to be killin you, but I'm not. Somebody

else can do that. The government, maybe. They're gettin pretty damn good at it.

Doctor D starts to laugh, and the laugh goes to a smile, and it's not a good smile, it's the Jinx smile, the wolf smile, the predator smile. And just as suddenly it's gone.

But, the Doctor says, it ain't done.

You ought to know that, the Doctor says. To me.

It ain't never done, he says to me. And then he says:

Who?

My eyes search the congregation and I see the first of them. The ones he wants. The shooters. The ones who killed Gideon Parks.

I nod at Quillen.

Him, I say.

Doctor D turns the four-five on Quillen, and there's this nervous shuffle among CK's guys but CK calls out: Stand fast.

I have to give it to Quillen, the guy puts a pissed-off look on his face, but he doesn't move, he doesn't blink, he's a professional to the very end.

Which comes in less than a second, because:

Blam. Doctor D plugs Quillen.

A scream from a woman somewhere in the back. Quillen falls, but it's a sweet shot, the guy's dead before he chews the carpet. Meredith Berenger flinches, at the sound of the gun or the sudden violence, it's not clear. Her wet eyes are blank. Maybe she's finally seen some truth.

Who else? Doctor D says to me.

I look for Dawkins and it takes awhile but I find him, over there, twisted into a broken pew, his body curled and limp. Dawkins always preferred the long-range action. Somebody got him close in, and they got him good.

Him, I say.

Doctor D turns the four-five on Dawkins's corpse. He says:

Can't get him no deader than that. But what the fuck.

Blam. He shoots the body. Then:

Who else?

I take a nice long time letting my eyes pick over the remains of that sanctuary, looking anywhere and everywhere but not at CK. And after that nice long time is up, my eyes come to rest on CK and that's when I say:

Nobody.

They're dead, I tell Doctor D, and I don't stop looking at CK. I tell the Doctor the same thing I told Renny Two Hand:

Every last one of them is dead.

Yeah, Doctor D says, and it's a lazy kind of yeah and I don't know if he believes me, but right about now I don't care if he believes me and I'm not sure he cares either. His business is done, and the law's looking for him and they're going to be looking harder now.

Come on, he says to his set. Let's get the fuck out of Dodge.

One by one, the U Street Crew moves out, AKs trained on the crowd as they back away across the altar and through the door to the sacristy. They carry the bodies of their wounded and QP Green, their dead. Soon only Doctor D and Ray-Ban are left, and Doctor D has one last thing to say to Jules Berenger, to the whole congregation:

Maybe y'all figured it out by now, he says. But I'm gonna tell you anyway. You folks made one hell of a mistake today. Because you went and killed the wrong nigga.

Then: U or Die, he says.

Doctor D vanishes into the shadows of the sacristy, and there's this frail moment before Ray-Ban calls out to Jinx:

Yo, homes. Let's get gone.

Jinx tucks his pistol into his belt. As he walks away, he doesn't even look at me, he just says:

Peace.

body count

Peace. It's the last of my pal Jinx, but when I bend forward, trying not to puke, it's only the first of the voices I hear. Words words words are pounding at my head and after a while I let them in.

Daddy? That's Meredith Berenger. The blood-stained bride, with the U Street Crew for groomsmen. What a wedding. At least she got to say I do.

Let them go. That one's Jules. The guy's finding his way back to Main Street USA and doing what he does best: Giving orders. Just like that.

Get CK, he's saying. Get CK down here now.

Footsteps, hard and heavy. Someone running. A radio squawk that's answered with white noise, and from somewhere, I kid you not, the sound of a baby crying. That cuts things loose. Suddenly there's a muddle of mouths and movement and I do think I'm going to puke.

I try to hold my breath and I stare for a while at the sluice in my left armpit, the place where coat and shirt and Kevlar and skin and muscle and fat have been torn away by a few millimeters of flying metal, and I feel nothing, nothing but the need to vomit, and it's shock, sometimes it's the shock, just the shock, that kills you. I keep staring at the mess in my armpit and I manage to holster my Glock and then there's nothing else to do: I stick my index finger into the wound, and when I don't feel a goddamn thing, I push it farther, farther, up to the second knuckle and that's when something starts to hurt. So I dig that finger in there, dig it hard, and by the time the tip of that finger pokes out the other side of my arm, Christ, it hurts, and that's when I know I'm going to be okay, I'm going to be just fine.

Ah, Chopper Two Niner this is Top One, over. Chopper Two Niner this is—

Daddy?

Let them go, goddamn it. We need— I told you to get CK down here. And McCarty. I want McCarty too.

This way, Senator. Another voice, but it's one I don't know. Please. Senator? Mrs. Blaine?

And then it's McCarty: Mr. Berenger, uh, sir, we're gonna get these people out of here. But what about—

Daddy?

Ah, Top One this is Chopper Two Niner, we read you, over.

Yo, Jules. That's CK, good old Clarence, at last. I manage to lose focus on the hole in my armpit and check him out. The guy is cruising down the aisle like it's an afternoon at the Safeway. The Magnum's loose in his fist. His belt is knotted around his right thigh. He wears the wound like a fashion statement.

Talk to me, says Jules.

Wait one, CK says to Jules, and he bypasses the old man and saunters over, bending down, huddling with me, to look at my shoulder, look at me, before he leans in close and whispers:

Thanks.

That's when he coldcocks me with the Magnum. There's an instant of bright light, the strobe of a flashbulb, and then nothing but pain. The impact takes me down to one knee. I fight the urge to put my hand to my face. Everything there feels broken: my ear, my cheek, my nose, my left eye. I can't see out of my left eye and then I can and it burns, there's blood, and there's something else, something blurring my vision, and slowly gently carefully I bring my hand to my face and I touch a thin rag of skin torn from my temple, a flap over my eye, and I tear that skin from my face and come away with more blood. The world looks like a television picture that's lost half its color.

CK strolls back over to Jules in time to hear him say: Clarence, you are going to have to do something with these people.

CK tells him: It's done. He pivots right and calls out to the chaos, the panicked press of bodies, pastel and white and black, at the exit, and in their midst, his soldiers:

All right, ladies, listen up. Teams of two. Get these fucking people out of here, then get your dead and wounded. Martinez, I want a perimeter, and the rules of engagement are simple: There are no fucking rules. You see somebody black, you shoot, and you shoot to kill.

Then CK's back to Jules.

Tell him, CK says to McCarty, and McCarty gets his face out of a walkie-talkie and, since he doesn't have anybody to pass off to, he tells him:

We got twelve dead, Mr. Berenger. Some of them civilians. And we got maybe twenty wounded. A couple souls ain't gonna make it—

CK finishes for him: Unless we get somebody in here stat. Then his voice goes soft, to McCarty: Get our wounded out but forget the civilians. If they can't walk, they're dead. We got to bury this one so deep it's in China.

Daddy?

Just a goddamn minute, Meredith. What do you mean, somebody?

Look, Jules, CK says. We got a window here. We got fifteen, maybe twenty minutes. Tell him, CK says to McCarty.

So McCarty tells him: The, uh . . . the blow in Old Town has Alexandria PD and Fire overextended, most of the duty units and backups are locked down tight. They're calling in mutual aid,

Arlington County and Fairfax County, Code 3, and our friends in dispatch are gonna try to keep the lid on things here.

Daddy, I—

Shut the fuck up, Meredith. Just shut the fuck up.

Chopper Two Niner, this is Top One, we have a situation, stand by. Change frequency to Code Bravo and stand by, over.

CK's right on top of Jules, and he says: So we got time, boss. Time to deal with things. So let's get dealing. Look: Murders in Manhattan, bombs and burning buildings. Now part of Alexandria's blown to never-never land. What does it take to connect the dots? Try this on for size: Maybe the U Street Crew wasn't satisfied taking down Gideon Parks so they go gunning for a U.S. senator and a respected businessman *and* their fucking families. At a wedding, for Jesus' sake. The niggers want to start a civil war, so hey, we're cool. I got a couple birds and a lot of friends incoming. We'll get you and then us out of here.

Jules starts to say something, but McCarty jumps in: Heads up, he says. Then:

Jules.

A new voice, and this one's unmistakable, courtesy of *Meet the Press* and *Larry King Live*, that mid-south baritone flavored with hickory and rehearsed sincerity. The junior senator from Kentucky. Everything the guy says is a sound bite.

My God, says Senator Anthony Blaine, and Jules gives him back full scripture:

Senator Blaine— Tony, my God. Let my men see you and your loved ones to safety. My God, sir, what has happened to this nation? No one is safe from these savages. I trust that you will help see that this act of terrorism does not go unpunished. But here, let my people take care of you—

I wonder, Jules, if we might not be safer on our own.

Cue a pair of earnest faces I've never seen before, preppie nightmares with Pepsodent smiles. The first one flashes the junior senator from Kentucky a leatherette wallet with an FBI badge before making a polite but insistent gesture toward the exit.

This way, Senator, Prince Charming says. Agent Smithee here will escort you and Mrs. Blaine outside. Ma'am? There is a helicopter inbound.

But Senator Blaine isn't finished. Jules, he says. Who is that man?

I raise my head, show the politician my bloody face. That ought to be his answer, but Jules says to him:

I wish I knew, Senator. I wish I knew. Come now, let these gentlemen take care of you. And take care of this dreadful affair.

But—

Prince Charming's partner sweeps in and steers the Senator and Mrs. Blaine off on their way back to Oz or wherever it is that Republican bluebloods go while CK picks up the pieces.

Chopper's gonna be here in under ten minutes, CK says to Jules. But you need to know something else. Tell him, he says to McCarty.

McCarty has his face in the walkie-talkie again. He tells the walkie-talkie: Wait one. Then he tells Jules:

We got beaucoup radio traffic out there. Not just Alexandria PD. We got Feds.

All eyes spin toward Prince Charming, who gives back nothing, not even a shrug.

McCarty has some words caught in his throat. There's this weird pause until finally CK says to Jules:

Not ours.

Then, to Jules, to Prince Charming, to McCarty, to the boys, maybe even to himself:

But listen, it's not a problem. If they get here first, we got them covered.

CK's eyes go over Jules's shoulder and into slits. He stalks to the front of the altar, where the priest is bending over the kid in the flayed tuxedo. The poor kid's dying and he's not doing it well. CK grabs the priest by the collar, drags him to his feet, and says: Get the fuck out of here.

CK shoves the priest down the aisle, past us, shoving and shoving, and he's off to do whatever it is he's going to do.

Jules says: What happened to you?

My mouth tastes like pennies. I want to spit but my tongue can't find anything wet. I don't know, just yet, that Jules is talking to me. Then he's saying my name and there's no doubt about who he's talking to, it's me, and Jules is saying:

What happened to you, Lane? What in the world happened to you?

It takes me a while, but:

I got shot, I tell him.

I look at the blood streaming out of my shirt cuff, dripping down my left wrist and falling. Wicked ink on the floor.

Yes, he says. I can see that. But I'm not talking about that. I'm talking about what happened to you.

Jesus, my shoulder hurts. My face hurts. Talking hurts. Just thinking hurts:

What happened to me?

Yes, he says again. You were a good soldier, Lane. A very good soldier.

Yeah, I tell him. Like all the good soldiers buried out there in Arlington Cemetery. Headstones in rows and rows and rows. Little flags on Memorial Day.

Jules tugs a white silk handkerchief from his tuxedo jacket, hands it to me. I press the handkerchief into the wound, watch it stain.

You let them in here, didn't you? Those . . . people. It was your idea. All your idea.

Oh, yeah, I tell him. My idea. You started this, Jules, remember? I was just trying to finish it.

The guy laughs. The guy fucking laughs at me. He says:

Sure. You want to know something, Lane? Maybe you're right. Maybe it is my fault. And you know why? Because I misjudged you. I thought you were a good soldier. But instead of doing what you were supposed to be doing, you had to start thinking, didn't you? You couldn't just do what you were told. You had to go and get yourself a conscience.

His head snaps left.

Take his guns, Jules says, and here's that new guy again, Prince Charming with the leatherette wallet and the FBI badge.

Prince Charming twists the Glock out of my belt and shoves it into the front of his pants. He swipes into my suit coat, takes the Glock from the Bianchi holster at my back and pockets it. Then he starts patting me down. He pulls the magazines from my pockets, tosses them onto the floor. He dances over the small stuff, the pen and the comb and the change, before he slaps into my book and gives me a sneer. The frisk is less than professional, but Prince Charming finds what he's looking for, so the grand finale comes when he lifts the third Glock out of my ankle holster and shows it to Jules like it's the prize in the Cracker Jack box.

Then he backs off and Jules returns to center stage.

Not much without them, are you, son?

Jules turns on the high beams, and his words gather Prince Charming and the rest of his buddy boys closer. What he has to say is for them, not for me:

Give a man—any man—a gun, Jules says, and suddenly he's something. He can do what he wants. He can take what he wants. He can kill a man if he wants. And not just any man. He can kill a prime minister, a president, a king. He can kill a messiah if he wants.

A man with a gun can do all that, Jules says. But take the gun away, and what have you got?

Jules hawks up a gob of spit and lets it go onto my shoes.

You got nothing. And you know what, Lane? That sort of sums you up. Used to be, you had something. And now—well, now you don't. You got nothing. And you know what? When you got nothing, you are nothing. And that's you, Lane. You're nothing.

End of speech. So now maybe we get down to the short strokes. To business. The proposition. Because Jules is the kind of guy who always has one. And that's the reason I'm still standing, the reason I'm alive.

He says something to Prince Charming. Then to me:

Put your hands in your pockets.

Hey, Jules, I say, and try on a smile. What's the matter? You afraid of nothing?

Just put your hands in your fucking pockets, he says.

So I do what he says, as if I've got some kind of choice. And with a fist in each pocket of my suit coat, I follow Jules Berenger, and we leave Prince Charming and the rest of his buddy boys and we take a walk back down that aisle toward the altar. If this keeps up, I might get religion.

There's a new sound, the sound of spinning wings, and a rush of churning wind that rattles the ceiling. It's a helicopter and it's incoming and right about now I wish it was one of those eye-in-the-sky news guys, but I know better. It's the ticket to ride for the Berengers and the Blaines.

I could have let CK kill you, Jules says. His lips seem swollen with anger. I could have ordered him to kill you.

Even if I felt like talking, there's nothing to say. Nothing that would matter. He is going to talk his talk, and I am going to have to stand here and listen. Sooner or later he'll get to the point, and the point is the bearer bonds. After everything else that's happened, the guy still wants the same thing he always wants: The money.

What in God's name were you thinking? Jules says to me. Letting those . . . those *animals* in here?

Losing half your armpit and getting your skull

rung goes a long way to helping you look bewildered, and I'm wondering just what it is that Jules Berenger needs to hear from me, and the best I can do is to give him the straightest face I can and say:

It wasn't me who let those guys in here. It was you, remember? This was your deal, your run, not mine. You wanted me along for the ride. So hell, Jules, you got me. You could of left me out of it. You could of killed Gideon Parks without me.

No, he says. His eyes go off, following his mind somewhere I don't want to go. This is bullshit. I start to tell him this is bullshit when he says:

I couldn't, Burdon. I didn't have a choice.

Choice? I say.

No choice, he says. Then:

They wanted you, he says.

They? I tell him. *They*, Jules? Who the fuck are *they*?

The helicopter hovers outside the shattered east wall of the church, its landing lights strobing over the ruins, the haunted faces, the lines of departing automobiles, as it drifts down to the lawn. I see the helicopter and I see another helicopter, the one on television, the one grazing the roof of the Hotel Excelsior. The Feds who weren't Feds. Or maybe they were Feds. Or maybe—

How far does this thing go, Jules? How far up the fucking chain does it go?

Burdon, he says, it doesn't go up. It doesn't go down. It goes around. It goes around and around.

Jules—

Listen, he says. This is business, okay? I do what I'm asked to do. And I do what I'm told. How else do you think I could have stayed in business for all these years? Do you think it was dumb luck? Do you think the law never noticed? I was just doing . . . business.

Well, I say. Try telling that to Gideon Parks. Or that kid over there. What is this all about, Jules? It can't be just about guns.

Damn it, Lane. Use what's left of your head. Of course it's about guns. Maybe not for them. But for me? It's always about guns. You ever listen to that Gideon Parks? Getting nominated for a Nobel Peace Prize wasn't enough for him. The Reverend Parks, he actually wanted peace. He wanted to disarm the gangs, put those punks to work, put them in school. And the people, the kids even, they were listening to him. My God, the Mayor of New York was giving him money. Bills were being introduced in Congress, and these days real patriots like Senator Blaine, the ones who can stop that sort of nonsense, are in short supply. Disarming America? Disarming *us*? Imagine that, Lane, can you? What kind of world would that be?

So you killed him, I say. For his words, you killed him. For wanting peace, you killed him.

Blessed are the peacemakers, Jules tells me.

Isn't that what the Good Book says? Blessed are the peacemakers, for they shall see God?

Well, Jules tells me, we just speeded up his appointment.

And if there's something else to be said, it's not happening, because there's a shadow sweeping down on us and there's a voice to go with that shadow, and the voice says:

Boss.

It's CK, and CK says: Chopper's here. Let's get you and yours out of here.

Okay, Jules says, and he doesn't look at me again. He says to CK: You coming?

No, sir, CK says, and there's that blank face and he says: We got some unfinished business.

Jules sighs and says: Yes. Well, do what you have to do. But for Christ's sake, Clarence, do it right this time. And get those goddamn bearer bonds.

Then he's straightening his tuxedo and he's marching down the aisle and he's gathering in his latest blonde and Meredith and her beau, and there's Senator and Mrs. Blaine and a couple cronies, and that's Agent Smithee with them, and Agent Smithee ushers them into the narthex and down the yellow brick road to the waiting helicopter. Next stop, somewhere far, far away.

So now it's CK's show.

I stand there for a while with my hands in my pockets and CK stands next to me, and we watch the lights flickering through the broken cathedral windows, and soon enough the wings of that helicopter stir, speeding up, and together we watch that black dragonfly lift off the lawn and right about now I look at CK and CK is watching that helicopter like he's hypnotized, he can't take his eyes away from it, and I wonder and then I think and then I know why, and that's when I say to CK, I say:

No.

CK doesn't blink. He just says: Yes.

The helicopter hovers ten or so feet off the ground and its nose rotates slowly toward the ruined church. Toward us.

I say to CK: Who's flying the bird?

CK says: Hoyt Lindgren. Then: You know him?

Oh, yeah, I say. Flown with him. Steady guy.

The helicopter rises, completing the semicircle, angling toward the northwest and its flight path, probably to National Airport.

CK says: What a shame. What a crying shame.

The helicopter leans into a steeper angle and begins to climb: Fifty feet, a hundred feet.

CK says: I really hate to lose a good pilot.

Which is when the helicopter explodes, erupting into a frantic flaming junkyard that rains charred metal and vaporized lives back onto the lawn.

CK turns and shows me his teeth. Connect the dots, he says. Connect the fucking dots.

This is—

I start to say it's insane, but I think better about using that word, so instead I say:

This doesn't make sense. You can't sweep all this under the rug.

CK talks to me like he's passing the time of day. Come on, Burdon, he says. It makes perfect sense. Jules was everything the nigger said he was: old and in the way. So now he's neither of those things. And now, if push comes to shove, he's the fall guy. It's gonna make my friends real happy. And unlike you, I got friends. Lots of friends. And my friends, they're the best in the business. They're in those high places you might have heard about. They been doing this sort of thing for years.

CK sniffs that cordite air. Breathes it greedily, like a guy who's decided to start smoking again, taking his first new drag.

Lots and lots of friends, he says. And you know what? My friends, they got some mighty big rugs.

He leans into me. His hand grips my wounded shoulder and he squeezes. I try to shut the pain inside. No way he's going to hear me scream.

But you, Lane, you got nothing. He squeezes my shoulder again and my eyes wince shut; I wonder if it is possible to faint.

Old Jules was right about that one, CK says. You got nothing.

You're wrong, I manage to say through the

pain. My voice is ancient, but the words find their way out: I got something.

I do, I tell him. I really do.

He eases up on my shoulder. I try to stand steady. I get a deep breath, then another.

Look, I tell him.

I keep the movement slow, simple and slow, and what I do is bring my right fist out of my coat pocket to show him what I've got. Simple and slow and he's with me; he wants to see and I want to show him.

I raise that fist between us and I roll the curled fingers over and then, simple and slow, I open my fist and I show him.

There in the palm of my hand is what I've got, and it's all I've got: A nine-millimeter bullet. The one that was in Renny Two Hand's fist when I found his body in the ravine. I didn't know then why he was holding that bullet in his hand, but now I know.

Now I know.

I tilt my palm toward CK. The bullet rolls onto my fingers. I pinch the bullet between my thumb and forefinger. I bring the bullet close to CK's face, right to his eyes, and I say again:

Look.

He looks. He looks hard. He squints at that shiny hard-nosed cylinder and he sees but he doesn't see, because what I show him is there but it isn't there.

Because what I have is a bullet, just a bullet, and a bullet needs a gun, right?

Wrong.

I shove the bullet into his eye.

The sound isn't a scream, the sound from his mouth is a choked exhalation of air and astonishment, and my finger and thumb worry the bullet into the remains of his right eye, this goo, this jelly, this sticky mess, until he falls away from me, falls to the floor, and I'm past him and right smack into Prince Charming.

Whatever Prince Charming's trying to say, it's too late for talking, and he's good, he's fast, his right shoulder dips and he comes up with his pistol, but my fist slams down on his forearm, and the pistol spins away, clattering into the pews. I try to step back but my balance is gone. Prince Charming uppercuts me and I manage to duck my head, take the knuckles glancing on my cheek and above the ear, into the hard part of the skull. Still it hurts, Jesus it hurts, but Prince Charming yells too and now he's shaking his hand like maybe he broke a finger or two in the bargain. I can't back away, so I step in, punching into his gut and then raising up and butting my head into his face. I hear a nice crack, feel the bite of teeth against my hair and scalp, and he's dancing away from me. But not for long.

His arms take me into a bear hug and now I can smell copper, blood, it's my blood, it's his blood, I don't fucking care, I grab at my Glock in the front of his pants. Prince Charming's arms pull up to my neck and I've got the butt of the pistol but it won't come free, I can't get it free, so I just start pulling the trigger. The blowback kicks the Glock out of his belt and Prince Charming screams and screams and then he shuts up and falls down.

I dig into his pockets and repossess another one of my Glocks, scoop some magazines from the floor. Then I step over the body and start shooting.

People say that violence solves nothing, but they're wrong, they're so very wrong. I loose my Glocks on these killers and it solves them, oh, yes, it solves them.

I K-5 the first guy, single shot, center of mass, end of story.

The next guy's caught in the open too, and he spins like a dervish when I fire twice and put him facedown into the carpet.

Number three jerks a sawed-off from beneath his trenchcoat and starts down the aisle. I dive left, firing as I go, take him twice in the chest, and he's history. The fourth guy jack-in-the-boxes out of the last row and almost gets his weapon up when I spray him with death. Behind him the fifth guy, it's Martinez, he scrambles for cover behind a pew. He reaches his pistol around the wood and snaps a couple wild shots my way. Not even close.

I steady my grip and blow his hand off. He tumbles back and I finish him.

I empty the magazine into the next two guys and then I'm across the aisle, diving and sliding on the wood floor, my ruined shoulder taking the impact.

I crawl beneath the pews, feeling nothing but pain, getting my breath and my brain together. I lose the empty magazine, snap in a full one, and take inventory. Somewhere behind me is CK, still curled on the floor, no doubt, hand to his ruined eye. He won't have let go of that Magnum. But there's no one back there with him, which leaves five or six or seven guys between me and the door to the narthex.

Footsteps, coming from the left. I hug the carpet, watch highpowered rounds punch a ragged line of quarter-sized holes through the back of the pew. Count down the number of shots as the fool runs his magazine.

Then I stand, raising the first Glock and then the second, I stand and I offer them death with both hands, blasting my way into the aisle, blasting him and him and him and him and finally McCarty, who shouts something incomprehensible, his body undone, as he collapses into death. Then:

Silence.

Nothing.

But it's not over. No way it's over. I roll out of the aisle and it's back to GO: collect two hundred dollars and start reloading. But I need more than these pistols.

I look for what this is going to take: A shotgun. It doesn't take long. There are always more guns—always—because it's our right, our goddamn right to own them. And there, across the aisle, is the gun I need: An Ithaca police pump in the grip of a dead guy.

But where is CK? Where the fuck is CK?

I can't feature the voice. It's out in the narthex and it's barking names, probably putting the troops into position, somewhere beyond the door, getting ready for their version of the bounding overwatch, a little SWAT dance that goes something like this: Teams of two make the entry, alternating between point and cover positions. The point man boogies through the door in a low crouch or a dive. He flattens and starts rocking full auto while his partner scoots in to a better firing position and opens up while the point man advances, takes cover, and starts firing again while his partner moves. Like playing leapfrog. It's a tough act to pull the curtain on, and outside that door are lots of guys, but inside there's just me. They're going to come in pairs and more pairs, and there's . . . how many of them? Twenty, thirty, maybe more, with backup on the way. Oh, yeah, they're going to come, and they're going to keep coming.

And me, I'm laughing.

I'm laughing because I'm here and I'm alone and I am so very, very fucked.

I thought I had a plan. But it was just a script for a suicide.

I back off, the shotgun leveled at the door, and find the place I want, pick a pew, any pew, as if wood is going to matter with what they're going to be throwing at me, and I settle in about fifty feet from the door, which gives me some cover and enough distance to make whatever the point man shoots a Hail Mary. I set the shotgun down in front of me and check the first of my Glocks. It's been fired to lock-back, so I replace the magazine. I rack that pistol, stick it in my belt, and check the second one. It goes into the Bianchi holster at my back. Then I heft the shotgun. It's the best god-damn defensive weapon going. But it's only got eight rounds.

I wait and I wait, wondering if they've got fire-works or maybe tear gas to start the show, that would ruin my whole day, and when I've waited enough, I dry my hands on my pants and I aim the shotgun at the pair of doors and I count one, I count two, I count three, and that's when the shooting starts again, but the shooting is outside, the shooting is out there in the narthex, the alcove, the lobby, whatever, and holes are blowing in-ward, through the wall, through the double doors, heavy metal renovation that punches out fat chunks of plaster and wood. There are screams, too, the kind you don't think men can make until you hear them. Screams and gunshots and more screams.

The doors burst open and it's one of them, only one, and he's running and falling, running and falling at the same time, and I stand and let go with the shotgun and he's down and he's dead.

I'm into the aisle. I bob and weave toward the narthex, expecting the doors to go wide again at any moment with a rush of bodies firing full auto. I'm almost there when the doors burst open but it's the same routine, it's one of them, only one, and this time it's Prince Charming's partner, Agent Smithee, the smiley-faced Fed, and he's firing his handgun but not at me, he's firing back at the doors, into the narthex, and by the time he stops and turns and looks at me, he knows he's made a big mistake.

And he's right, he's made a very big mistake.

I blast the smile off his face and into forever.

And I don't stop, I pump and keep blasting, and the next shot tears those doors apart and the pieces are still falling as I pump and fire and pump and fire until I click down on empty. I toss the shotgun aside, pull the first Glock.

What's left of the doors swing, creak, swing, creak, shudder closed and into silence.

I kick through the broken doors and they collapse into pieces. What I find on the other side is not a narthex, it's a slaughterhouse. Somebody's spray-painted the place with blood. I count nine, ten, make that eleven bodies on the floor. All of them are dead, except for the one over there, in the corner, the one slumped with a bitter kind of smile on his face, a pistol in each hand and a couple bullet holes in his body.

The black one.

My old pal Jinx.

He drops the pistol from his left hand, then roundhouses the revolver in his right, tries to shovel it back into his shoulder holster, but he's not looking and there's so much blood on him that the pistol slides along the leather and falls clattering to the floor.

I come crashing to the hardwood next to him and I say to Jinx, I say to the guy:

Jesus Christ.

And he just says: Burdon Lane.

He looks at the bodies, looks at me, and he says:

I been a bad man.

From outside, at long last, comes the sound of sirens.

eighty f

Saved by the bell? I don't think so.

I think this is going to get a lot worse before it gets any better. If it gets any better.

My knees are burning. My pants are torn, my knees scraped raw from falling to the floor. Only now, looking at Jinx, do I feel the burn, the blood.

Took them long enough, I say to him.

He just says: Huh?

The cops, I tell him.

He just says: Oh.

There's a ragged mess of a wound zigzagging along his right leg, something else soaking his shirt. He's wearing blood. Some of it's even his own.

The doors, the wide wooden doors of the cathedral, are twenty feet away. It could be a mile. We're not going out that way. At least not on our feet.

Beyond those doors there's another sound, and it's closer than the sirens. It's the sound of men with guns, men who won't give up and go home, men who are going to kill or be killed.

The men beyond the door. They're coming. Oh, yeah, they're coming.

How many? I say to him.

Didn't have time to count, he says, out of breath. But you saw, they got a fuckin army out there.

His wet hands come alive, taking his Ruger from the floor. He works a speedloader out of his pants and reloads the .38. Then he lamps the bodies around us. He doesn't see what he wants.

He looks at me, says what I'm thinking:

Where's your friend CK?

He's— I start to tell him that CK's back there in the sanctuary. But he's not. He's not there.

Jinx looks at me and I don't like this grin. It's a new one, not the wolf, not the predator. It's an empty grin, the one that says something very bad is about to happen.

Doctor D could of shot him dead, Jinx says. But no. You had to be the one, didn't you?

Yeah, I told him. And you know what? I still do.

He's all yours, Jinx says. I'm done with my shootin.

I want to tell him that I doubt it, but that's when they pull the curtain on our little homecoming celebration. A salvo of high-powered rounds blows overhead and ventilates the wall behind us. It's a turkey shoot, nothing tactical, they're out there unloading anything and everything they've got.

I get my head down down down. The whole world rattles and the walls feel like they're coming apart. There's nothing to breathe but dust. And nothing to do but stay here and breathe it until the seconds that become hours become seconds again, and things go quiet. Except for the sirens. The sirens and the new but old sound, the sound of whirling wings.

They're out of time, Jinx says. He hasn't moved. He's still sitting there, still holding his pistol, still grinning that empty grin.

Help is on the way, he says.

Yeah, I tell him.

So we wait, he says. Wait long enough and let the police do their job.

No, I tell him. No way. That's not CK's style. They're gonna come, and they're gonna keep coming. And I don't know about you, but I'm not gonna die in a church. Not today. So I don't think we got a choice. We got to move.

Easier said than done, he says. He twists his right leg, shows me the wound. It's a nasty one that says he's not walking.

Hang on, I say to him. There's an Uzi on the floor that one of the dead guys doesn't need. Still cold. Hasn't even been fired. I slap the butt of its magazine and hear the magazine catch lock. Pull back on the charging handle and push the selector forward to automatic. Get my head down, chin onto the floor. Crawl through the doorway to the sanctuary. Check overhead. No light switches, but farther along the wall there's something better, the place where somebody's idea of a fire code forced the parish to mount one of those generic EXIT signs. A silver cable snakes out of the sign and into a junction box, and that might work. I steady the Uzi, it's not meant for marksmanship, and let go, subsonic hiccups sparking up that junction box, and there's a scrunch of shattered metal and a flickerflash of light and then everything in the sanctuary goes dark.

I slither my way back and tell him: What do you think?

Hey, he says to me. Don't know bout you, but I stopped thinkin round four this afternoon.

Yeah, I tell him. But what I'm thinking is we move.

I nod to the wound, the bad one, the one on his leg.

That's got to hurt, I tell him.

Yeah, he says.

If we stay here much longer, we're both dead.

Yeah, he says.

So, I tell him. I push my forearms into his armpits and get ready to lift. The way I see it, it doesn't matter if I move you. Except it's going to hurt even more.

Yeah, he says.

Okay. I tighten my hands into fists, bend my knees.

On three, I tell him. Okay? One, two—

That's when I yank him up and Jinx doesn't scream, doesn't complain, doesn't do a thing. He just leans into me and says:

What happened to three?

I swing his arm over my shoulders, take some weight on my back, and that's what screams, pain doing a line dance across my left armpit, over my rib cage, down my spine. We're side to side, like a cruel sack race, the three-legged man hobbling down the aisle for some healing. But we're making time, out of that morgue and onto the altar, finally into the sacristy and through another door, and the door opens to a long hallway where the lights are still working. There are doors and more doors and a fire door at the far end, and I choose the second door on the left and we're inside a small room.

I lean Jinx into the near wall and he does the rest, easing his way down to the floor. It's this pillbox of an office. There's a desk and a chair and a file cabinet and a crucifix on the wall and a picture of that dead pope, the pope before the last pope, that guy, and a little square window and maybe this is a priest's office, and with that thought I stagger over to the desk and it's locked but I kick the bottom drawer and it pops out a little, so I kick it again and drag the drawer open and inside there's a pint of that holy water known as Dewar's, and I say to Jinx, I say:

Hey.

He catches the bottle on the fly and looks at the label awhile before he unscrews the cap and takes a long hit. It gets him coughing, and a little scotch and a little blood leak from the corner of his mouth, but he's about the happiest wounded guy I've ever seen. He screws the cap back and sends the bottle my way. I grab that thing and right about now I start to believe, really believe, that we're alive.

The first taste of that scotch is like truth: It burns but it's good. I let it linger on my tongue for a while, then I drink it down. But I'm not greedy. I toss the bottle back to Jinx and I settle back into the wall on my side of the room, slide my ass down, and take a load off. I tug at the magazine on the first of the Glocks; it's latched.

More sirens.

I don't fucking believe it, I tell him. Took them long enough but they're here. Coming in like the U.S. Cavalry. Never thought I'd be happy to see the cops.

Jinx looks a long time at that bottle. Then:

Bout time we called it a day, he says, and he wants to laugh a little but he can't. He takes a quick pull of the scotch and now it's my turn again. To take a drink and to talk.

Yeah, I tell him. It's about time. But not yet.

The bottle comes to me. I take my drink, and the scotch is almost gone, so I save a little bit, for me or for him. It all depends. I wait for my stomach to warm and then I tell him:

I got to ask you something.

Yeah? he says.

Yeah, I tell him. See, something's been bothering me for a while now, but I wanted to wait for the right time or maybe the right place. Or until I figured it out for myself. But that didn't happen. So now, before little boy blue gets here, maybe you can help me out.

I hold that bottle of what's left of the scotch out at arm's length and I watch the glass bend the fluorescent light, make it blur and bloom, and I guess it's time to say it, so I say it to Jinx, I say:

I want to know why you shot me. In the garage. In New York. Why you shot me in the back.

But that's wrong. I know why he shot me, and I know why he shot me with a small-caliber pistol, and why he shot me only once and in just the right place, below the shoulder, above the kidney, away from the spine: To put me down but not out. So I try to say it again. I say:

What I want to know is what you were doing there. In the garage. And what you're doing here. Now. Why you came back.

There's a burst of gunfire, something automatic, and it's answered by pistols and more pistols.

Voices yelling. Voices in command. The cops are here, and they're closing things down.

Jinx isn't looking at me. His head rests back against the wall and it's like he's calm, suddenly calm. He's staring at the ceiling, or something past the ceiling, the sky, the stars, a dream, I don't know. But he's somewhere else for a moment and then he's back. That's when he says:

We were following you.

Something about his voice, it's wrong. It's different. Changed somehow.

That can't be right, though, because—

There's another exchange of gunfire. Closer. In the distance, above us, chopping wind, the sound of helicopters. Incoming. It's almost over.

You could of followed me to the hotel, I tell him. But then I realize what he said, what I missed: *We?*

It doesn't take long. I hear a shot or two from the direction of the chapel, and then the sound of boots, and then the voices:

Clear. Clear. Clear.

The sound of a door being kicked in.

Go!

Boots on linoleum.

Clear!

Coming down the hallway.

Go!

Door to door.

Clear!

Until they're right outside the office and I know they've got fingers on the triggers and they're going to shoot first, probably shoot second and third, and then, maybe somewhere around fourth or fifth, they might think about asking questions. So it's got to be smooth. Perfect.

Officer? I work for the right tone. Loud but not too loud. No threat. Compliant. I keep my Glock up, watching the shadow, the helmeted shadow, watching it thicken outside the door, and then the second shadow, hovering over and merging into the other one, and I say:

Here. In here. We're friendlies. Let me say that again: We're friendlies. And we're surrendering. We have weapons but we're giving them up, okay? So go slow. No más, okay? We give.

The first policeman swings in at a low crouch, service pistol out, very steady. Blue helmet, blue uniform, one of the District of Columbia's finest.

Drop your weapons, Helmet tells us. Then:

Now.

I look at Jinx.

No problem, he says. He takes the Ruger from his lap and palms it onto the linoleum, pushes it toward the cop. Then he goes into the moose: Hands over his head, right hand clutching his left wrist. He's wincing. It has to hurt. He's trying to say something.

I bring my hands out wide to each side. But I don't let go of the Glock.

Drop the weapon, Helmet says to me. And raise your hands. He flattens his foot on top of Jinx's pistol. Then he says:

Clear.

The second cop slinkies into the room, pistol pointed at the floor, and he's popped out of the cookie cutter, same chiseled cowboy face, same blue-on-blue. He settles in behind Helmet and I'm showing him my hands, nice and wide, but Helmet isn't happy that I'm holding on to the Glock and he starts to follow the nose of his pistol my way and that's when Jinx says to the cops, he says:

Eighty f.

Whatever the fuck it means, that's what he says, and he says it again and Helmet seems frozen in place, the second cop turning in slow motion, and Jinx comes out of the moose and he reaches toward his right ankle and I can't believe he's trying to pull something, go for a piece, what the fuck is he doing?

Eighty f, he's saying to Helmet.

That's when Helmet turns and starts emptying his pistol into him.

That's when the second cop spins toward me and fires, but his first shot kicks wide and he doesn't get a second shot because I blast back, two shots into his groin that fold him over and put him down. Helmet's still shooting Jinx when I blow off Helmet's left shoulder then spray his fucking brains across the far side of the room and I shoot him as I stand and I'm still shooting him when my pistol clicks dry about three feet from his corpse.

I bend over Jinx. I can't tell how many times he's been shot, but it's bad, it's real bad. Jinx looks at me, and if there are words to describe what happens to his face, I don't have them. It's the face of cruel knowledge. The face of death.

He speaks blood.

His mouth opens, his lips move, but it's blood that comes out. Blood, and at last: Aw, fuck.

Then:

Metro Police, he says.

Yeah, I tell him.

D.C. Police, he says.

Yeah, I tell him. But not anymore.

And he says: No, man. No no no. Not ever. Not here.

What?

D.C. Police, he says again. Aw, fuck. Don't you see, man? They may be D.C. Police. But this is Virginia.

Oh, shit, I tell him and myself, and I slap another magazine into the Glock, the Teflon-coated KTWs, and I head for the door and I'm right on time. Two more of them are shuttling down the hall. The same blue helmets, the same blue uniforms, the same white faces.

Maybe they're D.C. cops. Maybe not. But even real D.C. cops can't do shit in Virginia.

The first one doesn't have a rat's chance, doesn't even see me until I snap the Glock up and rack the slide, doesn't even get to react as I blow his chest out his back. The shots cut through him and then past him, twisting his partner into the wall, his head and helmet fractured into a messy stain. What's left of them flops onto the floor.

Then: Nobody.

I duck back into the priest's office and I look at Jinx and the guy's convulsing. He's spitting the blood off his lips but he's talking, he's still talking.

Eighty f, he's saying, and he's pulling at his ankle again, but there's no throwdown gun, there's nothing at all, and he's tearing past his pants leg, he's pulling off his boot, the man's delirious, he's pulling off his boot and finally he gets the boot into his hands and he drives the boot into the floor once, twice, like a hammer, again and again, and his fingers, curled with pain and slick with blood, so much blood, peel the broken heel away from the sole and a shiny rectangle, a piece of plastic, falls from the gap onto the floor.

He drops the broken boot and fades back into the wall.

I put my hand into the tarry black of his blood. I pick up the plastic card that was hidden in his boot. I wipe it off. I try to read.

Who are you? I say to him.

Some kind of laugh rattles and slurps up out of his lungs. Blood bubbles on his lips. He coughs, shooting phlegm and more blood from his nose. Forget what they tell you in the books, what they show you on the TV, in the movies. Dying is never a pretty thing.

I say it to him again: Who the fuck are you?

Eighty f, he says, and his hand reaches to touch the rectangle of plastic. His fingers trace through the blood and now I see his picture, there on the plastic, and at last I hear what he's saying:

ATF, he's saying. ATF.

He presses the plastic into my hand and I see the emblem. I see the shield. I see the words that read Bureau of Alcohol, Tobacco and Firearms. I see the words that read Special Agent. I see the name but I don't read the name, I don't want to know the name, I don't want to know what's behind the name, the wife and the kid, the mother and the father and the sister and the brother, I don't want to know these things, not now, not ever.

We had a man inside . . .

You fuck, I tell him.

No, he says to me.

No, he says. *You* fuck. Then:

Don't you understand? he says. Haven't you figured it out yet? Nobody's what they seem. Not me. Not your girl. Not your crew. Not your boss. Not those fucking cops. *Nobody*.

His breath is wet. His eyes wince shut. Pain nearly takes him into the dark. But the guy's a fighter. He may be down but he's not out, not yet, and soon enough he's back and he says:

So?

He holds me with those eyes, those dying eyes.

I tell him: So?

So who are you? he says. Who the fuck are *you*?

For about the only time in my life, I don't have an answer. Not one that works. I can only tell him what I know, which is nothing:

I don't know, man. I just don't know.

His eyes go shut and I think it's over. I think he's going to find sleep and never wake up. I wipe the blood from his ID and I slip it into his shirt pocket. I take his hand in mine and I wait. Time doesn't mean much, it could be seconds, minutes, it's a lost gap until he opens his eyes and he says to me, he says:

I do.

Yeah, I tell him, and I don't know why, but I want him to see me smile. So I smile, what I've got left of one, and I tell him: Yeah. I bet you do.

He blinks his eyes and he coughs more blood and he says to me: I do. So listen to me, Burdon Lane. Just this one time. Listen, okay? See, they say the Lord works in mysterious ways—

Oh, yeah, I tell him, and I want to shut up but I can't. I tell him:

And you know something? Out of all the things

they say, that's the one I can believe in. Because they're right. The Lord does work in mysterious ways. All the fucking time. He kills your mother with cancer. Gives three-year-old kids leukemia. Takes down airliners. Aims drunk drivers right smack into school buses. Sets retirement homes on fire for Christmas. Thinks up things like AIDS. Gives people different color skins—

Yeah, Jinx says. That's right. God does that. All the time. Those are His ways. Mysterious ways, terrible ways. Evil ways. But they're His ways. And you know what, Burdon Lane?

His hand tightens on mine, and he says:

Somewhere in those mysterious ways, I do think there's room for you.

He says that word again:

You.

I want to laugh now but I can't laugh. I can't do anything but look into his face. Because I know this face. It's my mother's face. At the end.

I can't leave him this way. I can't let him die this way. I need to say something, do something, but there's nothing left to do. Then I remember what I did for Renny Two Hand when I found him at the bottom of that ravine. I can give him that.

I let go of Jinx's hand, and I reach across the corpses of the cops who aren't cops, or they're the wrong cops, I don't know and I don't care, and I find what I need: Jinx's pistol, the Ruger, there on the floor. I wipe blood from its grip and I show it to him, show him that pistol, then press the grip into his hand. It's so wet, his hand, the gun, my hand, there's blood everywhere, so much blood, I can't wipe it all away. At first his fingers can't hold the weight of the pistol, but I curl his knuckles tight around the grip until he has it. He has it.

He looks at that pistol and he looks at me. He raises the pistol between us. His hand shivers with its unbearable weight.

His face goes calm, resolute, and he says:

I don't need this anymore.

With whatever strength he's got left in his body, he throws the pistol aside.

His empty hand reaches for mine, takes it, holds it, squeezes it. After a while his eyes drift closed.

I sit waiting. Trying not to let go. Until he's dead.

no exit

So this is the end: The big silence. The yawn that's the payoff for a lot of years pretending I had a life. Making my money and biding my time, waiting for something to show me that there was a point to making the money, biding the time, waiting and wishing and wanting and running and running but never getting anywhere but here, where there's nothing, nada, zip, zero, zilch.

No, make that less than nothing: It's a hole that sucks everything left of life into that blank space called death.

I'm thinking about a run. A run that was nothing special, the same old same old: Guns for money, money for guns. A run from Dirty City to Manhattan and back, count the dollars, drink myself to sleep, and wake up bleary and weary on another Monday morning. Business as usual.

But it was the last run. The run that would close down UniArms and all the spiderwebs in its attic. The run that Fiona and Jinx and the rest of the cops and the Federal agents worked so long and so hard to set up, to get inside of, so deep inside that they would own it, make it happen, watch its every move to the moment when the badges and the handcuffs would start to shine. The run that would end with arrests and convictions and maximum jail terms, that would take out the gunrunners and the gangbangers in one package wrapped so tightly and brightly that it just might look like Christmas.

And I'm thinking about another run. The run inside the run. The run that the cops and the Feds didn't know about, at least not most of them. Not Jinx, maybe not Fiona, maybe not even that grey ghost who was sitting in my chair, in my den, in my house.

It was the run that was about killing the Reverend Gideon Parks. Killing a movement, killing a dream. The run that someone in some high fucking place wanted, and that Jules Berenger and his mad dog CK, who wanted to stay in business and out of jail, were pleased to make happen . . . with a little help from their friends. The run that no one, cops or Feds, would investigate for very long, because they were inside the thing, it was their run, they had made it happen, and what the hell, they had the perfect patsies, very black and very dead, for their fall guys.

So I'm thinking about that other run, and I'm thinking about the cops and the Feds and the patsies and the rest of the pawns. The guys who did the running. The guys like Renny Two Hand and Juan E and Jinx. The guys like me. The good soldiers who did what they were told, at least until they got wise or got dead.

And I'm thinking about the other guys, the guys in the suits, the guys who sit behind those big oak desks in those quiet grey buildings, the guys who aren't the pawns or the bishops or even the kings.

They're the guys who move the pieces.

The guys who owned Jules Berenger. The guys who CK wants to own him. Who CK wants to be. Those guys. Those fucking guys.

I'm thinking about those guys, but my head hurts, my heart hurts, and motherfuck my shoulder hurts, and I'm so damned tired of thinking.

Somehow, someway, I struggle onto my knees. Force myself to stand. It hurts so bad, and it's not where I've been shot. It's the other wound, the wound inside. I want to stand, I just want to stand, and then I am standing, I don't know how, but I am standing, and when I stand I feel nothing, I hear nothing, and I see what's left of the light begin to fade.

I snap a fresh magazine, my last, into the Glock. I step over one of the dead D.C. cops. Another good soldier.

I don't look at him, and I don't look back. I just find the door.

Outside the priest's office is the hallway. To the right is the sacristy and the sanctuary. To the left is thirtysome feet of linoleum and then another door, a windowless metal slab with a red bar for a handle. A fire door. The placard on the door reads NO EXIT.

And that's right, that's the truth, the sign says exactly what it means:

There is no exit. Not for me.

There's nowhere left to go.

Nowhere but back into the sanctuary.

Because Doctor D was right. It's not over. It'll never be over.

We kill and kill and kill, and we'll kill again, for as long as the guns are in our hands. We will kill the sinners and we will kill the saints. We will even kill the saviors. We will kill and keep killing and we will never, ever stop.

As long as we keep holding on to the guns.

So I follow my pistol, and I follow the sound, the sound of footsteps, my footsteps. The path is marked in red. Blood is everywhere. It paints the walls, the floors, curdles in dull pools, trickles and pours and wets all the world with its stain.

The blood leads me down that hallway and through the sacristy, finally brings me to the altar, that silent place of vows unmade and vows that were broken.

Slim and twisting wisps of gunsmoke, mist, fog, rise around me and drift toward the shattered ceiling. Ghosts. Angels. No no no: dust. It's only dust and ashes.

Death. More death. Always death.

I wipe at my eyes. More blood on my hands. But I need to see. I have to see. And through the broken windows of the cathedral I see everything . . . and everything is dark.

I forgot it was night.

As if that would matter. The darkness is out there, in the night, but it's here, too. It's here. Inside. With me.

The sky's gone out. There are no stars. A false sunset fades over Alexandria, a shrinking bloom of violence where the city block of warehouses that was UniArms is a smoldering vacancy. Closer, fire shines across the churchyard and into the lawns of the bordering neighborhood, consuming the shrubs and wooden fences. Fingers of flame stretch to grasp at trees and finally the houses.

The parking lot of the cathedral is littered with the twisted wreckage of cars and people. At intervals on the pavement are bodies, sprawled where they fell or were thrown by gunfire or explosions. In their midst are men with guns, walking and shooting, walking and shooting.

They are two more of the cops, the D.C. cops, blue helmets and white faces, and they move through the smoke in what seems like slow motion, checking the bodies, shooting the wounded, making them into the dead.

They are CK's friends, summoned to clean up the mess. Sweep it under the rug. But they're late, so late.

Too late.

Lights flick flick flash: red and blue and red and blue, cutting through the smoke of this burning world. The first of the Alexandria police cruisers veers into the parking lot and slams to a stop, its tires spitting dirt and gravel. An Alexandria cop, a black sergeant as ripped as a power lifter, boils out from behind the steering wheel. He pulls his service piece and says something to the D.C. cops, and he says it again, he says it louder, and now I can hear him, I can hear the Alexandria cop say:

Holster your weapons.

The first of the D.C. cops waves to him—hey, hi, say what?—and takes a step his way, and the Alexandria cop says again:

Holster your weapons.

The first D.C. cop waves back, and that's when the second D.C. cop makes his move, swinging his pistol up, but the Alexandria cop shoots first and it's center of mass, he blows the second D.C. cop down and the first D.C. cop shoots the Alexandria cop and clips his shoulder but the Alexandria cop keeps firing as he falls and the shots take out the first D.C. cop and now they're all on the ground and more lights are dancing in the air, red and

blue and red and blue, a column of Alexandria police cars emerging from the smoke and the fire and
the darkness.

So now it's time.

He is alone. He sits in one of the pews, twenty
or so rows away, right next to that long center
aisle. One last and forgotten worshiper.

His head is bowed, but he's not praying.

He's waiting. Waiting for me.

It's CK.

Of course it's CK.

Because this is what it comes down to. This is
always what it comes down to. Two guys with
guns who are going to square off and use those
guns to solve everything. Or die trying.

CK stands with a drunken lurch and offers me
what's left of his face, a half-moon etched with
blood. His right eye is gone. The unblinking gap,
clotted red, gleams like a wet jewel. His teeth are
bared. They are jagged and yellow and seem
ready to bite.

About time, CK says. It's about fucking time.

Words don't seem to mean much anymore. Besides, I don't think I have anything to say to this
man. Not now. Not yet.

I told you, he says.

That much I hear. But not the rest. He tears a
fistful of wires, a headset, from his face, and casts
it aside. Then he moves herky-jerky into the aisle.

His walk is stiff, uncertain, favoring his wounded leg. He holds the .44 Magnum tight to his side.

Mine! CK cries out, weaving into the aisle, eighty feet distant. I wonder who he thinks he's talking to. He turns his back to me, swaggering and swaying all at once, his pistol tracing a circle through the hazy air.

Mine! he calls again, stumbling in his drunkard's dance, voice cracking into the plea of a child.

His mind is gone. I want to say that the guy is crazy. Meaning crazier. But maybe he isn't crazy at all. Maybe, in a world where weddings bleed into funerals, where D.C. cops shoot Virginia cops and the Virginia cops shoot right back, he is the one person who is totally and completely sane.

Then, with an effort, CK reels back to me.

Hey, he says. Hey. The guy is talking to an empty church. To that darkness.

Look what we got here, he says. Burdon Lane. A real soldier. A stand-up guy. A piece of the rock. So what's the deal, Lane? Huh? You talked, didn't you? You ratted us out. Who did you talk to, Lane? Who did you tell? And . . .

And . . .

The word seems stuck. An old vinyl record album, the needle caught in the groove.

And . . .

Before it kicks loose and he says:

And who the fuck made you the honorary nigger? Huh?

I get what's left of the CK smirk, and it's not for effect. The guy does nothing for effect. He wears the face of madness, and part of the madness is the desire, the urge, the need, to kill. The pleasure of taking life because it's there for the taking.

I know it because I feel it too. My finger strokes the trigger of the Glock. I want it to happen. Oh , I want so badly for it to happen. But I have to try to stop him, even though I know it won't work, that it's going to happen as surely as if it was written in a book.

I drift down the altar stairs, one and two and three, and I stop, as if I'm waiting for him. Keep the moves steady, nothing abrupt, nothing sudden. And keep him talking; most of all, I need to keep him talking. So I breathe out the words:

You did.

He likes that one. He likes it so much he goes to work on it. He starts chewing those words like a steak. Tries to decide whether to swallow or spit.

A helicopter swoops in low. The sound of its wings batters the broken ceiling. Its searchlight lances into the ruined interior and is blunted by the smoke, the darkness.

I wonder what it sees, and as I wonder I hear the voice, the voice in the night, the voice that growls out of the hailer, that caroms off the thumping wings, that echoes into the sanctuary, the voice that says

Inside

The voice that says
This is the Alexandria Police Department
The voice that says
With agents of the Bureau of Alcohol Tobacco and Firearms
The voice that breaks suddenly into a whisper, a whisper at my ear, and *Eighty f*, it's saying, *eighty f*, until the other voice returns, the voice in the night, the voice that says
Put down your weapons
The voice that says
And come out with your hands up
Before the whisper at my ear again:
Who? That's what it whispers. *Who the fuck are you?*
And I have to say something, I have to hear my voice, my own voice, so I say to CK, I tell him:
Put the gun away. The cops—
The cops, CK says, and he blows what's left of the smirk off his lips. Then:
Whose cops? he says. Mine? Yours?
They're here, I tell him.
Oh, yeah, he says. They're here.
He starts toward me again, his body shambling forward like a wound-down machine that wants to stop but can't. His left leg drags behind the rest of him and when it catches up, the whole damn thing starts over again.
A pained gasp, maybe it's a cough, maybe it's a

laugh, rattles from his throat, and then more words:

And what are they gonna do? he says. Send me to Vietnam?

A flicker, a tiny shimmer of light, steals like silent lightning across the darkness behind him, and I blink, I try to blink the blood from my eyes, but there is nothing else to see, nothing but the darkness and CK and the gun in his right hand.

His sick laughter ratchets on and on until he says:

Fuck the cops. This isn't about them. And it's not about guns, is it? Not anymore. It's not about money, either. Ten million dollars, Lane. Can you even think about counting that kind of paper? Ten million dollars you pissed away today. But it's not about that. No way. And you know what? It's not even about dead people. It's not about Gideon Parks. It's not about Mackie or Two Hand—

His shuffle ends about twenty feet from me, and so does his speech, because that's when he says:

It's about nothing.

CK straightens, shifts his grip on the Magnum, and says:

Nothing but you and me.

I look at CK but I don't see CK. I see the Reverend Gideon Parks, but he's just a man, a man with a dream, maybe, but just another man. Now he's dead. I see a young man, they called him

Juan E, I see Juan E and his friends, his crew, and they're dead too, all of them dead. I see an old man, standing with his wife, she called him John, John Henry Mason, lost and so very afraid in a building that burned down around them. I see Renny Two Hand in the ditch and Lauren in the trunk, and I see Jinx on the floor of that office, and finally I see CK, I see CK standing there in the aisle and I tell him:

You're wrong.

I tell him:

This is about everything.

I raise the Glock on him.

The darkness behind him blurs, flutters like the wings of a waking bird. I push the thought, the impossible thought that the darkness is alive, back down into the basement of my mind.

He answers with the Magnum, and then these words:

Well, then, he says. Fuck everything. And most of all, fuck you.

My Glock is loaded and it's got fifteen rounds of hollow point. His Magnum's a roundhouse, so that gives him maybe six shots of what are probably cast-bulleted hunting loads that'll cut through cinderblock, not to mention Kevlar, like it's toast. But CK doesn't shoot. He doesn't do anything. He just holds that hand cannon on me until I realize that he's waiting, waiting for me to say something, do something, that will bring us to that moment when I shoot him and he shoots me.

The darkness behind him shifts. The darkness shudders. The darkness moves.

So that's when I say it, when I say the one thing, the only thing, that there is left to say. I say:

Tell me, CK. What was it like?

The last word comes right back to me: Like? he says.

Yeah, I tell him. What was it like? How did it feel . . . to do what you did? In New York?

How did it feel? CK says. When I killed the Reverend Gideon Parks?

His face twists into another agonized smirk, and he swings the Magnum to the right, where the cross, fallen from above the altar, angles against the first of the pews. CK squeezes down, and the Magnum roars. The shot blows the top of Christ's head into oblivion.

Then CK and the pistol are facing me again, and he says:

It felt just like that.

And it's then, watching him close on me, his finger curling back onto the trigger, that I smile. I smile for Jinx and what he showed me, and this is what I know:

I don't need the pistol anymore.

I show CK the Glock, and I show him what Jinx showed me.

I show him what to do with the gun.

I pull the magazine and I flick the bullets, one by one, onto the floor.

CK starts to laugh, but stops when I tell him:

I didn't talk, CK. But you did. You just did. You broke the rules. Like Mikey. Remember Mikey? Another guy I watched you kill. But you screwed up this time, CK. And it's the last time. You know why?

The magazine is empty, and I toss it aside.

I look at him and I look right through him and I know, I know, I don't need the gun. Not anymore.

I let the pistol slip through my hands. I feel its weight, so heavy, leave me forever, crashing down onto the floor. Gone.

You talked, CK. And you know what that means, don't you? It means: You die.

CK looks at me, looks at the discarded gun, looks again at me. Disbelief melts into a hideous smile that wants to match mine, but he does not know, he cannot ever know. He forces a laugh, and then there's nothing left for him to do but call my bluff.

He locks his elbow and points that Magnum at my face. Ten feet away, but it looks and it feels like ten inches. That one eye stares down the shiny barrel, over the sights and into my head.

Another sick laugh. It ends with a cough, and CK spits out blood and finally the words:

Forget those fucking fruitcake poets, he says.

This is the way the world ends, he says.

With a bang, he says. With a motherfucking bang.

Then:

Silence, startling silence.

He thumbs back the hammer and the sound of the action is like some cosmic gear shifting into overdrive.

That's when the center of his chest expands, erupts, explodes, geysering shirt and suit coat and Kevlar, tissue and bone and gristle, muscle and guts and blood and blood and more blood.

I feel the red rain on my face, my hands, a spray of heat that quickly goes cold.

I see the fist-sized gap in CK's chest, and I see the shadow, the shadow just past his shoulder, the shadow with the gun.

I see what's left of CK topple forward, onto his knees, the look of sadness turning to one of surprise and then to the slack sigh of death. His lips can't quite form that one last word.

Who? Is that the word, seeking some final knowledge, the answer that could take him, satisfied, to the grave?

Thin beams of crimson pierce the darkness, crisscrossing and then merging into a halo that circles his head. He wears, for one fleeting moment, a shining crown. Then the strings that hold him upright are cut. His body tumbles onto the floor.

Is it who or . . . what? Or why?

As if the answer to each question isn't the same.

It's always the same, and it's coming now, coming out of the darkness.

In the far corners of the sanctuary, the shadows begin to move. The shadows rise, the shadows stand, the shadows walk through the ruined cathedral, silent and certain. They wear black uniforms, black helmets, black masks. Their weapons shine ruby lines through the smoke, the darkness, laser aimers that dance around me, over me, painting my bloody clothes a deeper red. Their bodies are armored and carry the tools of their trade: flares and grenades, ropes and batons and handcuffs and all manner of authority and death.

The first of them, the one with the handgun, steps over CK's body, settles back into a Weaver stance just a few feet from me. Its masked face peers down the snout of a Glock .40. A metal chain circles its neck, dangling a black rectangle of fiber that frames a gold police badge. Another shadow joins it, kneels for a moment over the corpse, touching nothing. Then another, and another, to the side, all around me, their machine pistols and combat shotguns and sniper rifles pointing into me.

Beneath their black helmets they wear night vision goggles and masks and respirators. I wonder why they wait, why no one shoots, why it isn't over, and as I wonder, the shadows give way to another shadow, the one who is their leader. Its gloved fist clutches a Sig Sauer nine-millimeter, the P-226, another government handgun. In its other hand a Sure-Fire CombatLight flickers. White light burns into my face, across my body, and is gone.

The leader whispers something into the microphone that curves from its helmet to its lips. Then it holsters its pistol, and its hand, now free, tears away the black Velcro tab above the pocket of its flak vest, reveals the embroidered yellow letters that read A and T and F.

Eighty f . . . eighty f.

The other shadows do the same, and I see more yellow letters, ATF and ATF and ATF, and then I see ALEXANDRIA PD.

Those letters are printed on the flak jacket of the one with the Glock .40. The one that shot CK. Its gloved left hand tugs at the strap of its helmet, pulls the helmet and hood away to show me a cropped haircut and a forehead sheened with sweat. Off come the night vision goggles, the respirator, the balaclava, and the shadow becomes someone, a face, and it's a face I know.

Her face.

Fiona.

Or whatever her name might be, it doesn't matter, it will never matter, because she is Fiona, of course she is Fiona, and her smile, that smile, breaks across her face as Fiona, my Fiona, my sweet Fiona says to me:

Don't you fucking move.

I—

And don't you say a word. Not one word.

Then, to the shadow beside her:

Bruce, do me a favor and cuff this clown.

The next of the shadows flicks the mask from its face, and it's the Alexandria cop who was with her at my house, the Asian guy, and he tugs a pair of handcuffs from his belt and he starts my way, which is when I say:

I—

To which she says: Not a word.

But someone else has a word. Someone else in black. Someone Federal. It's the guy with the Sig Sauer and the letters ATF embroidered into his flak jacket, the leader of what ATF calls a Special Response Team, and he's got more than a word, he's got lots and lots of words, and the words go something like:

Wait just a minute. This is our jurisdiction now, officer. We'll be taking it from here. Gentlemen—

No.

That's all she says. The word hangs there for a moment, and then she says: Bruce, cuff him.

To which the ATF guy says: Hold on, officer. What do you think—

No, she says, but the ATF guy keeps talking:

You're doon.

That's how he says it, one syllable, like a big pile of sand: Dune.

And then I know him, oh, do I know him, and it's Mr. Branch Manager, the guy who came to the garage, the garage in New York City, the guy who brought the paper, who came to pick up the guns. Little voices start singing a song in my head, the one about it being a small world after all, and I shut them up, I shut them right up by saying:

Hey, I'm doon just fine.

Fiona looks at me. Bruce looks at me. The ATF guy looks at me, and the best he can do for his witty response is to tell me: No, you're not.

And neither are you, Fiona tells him. She nods at CK's corpse. You heard that man, but you didn't need to hear him. You know the score and so do I. Some Feds are dirty. Maybe not you. Maybe not even the ATF. But somebody's dirty and this needs to be clean. And right about now you're standing in Alexandria. As in Virginia. And those, my friend, are the words on my badge, not yours.

And anyway, she says, and she sighs and it's a good one. I've been living with this asshole for four months. So this is my collar. Mine.

The ATF guy shrugs, takes a slow gander at the air to the left of her, shrugs again, and says: Look, officer, we ain't got time for this shit. I'm going to secure this crime scene. But come the sunshine I'm going to have a little chat with your supervisor.

You do that, she tells him, but it's to the ATF

guy's back. He whispers something into that microphone on his helmet, and then his fist knocks once at empty air, and the SRT fans out across the sanctuary, moving in studied silence down the aisles, spaced in long intervals, shadows melting back into shadows, until it's just Fiona and Bruce and me.

Bruce, she says again. Cuff this guy, okay?

Fiona still holds that Glock .40 on me, she's got a nice two-hand grip, and this Bruce guy does the business, starts to pull my arms behind my back. I try not to wince, but she notices.

Hold on, she says, closing in, taking in the blood on my hands, my jacket, then seeing the mess in my left armpit, and she says the obvious to Bruce: He's been hit.

Then she says to me: How bad?

Not bad, I tell her. Considering. One shot. Went right through me. Most of the blood's . . . not mine. I was lucky.

Oh, Burdon Lane, she says. You are lucky. You are one lucky man.

Bruce, she says. Tell you what. I'll do the cuffs. You go out and see if we have an ETA on the ambulances. And get me some compression bandages, okay? And hey, Bruce, she says, her voice going a shade to the soft. A whisper, but a whisper I can hear:

Take your time, okay? This guy deserves to suffer. And besides, I've got a little something to tell him. Off the record.

Bruce smiles and Bruce nods and Bruce does what he's told.

Fiona waits until he's gone before she says: Here.

She holsters the pistol and shrugs off her over-sized black SWAT parka. Takes off my suit coat. Checks the wound again. Shakes her head. Grips my left wrist, lifts it gently, tucks my wrist and then my arm into the sleeve of the parka. Then the other arm.

It's the warmth of the parka, the heavy cloth, the weight of the body armor, maybe, but I realize that I feel cold. So cold. She finishes with the buttons and the zippers and then she says to me, she says:

You have the right to remain silent.

I know what—

Not a word, Burdon Lane. I'm telling you for the last time. I don't want to hear one more word out of you. Because whatever it says on that laminated card in my pocket, you don't have the right to remain silent. What you've got, Burdon Lane, is the obligation to shut up. You are going to listen to what I have to tell you, and you are not going to say a word. And then we're going to be done.

So I don't say a word. Not a word. But neither does she.

She stands there for a while, looking at me. And

after she looks at me for a while, she backs away, into the aisle, and bends to fish her helmet from the floor. She pushes the gas mask and the night vision goggles and the hood into the helmet, cradling the whole thing in the crook of her arm like a football. Then she comes back to me and starts with the looking again.

Now listen, she says. I'm going to tell you something, Burdon Lane. I shouldn't tell you this, but I'm going to. It's something you never, ever, asked me about. In all those months we lived together. Not once. You never asked. But I'm going to tell you now, and you . . . you are going to listen.

There is no other word for the breath she takes but deep.

And what I'm going to tell you, Burdon Lane, is what I think.

I get the look again. I have no idea what it means. Until she says:

And what I think is this.

She throws the helmet at me. It hits my chest, hard. My right hand catches it on the rebound. The gas mask and the goggles and the hood fall between my feet. Look up at me. An empty face. Anonymous. One of the shadows.

And Fiona says to me:

I think you'd better run.

the open door

Seems like a long time ago that I told you: I'm not the good guy.

And I'm not. No fucking way.

There are no good guys. Not really. Not anymore. All the good guys, at least all the ones I've known, are dead. Like Gideon Parks. And the man back in that priest's office. Jinx. They're dead and they're gone, and maybe it's because we didn't deserve them.

So I'm not the good guy. But I wonder, now, what that means. Because maybe, if it's not too much to think, maybe I'm not the bad guy either.

The white and the black, the light and the dark, the good and the bad: All lies. We're all those things. All those things and more.

Who are you? That's what the good guy, the one who took the name Jinx, asked me. *Who the fuck are you?*

And I told him the truth: I don't know. I really don't know.

But that's okay. Because if I don't know the answer to that one, if I don't know who I am, then no one else knows either.

Not those guys in the suits, the guys who sit behind those big oak desks, the ones who pull the strings. And not the cops.

Especially the cops. Now that I look like them.

Now that I'm one of them.

I tighten the strap of the helmet. The mask fits snug to my face, and for a moment, as I square the night vision goggles, see a world suddenly gone green, I smell her, I smell Fiona, sweet and tangy all at once, and then all I smell is rubber and my own sweat.

I hear my breath, I feel its wet heat, and the words, the words that I offer, the words I try to tell her, sound dull and distant. Fading into the shadows. Like me. Just like me.

Fiona—

Her eyes wince shut, but only for an instant. Then they're seeing me, behind that mask, seeing me and then not seeing me, seeing instead the cop all dressed in black who rises up off that altar, the poor man's Lazarus, and Fiona says the words she always seems to be saying to me:

Burdon, she says. You got to go.

So I tell her what I've always had to tell her:

Yeah, I tell her. I got to go.

But I won't run. I will never run again.

I will walk.

I will put one foot in front of the other foot and I will walk down that long center aisle to the great wide door of the cathedral. The open door.

I will walk, I will simply walk, as steady and as certain as I can, out that door and down the stone steps, strolling through the smoke and confusion and into the night. Past the phalanx of cops and Federal agents, past the police cruisers, past the ambulances and the fire trucks and the news units. To the van that is parked somewhere out there, the van that is painted with the words FLOWERS ETC, where I will wait for the moment, the right moment, when, justified by probable cause, I will make my search and seizure. I will reach inside that van and retrieve the leather satchel, my get-out bag, and then I will walk on, carrying that satchel and myself on our way.

No one will notice. No one will care. Because I'm no one special. No one at all. Just another cop, another part of the background, part of the scene. An extra. You know. That guy. Yeah . . . him.

And that guy will follow the curve of blacktop down the low hill and he will walk across King Street, but he won't have to walk far. Because there, beyond the rail viaduct, is a Metro station, and at the front of the Metro station is a taxi stand.

He will lose the helmet and walk on. He will drop the gas mask and the goggles and the hood behind a stand of evergreens and walk on. He will stuff the black SWAT parka into a trash bin and walk on. He will take the washcloth from the leather satchel and he will dab the blood from his wound, it's bad but not that bad, he's going to live long enough to go where he needs to go. He will stuff the washcloth into his armpit. He will take the houndstooth jacket from the leather satchel and he will wear the jacket, and the pair of glasses in the jacket pocket and a tight kind of grin, and he will walk on.

And as he walks toward the Metro station he will wave, he will wave at the first of the cabs in front of the station, and the cabbie will look and he will see someone who is no one, this guy in glasses and a houndstooth jacket with a satchel, an impatient business guy or a schoolteacher, maybe, this harmless soul who will tell the cabbie he wants to go to National Airport, a decent fare on a Sunday night, and it will take less than ten minutes, and the cabbie will drop the impatient business guy, the teacher, whoever, at National Airport, where the guy will check the flights and he will stand in a line for a while and he will buy a ticket with a picture ID and a credit card, and he won't have to wait long before they call the flight for Chicago or Memphis or maybe Kansas City because he won't be flying directly, he will be making a stop, at least one stop, because you can never be too sure. So he will make that stop, and he will do another little dance, buy another ticket from another airline with another picture ID and another credit card, and then he will board another flight and he will be gone, forever and ever, and maybe even for longer than that.

I know all this in the moment it takes for me to say those words to Fiona:

I got to go.

I know all this because I know that there is one place, only one place, where I will be safe. Where no one will even think to look for me. And, if they do look, well, they will never see Burdon Lane.

It's not some sunny somewhere, a faraway beach, a foreign land, or even a place that's big and busy. It's the one place I've been where no one knows me, no one remembers me. Where no one cares.

I'm going home.

But before I leave, there is one last thing to be done.

My hands press against the front pockets of my pants, feel their emptiness, then find the book. Stuffed into my hip pocket.

My book.

My mother's book.

I take the book from my pocket. Look at its pages, wrinkled and torn, smeared with ash and blood. The words have run out. It's finished. I don't need it anymore.

I don't need the book, or the slips of paper,

those bearer bonds, that mark my place in it. A place I've read, a place I've been, too many times.

I hold the book for a long moment, remembering, never forgetting, and then I put it into Fiona's hands.

You saved me, I tell her.

No, Fiona says. You did, Burdon. You did about the only thing a person can do in this world. You saved yourself

I let the book go.

And I begin to walk.

ACKNOWLEDGMENTS

No book is written alone. Although some of my sources must remain nameless, I am grateful for the technical advice of Lieutenant Steven Mason, Alexandria Police Department; Special Agent Tom Walczykowski, Federal Bureau of Investigation (retired); and Andy Stanford, Options for Personal Security. Special thanks are owed to my editor at Alfred A. Knopf, Jordan Pavlin, for her enthusiasm, honesty, and insight; to Doug Grad at New American Library, for his persistence; to my agent, Howard Morhaim, for waiting out that final draft; and to my wife, Lynne, for being my best critic and best friend.

This book is dedicated to John S. Hummell, Special Agent, Federal Bureau of Investigation: My son. Walk calmly in the shadows, fearing both the evil and the good; all too often, they are the same.

PENGUIN PUTNAM INC.
Online

Your Internet gateway to a virtual environment with
hundreds of entertaining and enlightening books
from Penguin Putnam Inc.

*While you're there, get the latest buzz on
the best authors and books around—*

Tom Clancy, Patricia Cornwell, W.E.B. Griffin,
Nora Roberts, William Gibson, Robin Cook,
Brian Jacques, Catherine Coulter, Stephen King,
Jacquelyn Mitchard, and many more!

**Penguin Putnam Online is located at
http://www.penguinputnam.com**

PENGUIN PUTNAM NEWS

Every month you'll get an inside look at our upcom-
ing books and new features on our site. This is an
ongoing effort to provide you with the most
up-to-date information about
our books and authors.

**Subscribe to Penguin Putnam News at
http://www.penguinputnam.com/ClubPPI**